# DARKER BY DEGREE

A Maddie Pryce Mystery

## Susan Branham and Keri Knutson

**Anubis Books**

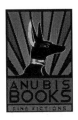

Cover design by: Keri Knutson
Printed in the United States of America

# PROLOGUE

She drifted away toward someplace safe. Time had lost its hold over her, become a contrivance by which normal people measured their lives, a scrapbook of still photos that had no relationship to the present.

Her arms were tied behind her and she could only move her head, which she leaned back against the carved wood of the chair, her eyes closed. There was music playing in the background, soothing and repetitive, Vivaldi maybe. If she didn't struggle, the pain went away, and she could almost imagine herself somewhere cool and green, somewhere years and miles away. Almost.

She tried to count backward, like when she was going under the anesthesia to have her tonsils out when she was nine. Maybe there would be ice cream there, all the cherry-chip ice cream she could eat. Her brother would let her have his comic books to read until she got better. But the thought of surgery, of the knife, was not safe at all. She drifted forward in time, and the cool air around her became a Montana night, on vacation with her parents under the dark sky filled with a jillion stars that glittered and winked like diamonds studding a swath of black velvet. She'd fallen in love there, not with a boy, but with a horse. And even though she was almost eighteen and knew that nobody kept a horse in fashionable Brentwood, she had cried and cried when she had to leave.

A light came on in front of her, invasive and insistent, and Montana disappeared. The light burned against her closed eyelids, turning her world red, and suddenly she was on a beach, watching the sun go down in a glory of gold and pink, setting the water on fire. His name and been Bobby, or Tommy, something non-threatening and middle class. He called her Jenny-Any-Dots, and read poetry on an old blanket on the sand. She tried to pull up his face, but it wouldn't come. There was just a wavery blur.

Bobby, or Tommy, was long gone, reading T.S. Elliot to some other girl on a beach that might as well have been on the moon. A tear spilled down her cheek, and she couldn't even reach up to brush it away. She didn't want him to see her cry, even though he'd seen her do it already. It made him angry.

The bruises on her arms felt hot as if the blood was pooling there under her skin, close to the surface and looking for a way out. Why would he do this, this man she hardly knew? What could she have done to make this happen, and what could she do now to make it unhappen? She felt the light growing warmer, as if she was a planet free of its safe and predictable orbit, moving inexorably toward the sun.

She wouldn't open her eyes, couldn't. Because then she would be pulled away from the safe place, from all the safe places, and she would be unable to hide.

She became aware of someone humming, just above the level of the music. She ached to brush the sound away, like a troublesome bee at a picnic, but the sound increased, adding an urgency, a tempo that outraced the tune. Vivaldi faded away and the silence when the humming stopped was much worse than the noise. Unbelievably worse. Then one word, whispered in her ear.

"Smile."

# CHAPTER ONE

I doubt I could remember the name of the first movie I ever saw, even with a loaded gun to my head. It was probably some classic from the golden age of Hollywood, perhaps one of the half dozen my mother had been in: the great Charlotte Corday, who had faded from the big screen and been reborn as the perfect '50s TV mother, forever smiling benignly.

Well, at least her dream had started. I was giving up the idea of ever seeing the name Madeline Pryce on the marquee, and this morning's audition was the most recent in a series of brief encounters that felt as awkward as blind dates and ended just as badly. For the past five years I'd subsisted on a diet of rejections, regional commercials, and one recurring daytime soap role that hadn't lasted half as long as the casting director had promised. The cachet of stardom attached to my family had not blossomed around me after my parents plunged off the seaside road and sometimes, mostly at night and mostly after a really lousy day, I wondered what cosmic fluke had kept me out of the car that night.

The emergence of a dark figure between two parked cars wiped out my thoughts of the audition and I slammed my foot onto the brake pedal, my '56 Chevy sliding to a stop with a sound like a woman screaming. I glanced in the rearview mirror to see the van behind me swerve sideways just in time to avoid my rear bumper. The Litigation Louie picked himself up from the street and skulked off in search of a mark with slower reflexes. If I wasn't careful, the cosmic scales were going to balance after all.

I started back down West Hollywood, past weed-filled, cyclone-fenced empty lots interspersed with cheap souvenir shops and trendy pseudo-celebrity hangouts. In places, Old Hollywood -- the one tourists look for and rarely find -- sparkles like a well-cut gem amid a tangle of costume jewelry. The Orpheus is one of those almost forgotten jewels, a 1930s theater hanging onto the dividing line where Hollywood is wedged against the galleries, shops and bistros of more affluent West Hollywood.

The theater was my day job, but something more than that. I had an abiding affection for the old art deco monster. Once I'd hit thirteen and had been deemed old enough to travel alone by cab or bus, I'd haunted the place like a ghost. The movies shown there seemed to appear at the whim of the owners: a film noir festival, lavish tributes to a single actor, sometimes just a mishmash of classics and foreign films with nothing to tie them together. I'd buy a pass and spend the whole day there, communing with the people in the dark. Strangely, the Orpheus had always seemed more real to me than my parent's house, where the sight of my mother sweeping down the staircase or of my father reading his paper in the sunny kitchen had always seemed like set pieces. More than any misguided emulation of my mother, it was the time spent in those red velvet seats that had driven me into acting. It was the only thing I could imagine myself doing. Irene Shoffitt, who had managed the theater for more than thirty years, had taken me under her wing when I was a kid and then given me a job after college when I'd started to worry about my dwindling nest egg. She was the closest thing I had to family now, she and the Orpheus, which was still part time machine and part secret fort, where I could slip sideways to a place where there were always happy endings.

But today romantic notions had no hold on me. The bad audition had put me in a mood, and I'd much rather have been vegging out in front of the TV than looking at long hours on my feet. I pulled onto the rotting pad of parking lot across the street, grateful to find a spot close enough to the lone streetlamp to assure at least a passing chance of making it back to my car alive.

Reproduction posters of tonight's triple bill studded the

theater's front window, night moths trapped under glass. Universal Monsters who once inspired terror in the movie-going public of the '30s and '40s now filled me with a different type of fear. I knew tonight's crowd was bound to be packed with mercenary youth and nomadic millennials, reckless kids whose spiral-bound theme book doodles ran more toward daggers through skulls than arrows through hearts.

The alley housing the theater's side entrance held the familiar smell of wet cardboard, a scent trapped by the high brick walls that formed a cut-out where the dented dumpster sat. I saw Irene leaning over the railing of the stoop, ensconced in layer upon layer of multicolored gauze, her white hair hidden beneath a bright scarf.

"Maddie!" she yelled.

"Aren't you hot in that get-up?" I said.

She jingled as she executed a slow pirouette. "Why, yes, thank you, I am." I waited through her giggles.

"Don't you get it? I'm Maria Ouspenskaya."

Again I waited. Maria who? Then I remembered. The old gypsy woman who sent Larry Talbot off to become the Wolfman.

"Irene, you never cease to amaze me. You don't think you're getting me into a costume, I hope."

"Oh, where's your sense of adventure? You'd make a great Bride of Frankenstein." Irene laughed again and descended the short stairway to offer a motherly hug. "I'm just kidding, sweetie. But you're too young to be such a fuddy-duddy."

*Not that young*, I thought. I gave her a quick hug back, taking in the scent of buttered popcorn mingled with gardenia perfume. I opened by mouth to tell her about the morning's failed audition when she took a step back and I realized she hadn't been looking for me.

"You didn't happen to see Jason, did you?" she said.

I hated the hopeful look that flashed in her eyes. "He's not here again? When was the last time he showed up for work, anyway?"

Irene's son had been an unwanted bonus that came with the Orpheus. We were contemporaries only in the fact that we were the same age. We'd nominally hung out together when we were younger, but once Jason had been able to drive he'd spent less time at the theater, unless it was to bring around a group of friends for a weekend showing. Irene spent those years fishing him out of trouble, and was still doing her best to keep him afloat. He was a prime example for the argument that it was nature and not nurture that make us the way we are. I tried to give him the benefit of the doubt most days for Irene's sake, but tonight he was just pissing me off. Four more hours added onto five I was already dreading.

"Maddie, I hate to ask you to stay late again, but I don't think he's going to show up and I'll need you here for the third feature. Jason will either straighten up or be out of a job. I'm tired of making excuses for him and tired of being embarrassed in front of my friends."

The last thing I wanted to do was make Irene feel worse. "Don't worry about me," I said, flashing a smile that I hoped look genuine. "I'll take care of it tonight. Jason can make it up to me later."

That seemed to pacify Irene for the moment and we went inside. She turned toward the lobby and I headed for the locker room that occupied a back corner of the building and always smelled like the inside of a latex Halloween mask.

The opaque glass of the single, narrow clerestory window threw the last rays of sunlight across the floor in an amber harlequin pattern. Dust swirled by my shoes as I made my way to locker number twelve to peel off my street clothes and trade them for the black fez and bolero jacket that made me look like an organ grinder's monkey. The uniform felt shiny against my skin, the tile floor cool against my stockinged feet.

Weak light bounced off the edges of the corner mirror where I stopped to straighten my jacket, creating phantom companions in the chairs behind me, indistinct reflections of faceless people. I stared into my own face for a moment: dark eyes, full lips, cheekbones the less fortunate would pay good money for. I'd grown accustomed to the fact that my beauty did not startle me. I was a pretty girl in a sea of pretty girls, and my looks had yet to open doors for me. My dark hair blended with the uniform, leaving my face floating like a disembodied spirit in the warped changing-room glass.

~~~

At 7:30, Bela Lugosi was telling his dinner guests that he didn't drink wine, and I was giving up any hope that Jason would show tonight. I gripped the over-sized chrome flashlight until my fingernails dug into my thumb and glanced to the right entrance where Pete leaned against the wall. His deeply grained face held a broad smile that trapped the black and white movie flickers for a second before letting them go. Every few moments I would see the detail in his cap, the red cording, the gold insignia centered over his forehead. Pete Torrence, world's oldest usher.

The crowd that spilled out after the first feature hadn't lived up to my expectations. Scrubbed college students, young professionals, blue collar workers who hovered just above minimum wage, punctuated here and there by the blood red lips of a passing goth. Half the crowd had bought all-night tickets, and they moved toward the smooth deco curve of the concession stand, streaming and flashing like a school of fish. The others passed the red velvet ropes, their feet whispering across scarlet and gold carpet laid in 1982 as part of the Orpheus' long period of restoration, a graceful nod away from the oranges and browns of the '70s. Their voices echoed into the ornate barreled ceiling as they opened the doors onto the night.

I could see Irene looking like a gypsy fortuneteller in a penny arcade, trapped by the round glass of the ticket booth, surrounded by black-laced teens in engineer boots. Glittery studs and gold hoops sprouted from noses, cheeks, eyebrows, and the pack passed through the lobby in a cloud of clove cigarettes and patchouli. I hoped they were only trying to look dangerous.

The crowd was getting darker by degree, and larger too. I knew by the time midnight rolled around we'd be looking at a full house. Good for business, bad for me. I started mentally counting the minutes, pacing through the last thirty minutes of *Frankenstein* as if I was the one waiting for the villagers to storm the castle.

In the break before the final feature, I headed for the alley entrance with my cargo of candy boxes and greasy popcorn tubs, the night air cool against my skin after the stifling press of bodies inside the theater. I tossed the bags into the open dumpster and walked to the mouth of the alley, drawn by the citrusy scent of oleander bushes that grew along the grassy front courtyard of the Orpheus. The ornamental gaslight at the corner of the building cast a protective circle around me as I glanced toward the parking lot to make sure my car was intact.

A red Cabriolet heading east on Hollywood made a careless turn into the lot, stopping just beyond the reach of the streetlamp. The headlights died. Nobody got out of the car. I caught movement and turned to see a running figure split the headlights of three oncoming cars. I recognized it. Jason.

He crouched by the driver's door and I caught the glint of the window sliding down. Jason punctuated the conversation with furtive glances, and then turned his shaggy head and looked straight at me. He stared for a beat, and then sprinted around the front of the car and yanked open the passenger door, cutting me another look before disappearing behind the tinted windows. The car shot backwards and took off down the boulevard, and I watched until it disappeared around a corner, unsure of what I'd just witnessed and what, if anything, I would tell Irene when I got back inside.

The midnight crowd looked like trouble. Posers had given way to gang girls with hair sprayed into shapes as threatening as Stephen King's topiary animals and boys pretending to be men strutted around, big pants slung low on their hips, hiding switchblades and crack pipes. I said a silent prayer and stood in the darkness long enough to make sure they were seated and not scaling the velvet drapes before heading back to the lobby to find Irene.

She was sitting behind the oaken desk in the small office off the main floor of the lobby looking wilted, her cheer from earlier in the evening nowhere in evidence. I positioned myself in the doorway so I could keep one eye on the closed doors to theater.

"Irene, I just saw Jason take off in a red Cabriolet, but I couldn't see who was driving. Sound familiar?"

Irene shook her head and slumped back into the chair. "I don't know his...friends."

I glanced back at the theater doors and imagined the chaos that could be occurring on the other side.

"I'd better get back. I just wanted you to know that Jason was around." I hesitated, unsure of what else to say. "Do you want to get together for an early lunch tomorrow? We could get spring rolls at Wong's."

Irene's shoulders lifted slightly at the suggestion. "That would be wonderful, Maddie." I turned to head back out the door.

"Maddie, wait," Irene said. "I want you to know that this is it. Jason's too old to be acting like a spoiled child. Next time I see him, I'm going to give him a piece of my mind. He's not going to be my problem any more, or yours either."

"Irene, really, it's okay," I started.

Her mouth was a firm line and her eyes flashed. She might be a little old lady, but she could be feisty when she needed to be. She had bounced more than one drunk out the door in her time.

"No, it's not okay. Not anymore. I just wanted you to know." She gave me a tired smile. "You go on. I'm going to finish up here and then head home." She waved me out. "Go on, you don't want them tearing the place up."

I knew she was right, but that didn't make leaving her any easier. I glanced back once before pulling the door shut. She looked small behind the massive wooden desk, like a child lost in the world of grownups.

On screen, Larry Talbot was undergoing his first

transformation, man to wolf, innocent to killer. The same metamorphosis did not appear to be affecting the audience, and the movie ended without incident, the crowd shuffling out to wreak their havoc elsewhere. Pete and the counter girl followed them, and I was alone with the Orpheus now except for Gene, a twenty-something teddy bear of a film nerd, who was tending his roost in the projection booth.

After forty-five minutes, everything was shut down and bagged up and Gene was downstairs leaning against one of the decorative columns smoking a joint.

I walked over and punched him in the arm. "Don't you have any respect for a landmark? You could burn the place down, you know?"

"At least then it'd look like the rest of the landscape. Besides, you don't want to be mean to me. I'm only hanging around to walk you out to your car."

"Well, don't think I don't appreciate it," I said. "Just give me five minutes and I'll gladly allow you the privilege of escorting me to my carriage. And don't drop any ashes on the carpet."

"You got it, babe," he said with a wink.

I changed as quickly as I could, glad to shed the black polyester skin, then grabbed my purse and pulled out my keys. Back in the lobby, I noticed the white bags on the carpet.

"Damn, I forgot the trash. Give me a sec, okay?"

I didn't wait for a reply, just grabbed the bags and ran for the side entrance. I fumbled with the lock and finally got it open, then kicked the wooden wedge under the door so I wouldn't lock myself out. I traversed a litter of empty popcorn boxes spoiled by yesterday's rain shower, and heaved one bag after another into the waiting mouth of the dumpster. Something gauzy and turquoise curved under a corner of the receptacle like a small river, glittering in the sodium lights, too unsullied to have been there long. In spite of myself, I walked over and reached down for it.

I could see around the edge of the dumpster now, into the brick corner of the alley alcove. I lost my balance and sat down hard on the cracked asphalt. It didn't matter; I didn't feel it.

Irene was crammed into the small space, her gypsy finery spotted with blood gone maroon in the shadows, her glassy eyes staring into the stars above Hollywood.

# CHAPTER TWO

I kept thinking tequila sunrise. Funny how the mind works. The sun was coming up, a tawny yellow against the deep red velvet of the lobby, and I was seated on the floor like an unwilling buddha at meditation.

Gene had stood with a protective arm around my shoulders as the officials arrived in waves, first two uniformed patrolmen and an unneeded ambulance crew, then detectives and crime scene technicians, finally a deputy coroner wearing a dark jacket over his T-shirt and sweats. A female detective in a navy blue pantsuit and flats led Gene across the lobby for questioning. She was nearly as tall as he was, and I watched her dark head bob in assent as he talked and she scribbled in a palm-sized notebook.

"What?" I focused on the man standing beside me, wearing a dark suit and a tie dotted with dancing cartoon characters. He was so square-jawed and clean cut he could have come direct from Central Casting.

"Could you go over exactly what happened?" the detective repeated, looking from me to the notebook in his hand with just a touch of impatience.

I went through everything I could remember, from when I'd arrived to that awful moment in the alley. I must have started babbling at one point, because he held up a hand and then wrote faster until he'd caught up with me. The second time I spoke more slowly, answering his questions like a robot until he was finally satisfied with my version of the night's events.

He handed me his card -- Kyle Oberman, Robbery-Homicide Division LAPD -- and his fingertips lingered on my palm. "I'm sorry for your loss. We'll be in touch," he said.

After he walked away, I looked for Gene, who must already have been dismissed. I couldn't blame him for taking off, but I was reluctant to leave Irene with these strangers, so I planted myself on the floor while they went about their grisly business beyond the quiet of the lobby. The sirens and flashing lights had been switched off hours ago. The urgency had passed. It was all over. Irene was over. I locked the side door as the coroner's attendants loaded Irene's body into the back of the station wagon to drive her, without ceremony, to the morgue.

Sydney was at the door when I got home, no doubt fighting back the urge to relieve himself on the hardwood floor. His compact French bulldog body was quivering with expectation as he raced ahead of me to the stairs that led up to the turret and the roof garden beyond.

Syd did his thing on the shrubs while I sat in a lawn chair, taking in the four-hundred square foot area filled with potted tea olives and ornamental figs, raised beds of fragrant herbs and perennial flowers that were just losing their luster to the summer heat. The city was coming to life below me, cars pulling out to clog the freeways, people setting off for suburban yard sales and sidewalk gallery showings or a Saturday trip to the beach. Lethargy overtook me and I leaned my head back against the cool aluminum frame of the chair, closing my eyes against the morning. Syd jumped up and began to lick my face, little wet kisses that propelled me back to my feet and inside to make breakfast for him and Catherine before I took a nap.

I soon gave up the idea of sleep and made myself a drink, chilled currant-flavored vodka. The last time I'd opened the bottle had been the night I broke up with Rick. He'd sat there holding his drink, his lower lip trembling as if he couldn't believe I'd had the audacity to dump him, Rick Swenson, who'd been a corpse on an episode of *CSI*. That was six months ago and I hadn't had a date since.

Cat walked over to my perch on the living room sofa, twisting her diamond-shaped head from side to side, as if she were studying me for the first time. After coming within an inch of my face, she suddenly broke off, bored with me, and headed for her food bowl. Deaf cats are different. Cat had come with this place, a permanent tenant. I hadn't been looking for another pet when I found the apartment, but I didn't have the heart to evict her. She was just another of the many oddities that came with living in the former residence of Otto Von Strasser, mad director.

Otto had built the Spanish-style castle in 1927, and paced the tiled hallways for fifteen years after that, terrorizing the maids and a succession of actress wives before his death in 1943. It had been reported as a suicide, but no one had ever explained the bloodstains left beneath his hanged corpse. Amid scandal and controversy, the estate had fallen to his last wife, who pieced it off to developers until all that was left was the house, which she then chopped up into the six apartments that exist now. The grounds had been reduced to a large, walled back yard, replete with aging statuary and tended on a hit-and-miss basis by various tenants. While my job at the Orpheus paid for groceries and car insurance, my parent's legacy had been able to provide me with the means to afford the home I'd fallen in love with. Living with the echoes of the late Otto seemed a fair trade for my roof garden.

Thinking about bloodstains was dangerous territory, so I downed the vodka and refilled my glass, the alcohol starting a hollow burn in my stomach. I couldn't remember when I'd last eaten, but the process of making breakfast seemed impossibly complicated and there was nothing in the refrigerator worth cooking anyway. The market would be my first stop before I opened the theater for the matinee.

The short, heavy glass slipped from my fingers and hit the floor with a thud, causing a divot that would no doubt remind me of this morning whenever I ran my bare feet over it. There would be no matinee today, and it didn't matter how much vodka I drank or if I never returned to the Orpheus again. Irene had filled those spaces my own family never had, those snapshot moments that never made it into my childhood albums. She was an impromptu celebration when a good thing happened and a hot cup of tea when it didn't. Now she was gone. No take-backs, no do-overs.

I wiped up the spilled drink with a dishtowel and carried it to the clothes hamper in the bathroom, which was full to overflowing from a week's inattention. Since I didn't feel like sleeping anyway, I carried the hamper down two flights of stairs and out into the back garden. There had probably been an interior entrance to the cellar at one time, but Otto's wife had doors walled up willy-nilly during the renovation, and the laundry room could only be accessed by a black metal door set into the back wall of the house. It was inconvenient, but it was quiet and there was never a line. The rooms below housed two coin-operated washers and dryers. Everyone in the building used the extra space for storage, so I passed sealed boxes and cast-off furniture, holiday decorations and barbecue gear. I filled the washer and paid the money, then stood and listened as water filled the drum with the cadence of a distant ocean. When the rhythmic thump of agitating clothes replaced the soothing rush, I headed back up.

The phone jangled as I re-entered my apartment and Sydney barked at it furiously. He had a thing about phones and doorbells. Cat slept on, blissfully unaware at the other end of the couch as I picked up the receiver. Sydney fell silent.

"Miss Pryce? This is Detective Oberman. Sorry if I woke you." His voice was soft and apologetic.

"No, no you didn't." I didn't tell him I hadn't been to bed yet.

"We've had no luck tracking down Jason Shoffitt. We're waiting on a warrant for Ms. Shoffit's house, but in the meantime, I was wondering if you could think of any other likely place we might find him."

I examined what I knew about Jason's life, which wasn't much. Ever since his band kicked him out for missing rehearsals, Jason had been living with Irene in her small Culver City bungalow. I knew he kept late hours and questionable company, but Irene and I had never been privy to the specifics.

"I'm sorry," I said. "Even though we worked together, outside the theater, I didn't have much to do with him."

"Okay. If by some chance you do come into contact with him, would you let us know?"

I told him I would.

I fell asleep with a dull, silver pain behind my eyes, promising myself that when I woke up, my trip to the market would extend itself to Culver City. Jason might hide from the police, but maybe he wouldn't run from me.

~~~

Irene's bungalow sat beneath a protective canopy of old oak and walnut trees, in a neighborhood yet to be scarred by gang graffiti and random acts of vandalism. Up and down the street, people tended flowers, mowed grass or simply sat on the porch enjoying the cooler air of early evening. There was no activity at Irene's.

I tried the front and back doors, but there was no answer, not even a yowl from Irene's cat, Chauncey. After one more pass by the kitchen windows I was going to give up, then I glanced at the aging garage set to the side of the side of the house, connected to the street by a gravel driveway. The door was open just a crack. I looked up and down the street, noting a figure in older metallic green sedan with a crushed quarter panel parked a few houses down. Hopefully he wouldn't report me for breaking and entering.

When I peered through the three-inch crack into the cool, musty darkness of the garage, I could only make out the skeleton of a hall tree against the opaque back window, partially coiled garden hoses dripping like tree snakes from the ceiling, and a landscape of sharp corners and hulking shapes. The rain-warped door resisted at first, but I threw a hip into it until it slid sideways. Jason's rusty Camaro huddled inside, amid boxes and crushed Christmas ornaments dislodged from their protective packaging in a snowfall of Styrofoam peanuts. I heard the tick of the cooling engine and reached forward to touch the hood. It

16

was still warm.

I returned to the kitchen door and knocked vigorously, calling Jason's name softly at first, then with more urgency. Finally the bolt slid back and Jason appeared, looking as if he'd been sleeping in the same clothes for days, the lines that drew down the corners of his mouth giving him the appearance of a ventriloquist's dummy come to life. He brushed his lank brown hair back from his forehead and squinted at me. He'd never had the confident good looks of the varsity jocks, and the years since had only hardened his already sharp features, making him a caricature of the future drop-outs who spread themselves against the back wall of the high school like graffiti.

"What're you doing here, Maddie?" His voice sounded thick with sleep, but I knew he'd just gotten home.

"Looking for you," I said. "Where've you been, Jason?"

"Nowhere. I've just been trying to sleep off this cold." He passed a shaky hand over his face. "That shit just knocks you out, you know. Sorry I didn't make it last night."

One more lie. "Have the police talked to you yet?"

His eyes widened in what seemed to be genuine surprise. I waited for his answer, but he seemed stumped.

"Jason, Irene's dead."

He took a step backward. "What?"

"I found her just after two this morning when Gene and I were closing up. Somebody slit her throat in the alley beside the theater," I said.

"Oh my god." Jason's eyes grew large, and I tried to read the thoughts behind them. He sputtered like he was choking, then turned and stumbled back into the kitchen and I followed, wondering if I should comfort him or call the cops. He seemed to be in total shock, and I regretted now that I'd been the one to tell him, that I was stuck picking up the pieces if he started to come apart.

Jason fell into a chair at the Formica kitchen table and put his head in his hands. I touched his shoulder, but he flinched away as if I'd burned him and let out a sound somewhere between a sob and a growl.

"Jason, I know you're upset," I said. "And I'm sorry. But I think you should be prepared to talk to the police. I already told them I saw you last night."

He stared up at me with red-rimmed eyes and I could sense the betrayal he felt. "Get out," he said.

He rose from the chair and it overturned behind him, clattering on the yellow linoleum. He took a step toward me and I moved closer to the open door. Jason didn't advance any further and the anger seemed to drain away, leaving him deflated in its wake. "I'm sorry," he muttered.

He walked over to the chair and carefully picked it up, then placed it at the table and stood there with his back toward me, a dark, trembling exclamation point against the sunny yellow of Irene's kitchen. I walked out and closed the door behind me, leaving him alone with his grief or his guilt. Once I was in the car, I called and left a message with the police telling them were they could find him.

# CHAPTER THREE

The next two days passed in a dreamlike funk. The theater was temporarily closed, and I'd taken over Irene's funeral arrangements. Irene's lawyer was of the ancient family retainer type, muttering about safe deposit boxes and legal arcana while he tried to balance his lunch on a stack of tattered folders. Irene had left simple instructions in the event of her death, more evidence that she'd given up relying on Jason, so there were enough stepping stones laid out for me to navigate my way through her wishes. Even in death, she was holding my hand.

When Detective Oberman did call me back, it wasn't to let me know they'd found Jason, but to ask if I had a key to Irene's house. Since Jason was still playing invisible man, the warrant had gone through and Oberman thought it would be less trouble if he could procure a key. I was about to tell him that I didn't, but a glance at the glass dish on the table next to the front door made me a liar. I must have picked up the keys off Irene's desk that night and pocketed them when I'd finally locked the theater for good, and then dropped them in the dish when I got home without even registering it. I told the detective I'd meet him at Irene's.

As I picked up the keys on the way out the door, I noticed a little silver charm on the ring in the form of a grinning kitty face. Damn. I was so caught up in worrying about the dead I'd forgotten all about the living. I should have picked up Irene's cat days ago. Even if Jason was hiding out in her house, chances were he wasn't being a responsible pet owner. I stopped to grab Cat's carrier from the hall closet on my way out.

~~~

Irene's house had an air of abandonment, the difference between a home where the owner has just stepped out to run an errand and a place where the owners are gone. The detective had left me sitting across the street in my car while he served the warrant. I'd given him the carrier and warned him to be on the lookout for Chauncey, then handed over a foil package of kitty treats I'd picked up on the way over. When he'd asked if that usually worked, I told him it couldn't hurt.

It was something more than an hour and less than two when he came trotting back across the street with the carrier in his hands, empty. He handed over the keys.

"No cat, huh?" I asked.

"Sorry."

"Anything else of interest?"

"Nothing obvious."

I was getting a distinct Dragnet vibe all of the sudden, and wondering how long a sentence he could actually put together. I stepped out of the car.

"Mind if I go back in and try to coax him out? I mean, that's not breaking any rules or anything is it? I just feel so bad, forgetting about him. He's probably terrified."

He paused for a moment, whether to run legal scenarios through his mind or just because he was trying to pick the right one-word response I couldn't tell. "Nope, no problem." A pause again. "If you want, I'll stick around and help you look."

Maybe he was a softie after all.

"Besides, Shoffit might show up," he added.

So much for the softie.

We started in the living room and methodically made our way through the house, looking in cabinets and under furniture. I was impressed that there was no apparent carnage from the police search. On TV you always see them turning over drawers and throwing cushions around while some shifty-looking suspect or tearful girlfriend stands by helplessly. Maybe Oberman was a neat freak. Maybe I watched too much TV.

I tried not to see the ghost of Irene in every picture on the wall, in the afghan folded across the foot of her bed, in every detail that spoke of a life no one would return to. I was determined to be brisk and businesslike, but managed to knock not one but two boxes of shoes down onto my head from the upper shelf of a hall closet. To his credit, Olberman didn't laugh, just helped me corral the errant footwear and shove it back into place.

In the kitchen I glanced between the cat door and the door to the basement. The best bet was that Chauncey was outside, but I wanted to leave no stone unturned. "You searched the basement, right?"

"Yep. Your friend was the tidy type, not much down there. But we can look again if you think that would help."

He stood there with the carrier clasped in front of him, looking like he was waiting for a cab. I was starting to feel guilty.

"Just a quick look, if you really don't mind."

Inside the basement door, Oberman flicked a switch and a single, dangling bulb came on below. As we made our way down the stairs, I could see he was right: the expanse of the shadowed basement was uncluttered and organized. The water heater and furnace stood together next to an alcove that held an empty worktable beneath a pegboard studded with tools, and at the edge of the reach of light there were neat stacks of cardboard boxes sealed with yellowing masking tape, faded marker script ran across the sides the hieroglyphic clue to what was inside.

"Here, kitty, kitty, kitty," I said.

There was no answering "meow," but a muffled rustling came from behind the fortress of boxes.

"Chauncey, kitty?"

I glance at the detective and nodded my head. I moved toward the sound with Oberman behind me, carrier at the ready. I wasn't sure how Chauncey was going to react. I moved between two rows of boxes, pushing them aside to make a bigger space, and as I reached the wall what leapt out at me was not a yellow cat, but a mouse of rather modest proportions. This was still startling enough that I slipped backwards into a stack of boxes. I tried to pirouette, but the boxes were having none of that, and all I ended up doing was creating a domino effect that ended with Oberman doing his best to stop the tumble.

The carrier in his hand must have made that awkward, and by the time I had maneuvered through the rubble, he was sitting amongst a pile of semi-squashed cardboard and spilled pots and pans with a surprised look on his face.

"That wasn't a cat," he said.

"Wow, you are good," I replied. I pushed the carrier out of the way with my foot and reached to help him up. There was a fuzzy clot of dust on one of his lapels and I tried to brush it off, only managing to make it into a wide smudge.

"Oops."

He grabbed my hand before I could do any more damage. "That's what dry cleaning is for."

I figured that maybe it was time to end this adventure before he handcuffed me and drug me out. If Chauncey hadn't made an appearance after all that racket, he wasn't down here. "I'm sorry. I guess this is pretty much a wash. I should let you get going." He had the good grace not to glance at his watch.

We made our way upstairs and back into the kitchen. I searched in the cupboards until I found a bag of dry cat food and filled up the bowl next to the back door.

"I'm sure he's around somewhere," Oberman said. "Once things quiet down, he'll come back. Actually I was looking forward to watching you cat-wrangle. After all, you do so well with boxes."

I paused with Chauncey's water bowl halfway to the sink and turned, unsure if he was making a joke. I didn't know him well enough to judge his sense of humor.

He was smiling, and it did nice things to his face. He looked kind of cute there with his smudged jacket, the carrier bumping against his knees. I realized I'd just crossed the line where you stop seeing someone in a professional capacity and really notice them. I felt that first little shocking thrill of attraction and my mind blanked. This was turning into a weird day.

He sat the carrier down and took the water bowl from my hand, filling it up and placing it down next to the food. "There, all set. And since you've got the keys, you can stop back by and check until you find him."

"So it's okay if I just come and go, the house isn't under quarantine or lockdown or something like that?"

Oberman smiled again. "I won't tell anyone. But seriously, I don't see a problem with it. It's not a crime scene, and we didn't find anything suspicious. Just keep an eye out for Shoffit. I'd appreciate it if you'd call if you see him." He reached into his inner pocket. "I can give you a card..."

"No, that's okay. I've still got the one from the other night." And I did, somewhere. He stood there looking at me expectantly, but his face was still distracting me. I tend to fill awkward silences with babble, so I got Irene's keys out, grabbed the carrier, and thanked Oberman again for spending the last hour on a wild kitty chase. After we locked the house up, I sat in my car and watched him pull away from the curb, telling myself it was silly to wonder what he was doing the rest of the day.

~~~

After finishing the afternoon's errands I pulled onto my palm-lined street, my only thoughts of a quiet dinner on the rooftop with Syd, but the image of a rusted yellow Camaro parked mid-block stopped me cold.

My first instinct was to drive past. No. Jason was the one who didn't belong here, not me. I parked behind him and watched as he got out of the car, grateful that we would be out on the street. If he went ballistic, I hoped one of my neighbors would have the sense to call the cops.

Jason looked no better than the last time I'd seen him, and as I approached I caught a whiff of stale cigarettes and beer.

I stopped a foot away and tried to stare him down. "What're you doing here?"

"I need to talk to you," he said, the whine of the spoiled little boy creeping into his voice.

"Ever heard of a phone?"

"Shit, Maddie. Don't be like that." He glanced up and down the street, and then focused on the bag of groceries in my arms. "Look, you got something to eat?"

"No, Jason. What do you want? Have you talked to the police yet?"

"I don't have anything to say to the cops. Man, my mom just died, you think they'd let me alone." He looked down and kicked at the ground, shoved his hands in his pockets and hunched his shoulders. If he was trying to evoke my sympathy, it wasn't working.

"I'm sure they will once you convince them that you had nothing to do with Irene's murder," I said.

For a moment I saw that rage behind his eyes again. "Fuck you. None of this is my fault. Nobody ever gives me a fucking break."

"Fine, then. I have better things to do, Jason." I turned to walk away, then felt his fingers on my arm. I spun to face him.

He lowered his head. "I'm sorry, Maddie. Things just haven't been so good the last couple of days. Do you think you could lend me some money? I just need to get out of town for a while."

I gazed at him, open-mouthed. Of all the.... "Goddammit, Jason. Don't you get it? You're not a kid anymore, and Irene's not around to pick you up every time you blow it. It's time to grow up."

He took a step toward me, his hand balling into a fist. I dropped the bag of groceries strategically between us and moved out of his reach, ignoring the cat food can that landed on my toes. Before he could act on whatever evil impulse was flashing through his addled brain, the cell phone in my purse trilled. It startled both of us and Jason froze.

I slid the phone out and punched the button. "What?"

The voice on the other end sounded apologetic. "Miss Pryce, it's Kyle Oberman, if this is a bad time..."

"Not at all, Sally!" I said as brightly as I could, grabbing the first non-threatening female name that popped into my head. "I was hoping to hear from you."

"Pardon me?"

"We really should get together and catch up. You remember where I live?"

"I'm sorry, I'm not sure what you're getting at."

God, he was dense. "My apartment. I know it's been a while, but you have to remember where I live. Besides, I probably have any clothes you've been missing. I never remember to return anything."

If I was standing next to Kyle Oberman right now, I'm sure I would be able to see the light bulb going on above his head.

"Jason Shoffit's at your apartment."

"Yes."

"Are you in trouble?"

"Not yet, but things have a funny way of working out."

"Keep him talking. I'll send a car. And leave the phone on."

"Sure thing. Just stop by when you've got time! Bye, kiddo."

I pretended to hit the end button but kept the phone in my hand, feeling like I'd slipped inside an old episode of *Police Woman*.

Jason narrowed his eyes. I tried to affect the tone of someone talking to a frightened but possibly rabid dog.

"Why don't you tell me what's going on, Jason. Maybe I can help," I said.

I could tell this was the wrong thing to say, and the wrongness was only compounded by the distant wail of a siren. I ignored it -- you hear sirens around the clock in L.A. -- but Jason's paranoia had reached such a fever pitch that he bolted toward the still-open door of his car.

I wasn't about to fling myself in front of him.

He looked at me over the scabby roof of the vehicle. "You should have helped me. All I wanted was a little money. Not like you can't afford it." His lips twisted in an ugly smile. "I could always tell them you've got it, then what'll you do?"

He jumped in and slammed the door, and I watched him peel away and speed off down the street. I was still standing there when the patrol car pulled up a few minutes later, its siren going off with a funny little whoop.

I was explaining the situation to the cops when Oberman arrived in a midnight blue Toyota Corolla, not a department issue. He must have gone off duty. He'd changed from his dusty suit into faded Levi's, Nikes, and a navy blue sweatshirt that wasn't an advertisement for anything. I could see a rim of white from the t-shirt underneath.

He ran over to the sidewalk.

"Shoffit's not here?"

"Nope, he took off when he heard the siren."

Oberman turned toward the patrolman closest to me, who looked like one of the fat kids who always gets picked last in gym, resentful but hopeful at the same time.

"Nobody told me," the cop said.

Oberman dismissed the uniforms with a description of Jason's car, then cocked his head at me. In the glow of sunset, he looked even younger than he had before. I wondered if that was a plus or a minus in interrogations, if he either caught people off-guard or they just dismissed him out of hand.

"You sure you're okay?" he asked.

"Yeah. He was just giving me the creeps. He wanted to borrow money and I blew him off. Then he made some kind of vague threat and bolted. Do you guys have an arrest warrant out for him?"

A line creased his forehead. "No. For now he's just a person of interest. But this game of hide and seek he's playing certainly makes him seem suspicious. You said he threatened you?"

What had he said? The actual words were lost in the confusion. "Something about telling someone I had something. I honestly have no idea what he was talking about. Before I talked to him at Irene's the other day, we'd barely said ten words to each

26

other the last few months. I saw him at work, but that was it."

Oberman glanced down. "Well, at least the only casualty seems to be your lettuce."

I followed his gaze down to a head of romaine at my feet. At some point I had apparently stomped on it and it was looking definitely worse for wear. Luckily the fruit and candy seemed unscathed.

We began picking up the remains of my shopping and shoving it back into the bag. The single filet of salmon had slid from its brown paper wrapper and looked crumpled and lonely on the grass.

"I hope that wasn't dinner," Oberman remarked.

"I guess I'll just have mangoes and chocolate and pretend I'm in a French café," I replied, trying to sound witty and nonchalant. At this rate the only images he was going to be able to conjure up regarding me were falling boxes and squashed produce. Charming.

"Open a nice bottle of wine, very continental," he said, rounding up the last stray can of cat food.

I popped it into the bag. "Thanks again. I seem to have wasted most of your day and given you nothing to show for it."

"Hey, don't worry about it. As days go, this was a lot better than some. No shootouts, no paperwork. And now we know Shoffit's around and hasn't skipped town. Don't worry, we'll find him." He glanced at his watch. "Sorry, but I've got to be somewhere. You're okay?"

I waved him off. "I think I can manage to get this stuff upstairs. Maybe. Thanks again for getting here so quickly."

He gave me a half-salute and loped back to his car. For the second time today I stopped myself from wondering where he was off to. Definitely a complication I didn't need. I stopped on the doorstep and looked back, but his car was gone. The only car I did see was a metallic green Olds with a crumbled fender, driving the speed limit. It seemed familiar and took me a second to place it as the one that had been parked across the street from Irene's when I'd confronted Jason. I thought briefly about

27

calling Oberman back and telling him, but it sounded ridiculous. Twice could be a coincidence. If I saw it again, I'd take the risk of looking like a hysterical conspiracy theorist and call it in.

# CHAPTER FOUR

Irene's funeral was a small affair, short and to the point. I'm not what you would call a religious person by nature, so when the minister switched focus from Irene to heaven, I chose to stare up into the old live oaks overhead. Let them all think I was looking at the great beyond.

Barely five lines had been uttered on Irene's behalf, and there was no hint of her presence, no whiff of her gardenia perfume. There was just the lacquered cherry box and the dry earth waiting to receive it. Had my proprietary anger not stepped in to balance my emotions, I would no doubt have lapsed into a prolonged crying jag. As it was, I walked away from the graveside service embittered, with the peppery scent of pink carnations burning my nostrils.

A few hundred feet away, under the spreading shade of one of the larger oaks, I caught sight of Detective Oberman. His feet were slightly apart and his knees locked, his hands clasped in front of him. It was an oddly military stance that relaxed as I walked over.

"I didn't know you'd be here," I said.

"I try to attend the funeral of every victim I deal with. A superstition, if you like." His soft smile did not reach his eyes. "Sometimes I'm the only one there."

I looked down at the roots of the old oaks reflexively. How horribly sad. Luckily before I began to weep over that, over so many things, the far off meaning in his words caught up with me. Good police work. Those television cop shows also taught me that the villain often shows up to catch the final act of his evildoing.

I looked back over my shoulder as the forty or so people trailed off like ants to their waiting cars, then turned back to Oberman. "I appreciate you coming."

He nodded his head and seemed unsure what to say next. I was used to this part, the place in the conversation over the dead where people run through all the things they knew it was okay to say before breaking into virgin territory. It was hard enough when they knew you. I felt sorry for the guy.

"Would you like to go have some coffee, someone to talk to?" he said. Sensitivity training to the rescue.

"That's very kind, but I'm afraid I can't. I've decided to hire a security guard at the theater and I'm interviewing someone for the position this afternoon."

"I think that's a good idea," he said. "I could give you some names if you'd like. A lot of ex-police work security."

I waved him off. "Thanks, but I found a guy's name in Irene's old Rolodex, so I assume he's familiar with the Orpheus." And Irene. There came the ammonia again. That sharp, stinging feeling you get before you lose control. I made a big show of checking my watch. "I'm sorry, but I really should get going." Even I heard my voice crack.

I don't remember if he said anything else. I was past the part where I had sure things all lined up to think and say. My mind didn't have to go far to leave safe territory. I know we walked to our cars and said something inane, something forgettable to fill up the space between right now and all the rest.

I glanced back once more toward Irene before getting into my car. There was already another tent popping up in another corner of the cemetery. A new hill for new ants to climb. The time set aside for my public grief had obviously run out.

I shifted the Chevy into gear and headed back to Hollywood.

~~~

I don't know what the old theater thought, if it thought anything at all, when I let myself in through the massive glass doors and made my way to Irene's office. The security prospect wasn't due for a good half hour, so I set about doing the mundane tasks of beginning to breathe the Orpheus back to life.

I punched the answering machine button and was greeted with some matter-of-fact male voice I didn't recognize telling me that the theater would be closed indefinitely and that when it reopened, I was expected to step in and manage the place in the interim. What the hell did that mean? The words "indefinitely" and "interim" brought something into sharp focus that I had yet to take into consideration. This job, though it seemed I still had it, wasn't going to be the same. I looked around at the walls of this room now as familiar to me as my own living room. It was like I'd come home and everyone was gone; a house but no family. No, goddamnit, you freaking do not do that.

I slapped my palms down on the desk. *What assholes! Don't even send a card, leave a note on the desk.* I sorted through all the neat little stacks on Irene's desk until they weren't neat any more. "Fine, if that's the way it's going to be, then fine!" Focusing on my anger, I was happy with myself for the first time today.

Over the course of the next half hour I divined uses for all of Irene's keys, save for one. Maybe it was useless, more of a charm than anything else. I had one like that. I'd found it in the yard one summer, my own mysterious bit of buried treasure, and it graduated from key ring to key ring until it wound up on the one I carry now.

As I passed through the stray sunlight that had split the clouds and found its way in, I glanced at the door across from the office. The old balcony hadn't been open to the public since the early '80s. I'd been up there a few times when I was a teenager, when Jason had been able to sneak his way in, one of the perks of being the manager's kid. Probably one of the few things that could make him seem cool to the scruffy crowd he ran with. I'd hardly thought of it since then, but as I inserted the stepchild of a key, the door swung open. I flicked the switch on the wall and was surprised to be rewarded with a yellow glow, allowing me to ascend the curving stairwell that opened up to the large curtained box.

The seats smelled musty, like moss-covered rocks near the entrance of a cave, as I pushed my between rows and circled the entire U-shape from rear to left and back again, placing my feet carefully, not wanting to stumble over whatever might be up there. I stood at the railing and looked out at the pale sweep of the screen.

Lands End. This was the landscape of my world, the near and the distant, windswept only by the passage of time. I'd somehow managed to dance along the edge of what I'd wanted, stayed just outside the circle of my mother's fame. I looked at the big, white ghost of a screen and tried to burn my image onto it, tried to wish myself ahead into a time when I would be up there instead of out here.

They say that those who can't do, teach, and those who can't reach the brass ring still ride the carousel. I suppose with Irene gone the Orpheus had reached out to grab a bigger piece of me like a big, white wave dragging me along then depositing me on the shore opposite the one I'd longed for. If I couldn't take care of Irene's cat, at least I could keep a vigil over this old place we both loved and bat away any vultures who might swoop in to claim the headlands.

I wound myself back down the corkscrew stairs, flipped off the light, and crossed the hallway. No sign of the security man, but by the clock above the office door, he still had five minutes to make it. Maybe I'm the only one who shows up early, anxious to every audition.

Crap. I punched up the calendar on my phone. Damnit, I knew I had something this Friday. Good thing the theater wasn't opening right back up or I'd never get a Friday night off.

The Screen and Theater Actor's Retirement Society had been created in the '60s as a stop-gap to fill the needs not covered by Actor's Fund and other groups. My mother and father had both been long-standing board members, and until his death my father had been the lawyer of record for the charity. They held regular fundraising events, including this Friday's cocktail mixer, that attracted both old Hollywood and new, and thanks to my parent's involvement, I could always count on an invitation. With all that had happened I'd all but forgotten about it, but this was one of the few big name parties I got a chance to attend, and I didn't want to miss it. My mind blew right past "the what will I wear" scenario as I tried to recall just what I'd done with the invitation. I made a mental note to check the glass bowl by the door when I got home.

I was still peering into the shiny black screen of my phone when I heard footsteps. In the doorway was the ugliest sport jacket I'd seen since Lawrence Welk went off the air. The man wearing the jacket must have been about sixty, his potbelly straining a yellow polyester shirt, wisps of wiry grey hair sticking out from under a canvas fishing hat fraying at the edges. I had sudden misgivings about Irene's Rolodex. Maybe it was a doorstop in disguise. The man was about to speak and I was afraid that would make things worse.

I spoke first, rising from behind the desk and crossing over with hand extended. "You must be Harry Gaines," I said.

"That would be me." He took off his battered hat, revealing just enough of a bald spot to catch the light from the single ceiling fixture. He was older than I'd expected and he seemed to realize that. I wondered how long it might take him to find his gun if I let him carry one.

"I understand you have a job for me," he said.

"Just general security. Keeping an eye on the place, tossing the rowdies out. After dark until closing, some weeknights, definitely the weekend." I paused. "Do you have experience?"

"Oh, yes, ma'am. Mostly in investigation, but I do the security bit to keep steady money in my pocket. I don't get around as much as I used to, but this should be a cakewalk. I always loved this old place. Used to come here all the time as a kid for the westerns. This is where I met Irene, oh, back in the '70s. Nice woman. Terrible what happened to her. I figured that was why you called me."

"Yes," I said absentmindedly, trying to buy enough time to

come to a decision. He wasn't what I had pictured, but he seemed sincere. He must have sensed my reluctance.

"I'll always show up on time, if that's what you're worried about."

"No, I'm sure you will."

"So, have we got a deal?" There was an almost desperate look in his eyes. I hate that.

"Sure," I said, hoping I wouldn't regret it. "I can't tell you exactly when we'll reopen, but it should be soon. You can take care of these in the meantime," I handed him the stack of tax forms and application papers. "I'll call you as soon as I have a definite date."

~~~

Cuppa Jo's is a little slice of nirvana in the guise of a coffee shop. And it's not even a proper coffee shop, per se, although I hear you can get a decent roast there. I am not a coffee person. No, what Jo's is known for is tea: black blends like Earl Grey, Ceylon Breakfast, Lapsang; gunpowder green and delicate whites; organic chai; a seemingly endless bouquet of fragrant herbals mixed in-house.

But the real reason I come to Jo's is for the scones. The "Jo" in Jo's is a Scottish lass brought to Cali by the owner's son, who fell in love with her and convinced her that she'd be happier in the sunshine. She might have been the shy, retiring type, but she could bake like a demon. A name change, a menu adjustment, a little celebrity word of mouth, and Cuppa Jo's went from borderline to mainline. There's was a baker's dozen of scone flavors, twelve standard and one rotating flavor of the day.

Today I was treating myself. It had been a stupid, draining 10 days, so I stopped by for a half-dozen variety box of scones, a half-pound of lemon-ginger pick-me-up tea, and a jar of double Devon cream. Then I was going to go home and talk myself out of eating them all at once while I watched old Hepburn and Tracy movies. Kate always cheers me up.

Confronted with the glass counter, I had a hard time choosing: lavender-lemongrass, cranberry, chai-pepper, ginger-current, and two of my favorite, hibiscus. I threw in a box of Cheese Nibbles for good measure. What the hell.

Everything smelled so good that once my choices were boxed, I added a chai latte and one of the daily specials, rosemary-pecan with lemon glaze, to eat in at one of the tables with a view of the street.

I made my way to alcove at the far end of the shop, a cozy little nook where they kept the creamers and spices to add to your beverage du jour. I was perusing the shelf for ground nutmeg when someone bumped my arm.

I turned to find a young guy of average height and build, his dark hair hanging in his eyes. He had no concept at all of personal space. I noticed his right hand jammed in the pocket of his windbreaker, which made me nervous. The intent concentration on his face as he stared at me indicated the bump hadn't been unintentional. I tried backing up, but there was little room between me and the counter.

"Where's Jenny?" he said.

"Pardon me?"

"Jenny Chandler, where is she?"

"Look," I said, stepping forward in an attempt to make him shift back, "I think you've got me confused with somebody else."

He wasn't budging, and now there was a scant few inches between us. Over the spicy scent of cinnamon and nutmeg, I could smell his sweat.

"I saw you talking to the cops, so don't play dumb with me."

Cops? "I've got no idea what you're talking about, buddy, but if you don't back off..." I left the threat unarticulated.

"I saw you talking to Jason Shoffit. Twice. I saw you looking in his garage. He had her car."

All the dominoes tumbled at once. The green Olds. The Cabriolet from the night of Irene's murder. So I wasn't paranoid, but this guy obviously was. He thought he had incontrovertible proof of...what? His hand was still shoved in his pocket, which I took as a very bad sign. Crazy people do crazy things, regardless of onlookers, and this guy certainly had a crazy look about him. Best to remain calm and try to diffuse the situation.

"I'm sorry, but you're mistaken. I don't know any Jenny. And Jason, well, I knew Jason's mom. That's all it was, really."

That wasn't the answer he was looking for. "You have to tell me..." his voice cracked and he grabbed my elbow with his left hand. I don't know if it was the desperation in his voice, the fact that I couldn't see his other hand, or the sharp and startling pain of his fingers digging into my flesh. Whatever the prompt, without really thinking about it I grabbed one of the heavy thermoses from the counter beside us and swung it at his head. Considering the distance between us, there was no way I could miss.

The dispenser top of the thermos popped quite dramatically, spewing a fountain of 1% organic milk all over the alcove, me, and the would-be assailant. He let go of my arm, so I had that going for me.

"This isn't over," he cried, finally removing his hand from his pocket and grabbing the side of his head theatrically. I'd opened up a gash, and the blood mixed with milk painted the side of his face pink. He turned and ran with his hand still clutched to the side of his head, like the Phantom of the Opera fleeing the stage, but instead of a mask what fluttered to the floor in his wake was well-worn picture of a girl, blonde and pretty, smiling as if she were startled by the camera.

~~~

A little more than 40 minutes later, I was sitting at that window table talking to Kyle Oberman, my scone crumbling in front of me and my second cup of tea gone cold. The counter person had insisted I drink up and then given me a second cup on the house, as if hot tea cured all ills. An intrepid customer had rushed out after the Phantom, confirming that he had indeed gotten into a metallic green Olds to flee the scene, but was unable to confirm the license number.

"We've got to stop meeting like this," Oberman joked. The look of amusement on his face would have been charming under other circumstances. I poked my scone and burst into tears.

Oberman's amusement turned to concern. "Hey, I didn't mean..." he began.

"No, no. I just realized I've spent more time with you the last two weeks than I've spent with anybody else." Okay, that came out all wrong. "I mean, you're going to think I'm like some Typhoid Mary of crime, leaving disaster in my wake wherever I go." I reached up to touch a stiff spot on the side of my head where the spouting milk had turned my hair to straw.

"How bad do I look?"

"Not bad at all," he lied.

He offered a napkin and I dabbed at my eyes. "I'm sorry, really. I'm not the hysterical type. It's just...damn. I hate being not in control of things. It's like I've got a few pages from the middle of a script and I have no idea what's going on. The plot's just going on and on and I don't know who I'm supposed to be..." I trailed off. My analogies suck.

Oberman reached over and took my hand. "This isn't your fault. Just think of it as a break in the case. We've got a description of the guy, a description of the car, we'll find him. And once we've found him, we'll start putting it all together." He tapped the picture of the girl. "And we've got this. Really, this is a good thing."

"If you say so." I wasn't convinced. I was still trying to put all the pieces together, like a thrift-store jigsaw puzzle. "Do you think this has anything to do with Irene's murder?"

"Too early to tell. Officially, we're looking at it as a 'wrong place, wrong time' type of crime. We don't have anything yet to tie it to more than that. But every piece of information is vital. Trust me, I'll stay on top of it."

"Thank you," I said. "I appreciate that. I didn't' mean to imply that you weren't doing your job."

"This has been a rough time for you, I know. But trust me, we know what we're doing." He paused and his face turned serious. "I think it might be good if you laid low for a couple of days. I mean, you've been accosted by two guys that are still at large. I don't want to alarm you, but until we get a clearer picture of what's going on, it might be a good idea if you stayed at home as much as possible, don't go out at night alone, that kind of stuff."

I ran through my schedule in my head. Work as no problem, as the theater was still in limbo. Ah, but there was Friday night and the at-least-semi-glitzy benefit. That wouldn't break up until the wee hours.

"Well, I've got an event I have to go to Friday, but that's really it. It's an actor's retirement fund thing, and I'd really hate to miss it. My mom was on the board and I'd feel bad if I didn't go. Got to honor the family name and all that."

"Your mom?"

"Charlotte Corday. She was an actress."

I watched him flip the mental index cards.

"Oh, my god, *Home, Sweet Home*. I remember that show."

Everybody remembered *Home, Sweet Home*, right up there with *My Three Sons* and *The Brady Bunch*. I still didn't know if that was a blessing or a curse.

"Wow, how old are you?" Oberman asked with barely disguised wonder.

Damnit, I never failed to see that coming. "I was a late and only child, let's put it that way. She played a doting mother long before she actually was one." If she had ever been one. I left that comment unspoken.

"Do you have to be there?" Oberman asked.

Did I have to? No. But did I need to? Yeah, I did.

"Look, Oberman…" I began.

"I think at this point we should be on a first-name basis," he interrupted. "Call me Kyle."

"Okay. But look, Kyle, an actress can't afford to pass up any networking opportunity. It's few and far between I can wrangle a spot at a place like this, so I really can't waste it. You can make connections at these events that you can't make any place else.

38

But I'll tell you what, I'll be extra careful. Look both ways, blah, blah, blah." A ridiculous thought crossed my mind. "I've got two tickets, you can send a cop with me."

Without breaking stride, he took the silly suggestion to heart.

"You know, that's not a bad idea. And if Shoffit or the mystery guy shows up, we can get him there." He frowned. "But I don't think we'd be able to requisition an on-duty cop for a Hollywood party. I've got Friday night off, how about I tag along?"

And with that, I had a date for Friday with a cute guy. Go figure.

# CHAPTER FIVE

I got out my one $450 dress, a white strapless sheath with a satin-draped bodice that showed off my chest to its best advantage. The only jewelry that seemed appropriate was my mother's, one simple tear-shaped emerald between two small peridot points. It caught the light, seeming to flicker with green fire as I looked in the mirror. Apart from the necklace, I looked nothing like my mother. She'd been an icy, blond beauty with hair swept up in a chignon, shoulders often bare to accentuate her graceful neck. I had almond-shaped eyes -- a legacy of my father's family, the side we rarely discussed and never visited -- and my blue-black hair was a genetic throwback to my paternal grandmother. I was the exotic counterpoint to my mother's Aryan looks, like the Japanese doll brought back by a veteran to the chagrin of his stateside wife. Too much nutmeg in the spice cake. I used to pretend I was adopted.

A piercing shriek came from the turret stairs. Experience led me to believe that was Cat's way of communing with the spirit world. Her outbursts always began in the turret room and usually ended with some inexplicable damage to plants or crockery. Sometimes I blamed Cat and sometimes I blamed Otto. A supernatural excuse seemed cheaper than investing in a kitty psychiatrist.

The scent of old books and cinnamon enveloped me as I reached the top of the stairs and I heard a slight jingle from the wind chime just outside the roof garden door. Cat sat framed in a wavy glass window, staring into an undefined space somewhere in the center of the room. I had long ago lost the embarrassment of talking to Otto and spoke to him as one might to an invisible friend, if one was so inclined.

"No shenanigans tonight, Otto," I said. "You need to relax and enjoy your afterlife."

I passed my fingertips over the glass shade of my Tiffany-inspired floor lamp one last time, just in case I'd failed to convince him.

~~~

The Sunset Strip doesn't exist during the daylight hours in the same way it does at night. After dark, brilliant yellow fountains spring up at each median palm, fed by silver cans of iridescent light. Each passing car becomes awash with glittery shafts alternating with deep darkness. Celebrities jostle with runaways who live only on this street, dirty with the fragments of a broken boulevard, as much one-dimensional figures as the streetlights and shooting palms.

We were in the front seat of the Corolla, Kyle watching traffic and me looking out the window. I wasn't sure how much of this was a date and how much was a duty, and how much I wanted it to be one or the other. For now, it was all business.

Kyle had promised me information as we'd pulled away from my apartment and now he was doling it out.

"So, your mystery guy is Paul Saroyan, a college kid from Glendale. We tracked him down from a traffic ticket issued on the night of Irene Shoffit's murder. Seems he ran a stop sign and got tagged by a pickup truck. He wasn't at his parent's house, and they said they hadn't seen him in several days, but we're going through his friends until we find out where he's staying."

"And the girl in the picture?"

"Paul's girlfriend, Jennifer Chandler. She's in the system as a missing person. I read through her file. Had a falling out with her parents over the usual stuff: college, boyfriend, spending money. I'm not sure exactly what the argument was, but she moved out from under mommy and daddy's wing and was trying to make a go of it on her own. Her dad's a lawyer in

Brentwood and I guess her life plans were not quite meshing with their expectations. You know, the standard rebellion story: quit school, got a job as a waitress. A girlfriend said she had some drug problems. Whatever it was, she started doing some reels for a porn outfit called Bravo Productions near Venice Beach. Then nothing. Parents haven't heard from her, boyfriend can't find her. She goes into the system, but with no sign of foul play it's not a priority. The boyfriend's becoming increasingly panicky, calling in to tip lines, talking the ear off anyone who'll listen. "

"And he finds me."

"Jennifer's car was a red Cabriolet. Whether or not it was her car you saw Shoffit get into that night, Saroyan must have thought it was, and he just lasered in on Shoffit, followed Shoffit to you."

"So that's why he was so upset."

"Yeah, figures you show up a lot with Jason, so you must have something to do with Jennifer's disappearance."

"And you have no leads on her?"

"No. Once we find the boyfriend, we can maybe shed some more light on Jennifer's troubles and we can sort out whether or not he's suspect in anything."

"Oh, I've got a few things I'd like to pin on him."

"I will be sure to call you as soon as we bring him in."

"Gee thanks. I'll be sure to bring a carafe of fresh milk. Oh," I grabbed at his arm, "that's your turn right there. We'll go with the valet parking guys. No one wants to walk across the parking lot in these get-ups, right?"

"Yeah, no one in Ro-Ho would recognize me in this monkey-suit. At least I don't look like a detective ready to interrogate the honored guests."

"Oh don't worry, I'll just tell everyone you're a screenwriter and then no one will want to talk to you."

Once it was our turn in the long queue, we got out and Kyle pressed his keys into the valet's outreached hand. With a nod, we were ready to make our entrance.

The Hollywood Palms was decked out in gold ribbons and silver stars, and I grabbed Kyle's hand so I wouldn't lose him in the sea of starlets and producers on the make. We had an option between hors d'eouvres and drinks, but the food was across the ballroom and drinks seemed a better choice anyway. I found a quiet corner table, and Kyle took on the heady job of slicing the crowd to fetch the libations.

"Gin and tonic, right?" He shoved a glass at me.

"Gin is just glorified rubbing alcohol."

Kyle laughed. "Just kidding. Here's your Vodka Collins."

"I wondered when they started putting cherries in gin," I said. "What have you got?"

"Bourbon and Coke, the drink of real men."

"A real man wouldn't need the Coke."

Kyle glanced around at the well-dressed partygoers, clustered in groups, some sitting at tables, but most standing, as if they were afraid they might wrinkle or that something nipped and tucked might spring loose. "So, you know any of these people?" he said.

"Some."

"Anybody important?"

"Self-important maybe," I said.

"I guess it didn't dawn on me that you had these kind of connections."

"Oh please. I'm just a struggling actress. It if weren't for my mother's name, I wouldn't even be here."

Kyle raised his eyebrows. "I'm sure you're not giving yourself enough credit."

"Sure," I said, and changed the subject by pointing out a cool, leggy blonde in shimmering white leaning against the bar. "Recognize her? Gillian Sinclair. Toast of the Tabloids."

"Oh, yeah. She was in...."

"Everything."

"Well, she's got a great pair of...shoes."

"We were up for the same part once. I was surprised she could actually read the script."

"And the claws come out," he said with a grin.

"Honey, the claws are always out. Let's just say it's not always talent that gets you the part."

Kyle was still looking at Gillian's exposed back.

"Don't gawk," I said

Kyle turned back to the table. "Does that mean you won't be getting me her autograph?"

"Not hardly."

Kyle winked at me. "I'll just have to settle for yours then."

We finished our first round of drinks and Kyle got up and headed toward the buffet with the fortitude of a man going into battle. I lost sight of him in the press of dark suits and glittery gowns and decided to find some celebrity to impress him with. I'd had no luck when I felt a hand at the small of my back. I turned, fully expecting to be greeted with a plate of hard-to-identify delicacies.

The man was tall, in an Armani tux, his blond hair just disheveled enough to prove it was a $200 cut. He looked like the world's wealthiest surf bum.

"Maddie!" he exclaimed. "It's been too long."

"Wow, Evan, you look...great." And he did, but he always had. Evan Marks' family was old money turned new. His father had taken the piles left to him by his father and turned them into heaps. From what I remembered of college, Evan's goal in life had been to skate as far as he could on good genes and inherited good fortune, which was apparently a decent distance.

Evan maneuvered so that his arm was around my shoulder and his hand on my hip. "What have you been up to?"

I wanted to manufacture credits for his approval, but what would I say? I couldn't tell him I was an usher in a movie theater. "Well, I'm still auditioning," I said. "Waiting for the big break." As the words left my lips, I heard an insincerity that I couldn't erase.

He gave me an appraising look, as if I was the catch of the day in a glass deli case. "You know," he began. "I'm getting the financing finalized for a project you might be perfect for."

"You're just saying that." I'd heard the line enough at parties like this, and those evenings usually ended with a slap and a muttered apology.

"No. Really. We're getting ready to look at the casting."

"When did you decide you wanted to work for a living?" I laughed, "They did tell you that there's more to movies than sitting around in a chair and pinching the extras as they stroll by."

"Well, it was Erik's idea. You remember Erik Wellman? He's convinced me that I was born to be an executive producer. I'm depending on him to do all the heavy lifting."

"Well you were born with the money to be a producer, and in this town that is the heavy lifting."

Evan glanced over my shoulder. "Speak of the devil, there's Erik now." He removed his hand from my hip long enough to motion Erik towards us.

It was one of those instances where the warm-up act came after the main attraction. Erik was not as tall as Evan, not as well-dressed, and all his hair was naively in place. I had known Erik before college. His parents had been "cocktail party friends" with mine: not the kind you invite to an intimate event, but the kind you make sure to have around when the guest list is important. Erik's dad had been a top director in the late '70s, a wunderkind who made films that managed to be avant garde but still sell tickets. He'd been rewarded for walking that fine line with an Oscar before taking off to Europe to pursue art over commerce.

If Evan's family took old money and made it new, Erik's had rested on the old money and was awaiting what the next generation would bring. Both families were very well-respected, but there were camps who would always fall on the side of the current movers and shakers just as there were those who would remain more comfortably attached to the golden age of green.

"Maddie, you look fabulous," Erik said. He leaned in to kiss my cheek. "Depend on Evan to attach himself to the prettiest girl in the room."

"Geez, stop it, the both of you," I said. "This some kind of contest to see who can be the shmooziest?"

"Ah, Mads, I forgot how good your bullshit detector was," Evan said with an easy laugh. He turned to Erik. "I was just telling Maddie we're getting ready to cast. She's between jobs right now." Evan, always the diplomat.

It was Erik's turn to give the appraising eye. I was starting to feel like the prize heifer at a county fair auction. Not that that's necessarily a bad thing for an out-of-work actress.

"You know, that's a great idea," Erik finally said. "I can definitely see it."

Before they could gush any more about my possibilities, Kyle walked up bearing a plate of shrimp and vegetables.

"Sorry I took so long," he said. "Some guy thought I was a waiter and it took ten minutes to convince him otherwise. But I see you've found some friends."

"Erik, Evan, this is Kyle Oberman. Kyle, Erik Wellman and Evan Marks. We all went to college together and Erik's parents were friends of my parents."

"I would shake hands, but...." Kyle glanced down at two full plates.

"No problem," Erik replied.

Kyle looked at the plates again. "Maybe we should find someplace to sit before the hot things get cold and the cold things get warm."

It felt awkward to walk away in the middle of what might or might not be a job offer, but I didn't want to make Kyle stand there like a lawn jockey. "That's a good idea," I said. "Boys, would you like to join us?"

"No, we wouldn't want to intrude and we've already taken up so much of your time Maddie, but I do hope you'll call me about the project." Evan handed me a business card, which I slipped into my bag.

"Actually, there's someone here I need to talk to," Erik said. "Maybe I'll catch up with you later. Pleasure to meet you, Kyle." He leaned down to quickly kiss my cheek again, the default "aloha" of the Hollywood crowd.

46

Instead of getting another drink at the bar, I grabbed a flute of champagne from a passing server and we made our way to a table.

"Sorry if I cut your conversation short," Kyle said as we sat down.

"No, that's okay. I haven't seen those guys since college."

"So I guess they were friends of Sally's too," Kyle said, staring at me.

"What are you..." Then it caught me. Kyle did have a sense of humor after all. "She was an invention, remember? Now eat your shrimp." I bit into a crab puff and glanced over at Kyle, who looked about as bored as you can get drinking free champagne and noshing free food.

"You never did tell me why you called me that afternoon.""

"Well isn't it obvious? I knew you were in some trouble, so I called."

"Uh-huh. So now you're psychic."

Kyle let his head dip just a bit, then looked up at me. "Would you believe I was going to ask you for coffee?"

"Why detective! You sound positively interested in me."

Not only did he have a sense of humor, Kyle could also go quite red in the face and in a hurry.

"Well if you're going to pick on me, then maybe my interest is misplaced."

"It's okay. I'm just dancing around the fact that I would've said yes had that been you on the phone and not that bothersome Sally. Of course, we see how well things go when I stop by a coffee shop."

"Well in your defense, you did go there for the tea."

Maybe it was the two drinks, but I felt suddenly warm. I felt it on my face, and in my stomach. That hint of attraction I'd felt in Irene's kitchen and pushed away was back, spurred on by the fact that it apparently had been reciprocated. I ignored the brief flare of guilt that the image of Irene's kitchen brought to mind. I'd learned that the world is not a cosmic swap meet where you trade one thing for another, though I tended to forget that lesson

47

about as often as I remembered it.

"So what should we do with this new knowledge?" Kyle asked, a crab puff teasing his fingers.

"I don't know, there's no rule against dating a witness?"

"I think I'm old enough to use my own judgment. It's not like you're a suspect."

"Well, that's a relief."

"Only justice has to be blind. Law-enforcement is welcome to admire the view."

"You are a cornball. Cute, but a cornball."

"Well since I'm such a cornball, as you put it, then maybe you should come up with a plan for the rest of the evening."

"There's a rest of the evening, is there?" Suddenly I was less concerned with networking. Hormones are a dangerous thing.

"Once this fete is complete, we could continue our conversation about crime, punishment, and whatever else you want to discuss."

"What did you have in mind? A drive, a walk on the beach? Hey, you could buy me some herbal tea."

"Oh, right, I'm going to walk in some other joint dressed like this."

"Well, then we'll just have to find an herbal tea drive-through."

"In this town, anything is possible."

We stayed long enough to watch the beautiful people make a few circuits around the room and then by mutual agreement decided we'd had our fill.

Kyle went out to meet up with his valet while I took the opportunity to look around once more for Evan and Erik, but they were nowhere near my location. Just as well. I couldn't help but think all their talk was the same old boilerplate that Hollywood types trot out to girls in low-cut dresses. I'd give Evan a call the first of the week, just in case.

I practically ran out the door, feeling like Cinderella at one minute to midnight. Kyle was in the driver's seat, fiddling with the radio.

"Why don't we head down to Marina del Rey and walk on the pier?" he said as I slid into the passenger seat.

"Sure, I'd like that."

We drove to the beach with the windows open, the night wind ruffling our hair. The sand still held some of the day's warmth as we crossed to the pier. I was careful to hold the hem of my dress above aging boards gone grey with years of salt-water spray as we walked out to the edge, close to where the moon lapped with the waves in a luminous dance.

"I always loved looking at the ocean at night," Kyle said. "You can take it all in then and it doesn't seem so big."

"You like having parameters?" I asked as I turned from the water to look at him.

"Not always. Not in everything."

He leaned forward, his green eyes glowing like the moon, and his lips met mine, tentatively at first and then more insistently. I let myself fall into that kiss until everything else disappeared: the sound of people down the beach, the soft hiss of the waves, the feel of weathered wood under my bare feet.

It took a moment for me to catch my breath, and when I opened my eyes again, Kyle was looking at me with a lop-sided grin.

"Well," he finally said.

"Yeah," I replied.

We stood there like that for a while. I felt the need to say something, anything.

"So, what made you want to be a cop anyway?"

"That's not a first date story."

"So, you're assuming there will be other dates?"

He took my hand and squeezed. "A boy can always hope."

We walked back to the car then listened to an oldies station on the way back to my place. He kissed me again, briefly, before I got out of the car.

"So, it's okay if I call you again?" he said.

"I'd be worried if you didn't."

He waited until I disappeared inside the doorway before

driving away, a nice guy, one who seemed so unlike the dimly remembered parade of the last few years. It all seemed dreamy and unfocused.

I walked through the downstairs alcove, past the mailboxes and the spot where on Saturdays and Sundays the paper guy left the free entertainment tabloids. I bypassed the stairs up to my apartment and instead went out the back door that led into the overgrown garden.

That same moon was there, I thought foolishly, and I watched it reflect off the green orb of the obelisk in Otto's old yard. At times the tinge of light from that ball had thrown a pallor over the garden and had left me depressed. Tonight it did anything but. Tonight that green glow made me smile.

# CHAPTER SIX

I might never have heard the phone if Sydney hadn't made such a racket. I swear that dog hated the thing for some reason I would never fathom. Little sharp barks pulled me from sleep and I fumbled around on the bedside table. I couldn't seem to find the light or the phone but I was finally rewarded with a jingling crash and the pale green luminescence of the handset.

"Yes?"

"Maddie? Oh, god. You're home."

It took a moment for the voice, panicky and pitched wrong, to register. "Jason? What?"

"I don't have time. You want to know, I'll tell you everything. But you have to get over here. Now."

"Tell me what?"

Jason wasn't listening to me at all.

"I'm getting out of here tonight. This is all too freaky. It was supposed to be easy, but it's all fucked up now." He let out a sob. I'd never known Jason to cry, not even at his father's funeral.

"I'm outta here, Maddie. You want to know who killed my mom, I'll tell you. Take it to the police, whatever you want."

I was fully awake now, the sheet pulled up across my chest, the receiver gripped in my hand. "Jason, look..."

"No. You look. This is serious shit and I'm not going down for it. You liked my mom, I know you did. If you want to do something good for her, you'll get over here. No cops, or I'm a dead man."

Something crashed in the background, and Jason cursed away from the phone.

"Jason, what the hell is going on?"

There was silence for a moment and then he came back on the line. "Please," he whispered. "Just come. Please." He hung up.

Shit. Just like Jason, always waiting to be bailed out, always expecting someone else to clean up the disasters he created. Irene was dead, and now I had become the designated closer. Well, he wasn't going to run this time. I slipped on jeans and a sweatshirt and found my tennis shoes in the jumble at the bottom of the closet. I grabbed my address book from the hall table and found the page where I'd jotted Kyle's number. It seemed he had been sleeping just as soundly as I had.

"Kyle? This is Maddie. Jason Shoffit just called me, hysterical. He wants me to go over to Irene's and talk to him. He says he knows who killed her."

"Christ, Maddie. What time is it?"

"I have no idea. But I'm dressed, and if you want to beat me over there, you'd better get a move on."

"Call the police, Maddie."

"You are the police." What was the use of going out with a cop if you couldn't depend on him?

"I mean call 911. And do not go over there."

"No time. He said he was leaving town. He's practiced disappearing for years. You have the address?"

"Goddammit, yes. I mean no. You are not going over there."

I made a mental note that Kyle was cranky when awakened in the middle of the night. "Hey, consider it our second date." I hung up before he could yell.

~~~

I tapped the brakes as I rounded the corner and pulled onto Irene's street. Relief flooded me at the sight of Jason's car in the drive, the door open. Now Kyle just needed to show up.

My mom used to tell a story about my first swimming lesson. I must have been about three at the time, but I was fearless. She said I walked right up to the pool, past the instructor with the water wings in her outstretched hand, and jumped in. The "leap before you look" syndrome, my mom had dubbed it. I just don't deal well with hesitation. I still believed I wouldn't drown.

I looked in the rearview mirror before I stepped out of the car. No Kyle, not yet.

There was a single light burning in the front window of the bungalow, the curtains half drawn. No other cars in front of the house, no suspicious thugs, no sounds. I hesitated on the porch and listened again, then knocked gently. The door swung inward and stopped halfway.

"Jason?"

I pushed the door, but it wouldn't budge. I slipped through and stepped into the front room. The place was a mess. I don't mean a mess in the typical way, newspapers and old pizza boxes, half-filled glasses with a topping of scum, although there was that too. It looked like someone had systematically gone through the room and torn apart anything that could be torn apart. The couch was slashed, leaking stuffing in great gouts, chairs were overturned and ripped. Broken video tapes and shards of Hummel figurines littered the floor. Irene's TV cabinet was laying on its side, partially blocking the front door. I stood there in shock, wishing the police had already arrived, absurdly glad that Irene wasn't here to see this.

I heard a noise behind me, a soft swish, and my heart stuttered. The only light came from a floor lamp tilted into one corner of the room. As I turned, I saw Irene's rag-eared yellow tom, hair standing up along his back, fur spattered with something dark. He meowed pitifully. I walked over without thinking and picked him up. He was stiff for a moment, then settled against my chest as if he was suddenly safe. He emitted a rusty purr as I ran my hand over his coat. It came away red.

"Jason?" It must have been my voice, although is sounded wavering and unfamiliar, too loud in the silence. Where the hell was Kyle?

I picked my way through the detritus on the floor, still clutching the cat. Light came from beneath the kitchen door and I swung it open with my elbow. Jason was still here, all right. In the kitchen in a slowly spreading pool of blood.

This was getting to be a very bad habit.

~~~

Kyle was angry. I could tell from the firm line of his mouth, from the way he slashed at his notebook with the pen. He looked at me and looked away, opened his mouth and closed it like a fish that found itself unexpectedly on the bank.

We stood on the front lawn like strangers waiting for a bus, in each other's company only by accident. Morning was still a few hours away, but old people in slippers and housecoats huddled under the rain of light from street lamps, survivors on islands in the darkness. They looked as disoriented as I felt, and some held each other's hands like children. The trampled grass smelled of the end of summer and the flashlights bobbing around the sides and back of the house could have been fireflies, flickering away their existence. The rest of the team was inside, doing whatever it is they do, picking up things and putting them in bags, walking around and muttering to each other.

Chauncey seemed reluctant to leave me, so I held him, warm against the cold places inside of me. I'd looked him over, and it seemed none of the blood was his. I think he was just half-starved and missing his owner.

Kyle said something under his breath.

"What?"

He sighed and flipped the notebook shut. "Do you know how incredibly stupid this was?"

"Yes," I said.

That seemed to throw him.

"Well, it was. You out here playing Nancy Drew. I can't believe you came here by yourself."

"Wait 'til you know me better, you'll believe anything."

I was only making things worse.

"I won't get a chance to know you better if you get yourself killed," he said. "You knew that Shoffit was trouble, you found his

54

mother's body, for god's sake. You promised you'd call the police if he contacted you again."

"I did call the police," I reminded him.

"Yeah, and then rushed over here." He shook his head. "You could only have missed whoever killed him by a few minutes. Do you realize that?"

The problem was, I did realize that, and it scared me worse than I wanted Kyle to know. "I didn't think...." I started.

"That's right. You didn't think. And you could have gotten yourself killed. That's extra work I really don't need right now." Kyle crossed his arms and glared at me. "I think you should go home and stay there. Lock yourself in and give someone else the key. You can come down and sign your statement tomorrow."

We'd run out of words, and I was quickly running out of steam. "Oh, and I'm taking the cat home. I trust you won't need him for evidence."

"If we do, we know where you live." No smile, no indication that he was kidding. He stared at me with those green eyes until I looked away, back toward the old people and their air of frightened expectation.

Kyle didn't say much after that, although he did help me find a box for the cat. Chauncey didn't appreciate the accommodations and he howled from the seat beside me all the way back to my apartment.

# CHAPTER SEVEN

Kyle's partner, Detective Angela Ramirez, was a no-nonsense woman with a suit that matched the industrial green of the interrogation room too closely. It made me feel like she was camouflaged. She peppered me with questions and dutifully recorded my answers, then once my statement was finished, had me sign and date it. It was all very professional and business-like and after close to an hour, Kyle had yet to make an appearance. All my mental deliberations as to whether I should be contrite or ticked off that he was ticked off were going to be for naught if he was intent on avoiding me. Maybe I was stupid to expect he was going to make it a point to be here, and maybe that brief moment on the beach had been obliterated by what came afterward.

I shouldn't have worried: he was waiting in the hall when Ramirez was finished with me. She walked past him with a nod, taking my statement with her. Kyle didn't look mad anymore, he just looked tired.

"We found Paul Saroyan," he said. "He was hiding out at a friend's in Glendale. His car was parked on the street though, so I don't think he was trying too hard to disappear."

"You've arrested him?"

"He's just here for questioning right now. We're trying to establish an alibi for last night."

"Oh." That made sense in an abstract way, after all Saroyan had apparently been tailing Jason. Still, it didn't feel right.

"He wants to talk to you," Kyle said.

"Me? Why the hell would he want to talk to me?"

A smile tugged at the corner of Kyle's lips. "Well, I might have intimated that you were thinking of pressing charges for the

56

incident in the coffee shop." He shrugged. "Never hurts to have a little leverage to get somebody talking."

I felt a brief flare of anger. It didn't matter if I did or didn't want to press charges, I don't like being a token in anybody's game. I was about to say as much, then thought better of it. I crossed my arms over my chest. "So what do you suggest, Detective? You seem to have a plan."

There was a subtle shift in his stance. Whatever had been left unsaid last night was still between us.

"I'm not going to tell you what to do. It's apparent you don't listen to suggestions anyway."

A-ha, so he was still ticked at me. The truth was, I had no intention of pressing charges against Paul Saroyan. As far as I was concerned, I didn't need the headache.

"Well, if you're going to use me to threaten the guy, I might as well go let him off the hook."

I followed Kyle to another room, where Paul Saroyan sat alone at an empty table, looking at his hands. He looked smaller, less threatening, maybe because he was slumped in his seat, but also because he seemed deflated, as if whatever mania had animated him had leaked out like air from a tire. There were two flesh-colored band aids plastered to his temple, and a yellowed bruise extended down his cheekbone. I suppressed a twinge of guilt. He'd started it.

Kyle dismissed the uniform that was manning the door and pulled out the chair opposite Saroyan.

"You had something to say to the lady?" he prompted.

I sat down and Saroyan finally looked up.

"I can't tell you how sorry I am for what happened," he began. "I didn't mean to scare you." He paused. "That's not true. Maybe I did mean to scare you a little. But I thought... I guess I went a little crazy. I haven't really been sleeping."

He smiled crookedly, as if he'd forgotten the exact emotion that produced that particular facial expression.

"It's just been so hard since Jenny's been gone." He flicked his gaze toward Kyle and back to me. "The police don't seem to be doing anything. I just couldn't stand it anymore. I'd been driving around for days, everywhere I could think to. It was just chance I saw her car that night. I followed it." He stopped and rearranged the placement of his hands. "After they left that house, I lost them. It was the damned stupid stoplight." His voice broke. "After the truck hit me, the car was gone. It was just gone. So I went back to that house and waited. I looked through the mail and found out the guy's name, and I just waited. That was all I could do, you see that, right?"

I wasn't sure what he wanted me to say. I nodded.

"I called the cops about the car, but they didn't do anything."

It was my turn to glance at Kyle, but he remained unreadable.

"So when I saw you looking in Shoffit's garage, I just assumed... I mean, you might have known Jenny. You might have been looking for her too. I kept following Shoffit, and when he started arguing with you, well, I guess I just saw what I wanted to see. So I followed you. I figured if I was wrong about you and you were in on it, you weren't going to do anything to me in a public place."

He gave that crumpled smile again, and absentmindedly touched the side of his head.

"I was desperate. That's my only defense. I'm sorry." He

Ironic that the whole time I'd been worried about him attacking me, he'd been worried about the same thing. And then, of course, I hit him with the thermos.

"I'm sorry too. But I wasn't lying when I told you I don't know Jenny. I'd never heard of her until you mentioned her name."

He sank a little in the chair, as if I'd snatched up the last straw he had to grasp at.

"I'll just chalk it up to a misunderstanding and we'll forget about the whole thing," I said.

This didn't cheer him up, but I suppose that was to be expected.

"I hope you find her."

Ramirez was outside the door waiting for us and they traded off like tag-team wrestlers. Kyle and I headed down the hallway.

"Is it true that he called in the car and nobody did anything about it?'

Kyle stopped in his tracks and turned to face me. "There's something you have to understand. Saroyan had been calling multiple times a day, every day. He was always checking up, always leaving messages. Turns out, going back over the logs, he even called in a tip about you. After a while, I think they might have started treating him like background noise."

"No wonder he was desperate."

"I'm not saying it's right or fair or reasonable, but it happens. We can't give everybody their own babysitter."

"But now you're going to listen to him, aren't you? I mean, you've got actual bodies now."

"We're putting it all together. He's not off the hook for Shoffit's murder yet. He had motive, if he thought Shoffit was responsible for his girlfriend's disappearance. He says he's got an alibi for that night but we haven't confirmed it."

"And Irene? How does this all fit with what happened to Irene?"

"I don't know. But we're going to be looking at it, I promise you." He glanced up and down the hall. "You know the porn outfit I was telling you about, Bravo? Well, in addition to Jennifer Chandler, there are two other young women reported missing who did work for them."

"Well, that certainly should raise a red flag."

"Don't make too much of yet. Girls like that, they tend to move around a lot..."

I didn't like the tone in his voice, the easy dismissal that had crept in. "What do you mean, girls like that?"

Kyle sighed. "I don't mean it like that. But it's a fact that drug users and runaways tend to just pick up and go without leaving a forwarding address. It complicates things."

"I don't think Paul Saroyan thinks it's all that complicated."

"He needs to leave it up to us. You see what happens when

people just take things into their own hands."

I wasn't sure if he was referring to the altercation with the thermos or my near miss at Irene's house. Probably both.

"And you've got to understand that to people like that poor guy and me, the cops have a thousand Jennys and Irenes when we just have the one. And we've just lost them."

His face dropped a bit and I was glad. He needed to know how the other side feels. Maybe too many incidents with too many perps had blinded him to the pains of everyday people.

"I do understand that. The problem in this job is that you can never tell those people everything you know, everything you're doing to help them. Sometimes they just have to take things by faith."

"Sorry, I'm not much with the whole faith thing."

"Not like that. You know what I'm trying to say." He took my hands in his. "And if I was angry with you last night it wasn't because I was concerned that you might mess up my crime scene."

Oh great, now he shows his humanity. Thermos attacks I can handle in public places. I wasn't too sure about this.

"How about I just stay out of crime scenes altogether. It'll be my mid-year's resolution."

"Too bad you've already signed your statement. I'd like to get that in writing."

He left me at the door with a promise to keep me updated on the case. He didn't promise anything else.

~~~

When I got home, the message light was blinking a red dot on the Moorish window panes. I hit the play button and was rewarded with a voice I didn't recognize informing me of a "management" meeting at the theater on Monday.

"What the hell now?" I asked Syd, Cat, and Chauncey, wherever he was.

There was a resounding crash from the bedroom. Well, that

answered that question. Chauncey's arrival had been about as popular as a trip to the vet's. Things had apparently gotten worse since I'd been gone.

As I made my way toward the hall, I saw the broken fronds of the geranium that had resided in the recessed window overlooking the side alley. The leaves looked like imploring hands reaching out from the dark soil that poured across the Persian runner. I stepped over the terra cotta shards and pushed open the bedroom door.

I entered the wasteland that had been my sanctuary. A precipitation of clothes a foot deep littered the closet floor and my make-up table was awash with cotton balls and tiny brushes. There were compacts lying on the floor, where I picked up the beginning of a trail of cat feet colored Santa Fe bronze. I followed the trail to my dresser where my collection of Russian nesting dolls stood decapitated in their aprons. The Egyptian gauze wound around the top of the wrought iron canopy bed hung in tatters and the quilted ivory lace comforter puddled onto the floor. From beneath it extended a ratty, yellow tail.

"Oh, Chauncey," I said through clenched teeth. "You have been a very bad cat."

Before I could make a grab, Chauncey shot out from the other side of the bed, jumped and skidded across the polished surface of the dresser, sending more dolls crashing to the floor in his wake. He stopped and watched me with his ears flattened against his head, the arc of his spine stiff and bristling. His tail looked like a bottle brush.

I murmured comforting words to him, but Chauncey wasn't buying it. He sprang for the open doorway and I sprang too, with considerably less success. I got to my feet and charged off down the hall after him, not quite knowing what I would do when I caught him.

Sydney's hoarse little bulldog voice began to grind from the kitchen, and Catherine yowled from the living room, an eerie, piercing cry unique to cats who can't hear themselves. It sounded like she was being skinned.

I felt pressure building up in my skull like the beginning of a migraine, and I could hear a faint white-noise hum filling the room and making my teeth ache. From the corner of my eye I caught a movement on the wall. Either it was a minor tremor or Otto was making his displeasure known. The framed movie poster from It's a Wonderful Life shuddered against the age-worn plaster and then fell to the floor, the glass in the frame cracking with a sharp report, sending a spit of spider webs from the center outward.

"Enough!" I let the scream loose, both hands clamped over my ears. Blessed silence. I collapsed on the couch, a bundle of used energy. There was Chauncey under the coffee table, huddled and stiff, eyes glassy, panting hard. He'd had enough too. I returned him to the box by the front door, knowing that if I didn't get him out of here soon, one of us was not going to survive. But he was Irene's cat, and I couldn't just take him to the pound.

I knocked on the door across the hall and Mrs. Cullum peered out at me, looking like some small nocturnal creature, a hedgehog maybe. She wasn't a cat person. The second floor was also a wash. One or the other of the Lamberts was allergic, and Mr. Alexander had a mean-tempered myna that rasped obscenities at me as I backed out the door. The artist in Apartment #2 wasn't home, but then he never was. Sharon, who occupied Apartment #1, was probably the person I knew best in the building. She was a little younger than me, and a buyer for an upscale dress shop. I would have crossed my fingers as I pressed her bell with my elbow, but the box prevented that. I waited and pressed again.

"Maddie, you need something?" Sharon's sunny voice carried down the hallway from the door to the back garden. She had a handful of pale pink climbing roses, and there were faint green smudges on the knees of her jeans.

Chauncey picked that moment to poke his head from the open square at the top of the box. I explained the situation in a rush of words, and I must have struck the right note between desperation and sincerity. Sharon laid the roses by the door and reached in for the cat. It wasn't love at first sight, exactly, but it was close enough.

# CHAPTER EIGHT

Sometimes you just don't have room for dessert. I remember once when my dad insisted on sundaes after an outing at Chavez Ravine to cheer the Dodgers victory, and not just any sundaes, but the huge two-person dish that was the specialty at the old Movie Diner. It was more a feat of architecture than culinary skill, beginning with a foundation of eight scoops of your choice of ice cream flavors. Then there was a mezzanine of fresh fruits awash in caramel syrup and dotted with minced nuts. There was one big, flattened scoop of vanilla on top of all that, either for good measure or to hold it all together. It was all topped off with homemade chocolate fudge sauce, a mass of whipped cream, a dusting of more nuts, cherries, and multicolored jimmies. They called it "Cloud Nine."

The problem that day was I'd just spent the previous week home from school with a stomach virus and the hotdog and peanuts at the game were all I felt I could safely ingest. But Dad really wanted that sundae, and I remember the look in his eyes when they brought it out to our booth, big spoon handles sticking out from either side. I guess he wanted me to know that I was normal again. He always had a way of making me feel not special, but regular, just a girl with her ponytail through the back of her ball cap, laughing with syrup on her chin and whipped cream at the tip of her nose.

Today felt like a sundae kind of day. No job to go to yet, and thankfully no funerals or police interrogations either. It was a day in between. I'd powered through the cold hard facts of all the unpleasantness since that night at the theater: Irene was at peace, Jason couldn't threaten me anymore, Paul Saroyan seemed more like a victim than a menace, and poor Jennifer Chandler might just have slipped sideways for a while, sorting out her bad choices. Where my spoon got in trouble was the fluffy unknown of future possibilities.

Goodness knows it was warm enough for ice cream. The thermometer on the door to the roof garden read 91 when I had taken Sydney out there an hour ago. Strains of Van Morrison met us from next door, where the neighbors in the next house over were setting up tables and chairs for a mid-summer party. The 4th of July had passed and Labor Day was yet to come, but those were relative days. Literally the days you spend with relatives. Neighbors found the days in between to be more suited for their affairs. I had gotten the invitation in my mailbox downstairs but if I was going to stop by, it would be later in the day, toward sunset. They always put out those criss-crossing white bulbs that light up so pretty at night. That and it's a hell of a lot cooler once the San Gabriels eat up the sun.

For now I didn't feel like making the effort, having to make conversation, having to listen. My head was too full of all the things I hadn't planned to be pondering, like death and stalking. Or a real acting job and a boyfriend. It was all I could manage to keep those items on the correct side of that imaginary page I was authoring.

Sydney and Cat had gone to my bedroom to sleep because the window was open, letting a nice, even breeze fill the space between the mattress and the floor to create a prime napping spot. I opened the windows in the turret to let out any rising heat, and to let in the soft sounds of people talking, music, and laughter.

I flipped on the TV but muted it so that I could just watch the ballgame unfold. It was the bottom of the fifth inning and the Dodgers were up by two on the Padres. When they went to a commercial break -- I don't use the DVR for live events, bad luck -- I went to the kitchen and pulled out the scalloped glass dish I bought at a tag sale a few summers ago and loaded it up with pistachio-cherry-chip. I sliced a banana on top, then added some Greek yogurt and granola, a slightly healthier version of the Cloud.

The activity in the kitchen had alerted Sydney to the possibility of food and I found him on the couch when I got back to the game. The vet had warned me that he really should lose a pound or two, but she wasn't looking at his eyes right now. I offered him a dripping spoonful. Cat suddenly appeared on the sofa arm and demanded equal time. She really likes the yogurt, so I obliged. And we sat, our weird little family, watching the Dodgers play, sharing our sundae and the relative quiet of a nameless day in between.

~~~

You forget how good an afternoon nap feels until you awake from one. I sat up quick and board straight on the couch, trying to blink the room into clarity.

"Syd! I'm getting it," I shouted making my way over to the phone.

"Hello."

"Hi, Maddie. Did I wake you?"

How is it people think they can always tell when you've been asleep? And why do we always feel the need to lie about it? I briefly considered trying, but knew it was a lost cause.

"That's okay, Kyle. I was just taking a nap. Is something wrong?"

"No." He sounded hurt that I'd made the assumption. "I was just calling to check on the cat. Little guy seemed pretty upset the other night."

"Yeah, he did, didn't he," I said, way too sarcastically.

"Well sometimes they do get themselves into trouble."

"Uh-huh, curiosity, you mean?"

"Well you know what they say."

"He's fine. My neighbor took him in after he caused a ruckus here. I can give you her number if it'll make you feel any better."

He sighed. "Okay, I'm not calling about the cat. Or anything else that's happened. Well, maybe just one thing."

"Did I leave out an important piece of information in my statement yesterday?"

"No. I just think kisses like the one we had on the beach are like potato chips." His voice was soft and low.

"Oh, you mean all salty and bad for your heart. They certainly can be."

"Maddie, come on."

I laughed. "I'm sorry. I couldn't resist."

"Neither can I. So what do you say?"

"You want me to come over to the police station and kiss you again?"

"Well that would be one idea. How about something a little more formal?"

"You want me to dress up, come over to the police station and kiss you again?"

"You're just a regular mind-reader aren't you?"

"Actually, if you must know, my superpower is the ability to draw out the truth."

"That and wielding a deadly milk thermos."

"I do what I have to do."

"Well do you have anything to do tomorrow, superhero?"

"Let me check my calendar, no. What do you have in mind?"

"Why don't we go on a real date? Not a party where I'm your police detail and not a crime scene or an interrogation room. Someplace sane."

"Sorry, I don't have anything to wear for sane. How about casual sane?"

He chuckled. "The more casual the better, but it'll take most of the day."

"Sounds like you really need to practice your unbuttoning skills."

I couldn't tell if his momentary silence was because I'd shocked him or because he was painting a mental picture.

"I'm just going to let that one go for now," he said.

Oh, great. "Now I'm officially embarrassed." I hate it when I catch myself up in my own mistaken double-entendre. "Sorry, I got greedy."

"So, this friend of mine has a boat down at Long Beach and I thought you might like to take it out tomorrow. That is, if you like boats."

"I like boats fine. But I should warn you, swimming is another superpower with me. You'll have some catching up to do."

"I think I can keep up with you. How about I pick you up around nine? That'll give us time to stop for supplies on the way down."

We said our goodbyes and I set the receiver back on the cradle. "Well, Syd. What do you think? Mom has a real date."

At first I thought he was happy for me, then I noticed the low angles of shadow stretching across the room. He did his little dance to bring the point home.

# CHAPTER NINE

It was one of those perfect early fall days, the kind that makes living in southern California worthwhile, even when you factor in the mudslides, the earthquakes and the crime rate. The sky was a blameless blue dotted with cottony white puffs of cloud that looked like whipped cream along the top of the Santa Monica Mountains. Some writer once said that L.A. had the personality of a paper cup, but there is more there, a palette of colors and textures that you don't see in the movies, don't read about in books. It's a vast and remarkable place with a temperamental soul, but on a good day in L.A. it seems like you can start over, awash in possibilities.

We headed south down the Long Beach Freeway, surrounded by sleek convertibles, imports, and muscle cars in various stages of restoration. Whenever traffic slowed, I caught snatches of songs from passing cars, five-second symphonies that ranged from salsa to alternative to opera, the music of the cosmos carried on a breeze that brought a salt tang inland.

We passed through the industrial section of Long Beach to the oceanfront, where the skyline was an eclectic mix of sharp new buildings and more graceful remnants of the city's past. Kyle pulled into the lot of an open-air market to get picnic supplies. We walked among all the sensual fruits and vegetables with old couples, teen-aged sweethearts, and thirty-something parents pushing strollers, loading our basket with green grapes and tart plums, lacy green leaf lettuce and a pomegranate Kyle had to try. We also selected a bag of Kaiser rolls from an umbrella-topped cart, and pasta salad, spicy mustard, and meat and cheese from the deli.

At the marina, we split our provisions between us and wove past dozens of dockside craft. The Queen Mary stood sentinel across a shimmering blue finger of water, resplendent in red, white and black, as we made our way to the slip. Kyle stopped next to a single-mast sailboat that arched sleek and white out of the water and bobbed gently with the current.

"Is this your boat?" I asked. The admiration must have been evident in my voice.

"Unfortunately no," Kyle said, with a measure of regret, "I don't have the time or the money. Someday, maybe. This belongs to a buddy of mine and he lets me use it when he's not in town. Luckily for me this week he's not in town."

After setting sail for deeper waters, we unpacked and prepared the food in the small galley, then carried it up on deck and spread out a blanket. We ate roast beef and provolone sandwiches and munched grapes, serenaded by easy breakers and light jazz, filling in the blanks in our personal resumes.

"You ready to show me your superpower?" Kyle finally asked.

"Pardon me?" I was full of food and sun and realized I had at some point stopped paying attention to what Kyle was saying and instead just enjoying watching him talk.

"Wasn't there some tough talk about swimming?"

"Be careful what you ask for," I said.

He stripped off his shirt and jeans to reveal trunks underneath while I ducked into the cabin. He was seated on the side ladder when I returned in my yellow bikini. "Wow," he said.

I shot him a sideways glance and then took two steps and dove over the railing. When I surfaced, he was only a few feet away.

"I should have warned you I'm part fish," I said.

"What's the other part?"

"You'll have to find out."

Something about being half-naked and wet melts away inhibitions, and I found myself breaking the horseplay to roll in a watery embrace with Kyle. After our last swim of the day, I climbed up the ladder and reclined against the light oak of the topside benches. I laid my head back and squinted into the afternoon sunlight that sparkled across the water.

"God, you're beautiful," Kyle said as he walked across the bow toward me. He bent down and lifted me into his arms, giving me the warmest, softest kiss I'd had in a long time.

He swept me down the narrow steps to the cabin bunk, all light and gleaming, the wood the color of good claret. The sheets were cool as he laid me across them and when he kissed me again my pulse quickened, the rhythm of my heart picking up tempo. He pulled back and looked into my eyes, asking permission. I pulled him down with me.

When I woke it was almost dark and I was wrapped in Kyle's arms.

"Hey," he said softly.

"Have I been asleep too long?"

"Not long. Just a half hour or so."

"You've been lying here awake with me cramping your arm for a half hour?"

He ran a hand over my side and let it rest on my hip. "Seemed like only seconds."

We docked the boat and had dinner at a casual little seaside eatery where no one complained if you had sand in your shoes. I barely remember what I ordered, I just remember the reflection of the moonlit water in Kyle's eyes. I knew I wasn't technically in love with him yet, but there was a possibility where one hadn't existed in a long time.

We drove back home enveloped in that special sweetness that only comes at the end of a really fine day. I fought back the urge to invite Kyle up and instead ended the evening with a kiss at my door. I didn't want to use up all my good fortune in one night.

~~~

A few weeks ago my life had been uneventful, not necessarily the life I wanted, but one with definite edges, with a measure of comforting consistency. The way I felt now, uncertain and untethered, was the way I'd felt after my parents died.

I can still remember the call. A month past high school graduation, the lazy warmth of summer that stretched though the days and lingered after dark, the feeling that I was holding my breath and waiting for my life to begin. That night I'd fallen asleep downstairs, a book in my hand and the silky champagne-colored throw that half-covered me bleeding into the pale leather couch. It was dream-like, still, ten years later. My voice, so unfamiliar at that moment, echoing against the marble, asking, "What?" Eventually understanding, but not believing, that Leo Pryce had missed a curve on the seaside drive back from Santa Barbara, missed it so completely that the Caddy had kissed the sand below, rushed to meet it like a lover's embrace. My beautiful mother dead, but hardly scratched, and that had been the hardest part to accept, especially in the retrospectives that played during the days that followed. My father had left no clips behind, so I relied on memory to draw up his kind eyes, the way the skin around them crinkled when he was about to laugh.

Now I was sitting on my couch, thinking for the first time, maybe, that I had choices. Things had been in a simple rut the past few years. Maybe I hadn't been happy, exactly, but I was well-defined.

Sydney gave a small whine, and I looked into his liquid brown eyes.

"I know, I know. You're just the incredibly patient one, aren't you?" I rose to let him out and caught the blink of the answering machine out of the corner of my eye. I'd missed it when I got home, and the machine was usually the first thing I checked when I came through the door. I'm honestly not a technophobe, but the answering machine was something I couldn't give up. I don't like that cell phones make you instantly available, even though that's an anachronism for a struggling actress, and I rarely gave out my cell number. Even though I know I could set it up so that I have an answering service, or have calls go automatically to voicemail, I still liked the fact that there was a gate, a real physical gate in the form of a silver and black box, standing between me and the rest of the world.

I hit the playback and after a moment Erik's Wellman's voice filled the silence: so sorry he'd missed me, looking forward to getting together, give him a call when I got in. Sydney danced back and forth as I stared at the box. When I reached for the receiver, he barked sharply.

"All right," I said. He followed me upstairs, nails ticking on the steps, and darted out when I unlocked the door to the roof. I waited as he visited the flowers, trying to formulate what I would say if I called Erik back. Fact was, I'd temporarily forgotten my plan to get in touch with Evan, and Erik's call had taken me off guard. The prospect of a job was tantalizing, but I'd been around long enough to know that opportunities vaporized as quickly as they appeared. Their offer had sounded like a line from the moment I'd heard it, and I'd already walked the grass off that field.

Once we were back inside, I played back the message, and then impulsively punched in the number that Erik had left. Two rings and I hit his voicemail. Great, I make the plunge and ended up playing phone tag. I outlined tomorrow's schedule, such as it was, and left my cell number.

# CHAPTER TEN

The first thing I noticed as I drove up to the Orpheus was a little flag of yellow crime tape, fluttering forlornly from a wrought iron stay at the mouth of the alley. The second thing I noticed was the marquee. The neon scrollwork surrounded big red letters that spelled out CLOSED FOR RENOVATION. That was either good news or bad news, but I resisted the urge to figure it out and pulled into the parking lot.

It was cool and dim inside the building, and I followed the faint sound of voices to the office, where everyone else sat in chairs appropriated from the break room. The man behind the desk wore a lightweight summer suit that looked expensive. The collar of his electric blue shirt seemed too tight, but maybe that was an optical illusion caused by his fleshy neck and florid complexion. He wasn't fat, but solid, and his close-cropped curly red-gold hair put me in mind of a television evangelist. His too-white smile and a smattering of gold jewelry only reinforced that impression.

"Ms. Pryce, I trust? Burton Willis. So glad you could join us." The same slightly oily voice from my machine. He pumped my hand enthusiastically, then motioned toward the last available chair. Gene rolled his eyes as I sat down next to him.

"Thank you all for coming. I know you're eager to find out why I called you here, so let's get right to it." He looked like he wished he had a storyboard and pointer. Instead, he shuffled a stack of papers in front of him.

"Hollywood exists because of tourists," he began. "But years of neglect, the Northridge quake, and the, uh, recent unpleasantness, well, let me just say this: People don't always get what they expect when they come to Hollywood."

No shit.

Willis continued, the color shining through his even tan. I wondered what his blood pressure was like. I looked past him, at a crack in the plaster wall that looked like a jagged lightning bolt, while he waxed poetic about the resurgence of the theater district on Broadway; about Mann's, The Egyptian, Disney's El Capitan. Apparently the owners of the Orpheus were ready to cash in on the new demand for old things. He paced behind the desk, the rest of us forgotten, and I picked up phrases like "espresso bar" and "interactive video." So there was the bad news. He finally wound down, like one of those clockwork monkeys that bang the cymbals, then seemed to remember that he had an audience.

"Unfortunately," he said. "The renovation will be a time-consuming process. We want to maintain the character of the theater while endeavoring to provide state-of-the-art entertainment. We anticipate closing for at least three or four months, and that's if everything stays on schedule."

There was a collective sigh, and Willis seemed to realize we'd gotten the point he had approached in such a circuitous manner.

"Of course, you're all welcome to come back when we re-open." His pass-the-collection-plate smile turned as thin as cheap tin. "We can't pay you in the interim. The renovations will be expensive and we don't expect to recoup our investment for some time. We'll understand if you feel you just can't make those kind of arrangements." Or in other words, you aren't exactly fired, but it would sure be helpful if you quit.

Willis reclaimed his seat behind the desk and folded his hands in front of him. "In closing, we appreciate you coming in today, and I'll be glad to answer any questions you have individually." His smile widened, but his eyes were dismissive.

It took us a few moments to overcome the inertia that had descended on the room. A few questions about paychecks and we began to shuffle out. I was the last through the doorway, and Willis cleared his throat behind me.

"Ms. Pryce? If you could wait just one moment, there is further business I need to discuss with you."

Gene turned around in front of me and caught my eye. "I'll wait," he mouthed. I walked back in and pulled the door shut behind me.

"I thought this was a matter best handled in private," he began. I didn't like the conspiratorial attitude he'd suddenly adopted. "Due to the nature of your involvement, of course, other arrangements can be made."

"Excuse me?"

"Well, a buy-out, of course. Or there is the possibility of you staying on if you prefer. We could negotiate a salary until we re-open." Willis looked at me expectantly.

"Pardon me, Mr. Willis," I said. "But I have no idea what you're talking about."

"Your percentage in the theater, Ms. Pryce." He looked like he was losing patience with me, and the red blotches were creeping up from under his collar again.

"I don't know where you get your information," I said. "But I don't have any percentage in the theater. Until a week ago, I was just an usher."

Willis grunted through pursed lips and sorted through his papers until he found what he was looking for.

"According to this, Irene Shoffit left you her share of the theater. Twelve percent is not a majority, but legally, it still makes you a partner."

"This is the first I've heard of it."

Burton Willis sighed. "That figures. Look, I suggest you contact Mrs. Shoffit's lawyer." He unclipped a beige business card from the page in his hand and passed it over to me. "He can straighten this out and then you can get back to me so we can discuss the specifics." He reached into his jacket pocket and retrieved another card, this one with his name and a Burbank address.

He picked up a calfskin briefcase from beside his chair and began to stuff papers into it. He looked up again, as if surprised

I was still there. "And I am sorry. I understand that you and Mrs. Shoffit were close. My sympathies."

I took the hint and walked out of the office.

Gene, Pete and Harry were leaning against the counter of the snack bar, looking like modern-day cowboys after a long trail ride.

"He didn't hit on you, did he?" Gene said. He seemed to be only half-joking.

"No. Just some business stuff." I didn't want to explain that I'd somehow become one of them, the faceless theater owners out to gut the Orpheus.

"Guy's a jerk," Harry offered.

"Yeah," Gene said. "Hey, Maddie, we were thinking about going out and getting a drink. Kind of a send-off for the old place. Want to come?"

"Sure." I felt like a drink anyway. Or several of them.

~ ~ ~

Pete had offered a final toast before leaving, telling us that he'd be able to spend evenings with the missus from now on. He didn't seem that happy about it. I watched him shuffle out the door of The Grind, a semi-trendy bar with smooth chrome booths and an occasional minor-league celebrity. We had chosen it because it was a block from the theater and had a happy hour that lasted until eight.

Gene walked to the bar for another, and I watched him slide onto a stool next to a plainly pretty redhead. I was still nursing my second Black Russian, and Harry was way ahead of me, drinking bourbon in a short glass, no ice. He seemed to be taking it harder than the rest of us.

"I'd like to thank you for hiring me," he finally said, his eyes caught fast by the swirling patterns in his glass.

"Yeah, I'm sorry it didn't last."

"Nothing does."

That was my cue. I reached down and felt around for my

purse. I'd managed to kick it under the lip of the booth bench and now it seemed stuck.

"I knew something bad was going to happen," Harry said. "Bad begets bad. Whole damn town falling apart. What with Irene getting herself killed. And then her kid. His fault, anyway."

I stopped fighting my purse and sat up.

"Jason?"

Harry took a long sip of bourbon then fumbled in his suit pocket for a match to re-light his cigar.

"Knew that crap was going to get him killed. Shame his momma got dragged into it. I told her the last report I gave her that it was going to end bad."

I sat very still for a moment, then decided that maybe I should finish my drink.

# CHAPTER ELEVEN

"Wait. Back up a minute. You were following Jason? Have you gone to the police with this?"

Harry snorted. "Cops don't wanna hear anything from me."

He drained his glass and waved over his head to get the waitress's attention. I'd officially lost track of the number of drinks he'd had.

"His mom was getting pretty nervous and she wanted to find out exactly what he was up to. Like he would ever tell her anything. All's he did was sleep in her house and eat her groceries. Didn't think for a minute what he was doing to his mom."

Harry leaned over his fresh drink and gave me a wry smile, then laughed and took a gulp of bourbon. "Ol' Jason wasn't the brightest bulb in the string. He was strictly Charlie Potatoes, running drugs for lower-level Hollywood types, but he wasn't slick enough to go very far. Always drawing too much attention to himself. Figure he had some big ideas and not enough smarts and that's what punched his ticket."

"Did you tell Irene about the drugs?"

"Oh, I told her. I think she already knew it. But she wouldn't admit it, told me I was mistaken." He laughed again. "I even gave her the pictures."

"You have pictures? Harry, you've got to go to the police with this."

He leaned back in his chair and folded his hands over his gut. "I don't got to do anything. Let the cops do their own legwork. I'll be too busy looking for a job and they won't pay me anything for information."

"Give me what you've got and I'll take it to the cops."

"I suppose you'd like to have my dead wife's furniture too. You didn't make the payments on it." He was waiting for another drink that he definitely didn't need. "People think they just have the right to help themselves to anything, don't they. Public domain they call it. You know, like the Happy Birthday Song. Some poor sap struggled over it and now it's everybody's and he doesn't even see a dime."

"I think he's dead, Harry."

"And that makes it all the better, huh. Being owed is being owed, and I don't care how dead you are. Hell, I know what it's like to be told you aren't needed anymore, then your wife gets shot by some thug and nobody there to stop it. Cops my ass. Honey, I ain't taking shit to the cops."

It was obvious Harry wasn't a life-of-the-party drunk, and I doubted if he continued to drink all night he would change from his present condition. His mind was in that foggy place where things go wrong if only by imagination.

I decided to take another tack. "How about I pay you for the information?"

"How 'bout you hire me?"

"Hire you?"

The waitress set another drink in front of him and rolled her eyes. I couldn't very well yank it away from him, so I waited patiently while he finished it.

He squinted at me. "Fifty bucks a day plus expenses."

I wondered what a half-decent bottle of bourbon cost these days.

Harry reached into his inside pocket and produced a battered brown billfold. He fumbled the wallet open, his old, swollen fingers looking too fleshy to function. He pulled a card out and handed it across the table with a flourish, overcompensating and knocking three empty lowball glasses to the floor.

"'S my address. Work at home, now."

His hands shook as he pointed to the bottom line of the card and I nodded recognition.

That last drink was his break point. Practicing alcoholics hit a level when the next drink sends them to that other place, where only their warped internal logic functions. I thought briefly of the vodka bottles my mother had stopped trying to hide, the juncture at which she no longer cared and her public persona became only a dream. I knew there was no use talking to Harry any more tonight.

"How are you getting home, Harry?"

"Home?" He looked at me with unfocused eyes.

"Why don't you let me drop you off?"

"Sure, sure. Drop me off."

I threw a twenty on the table and helped him to his feet.

The address was easy enough to find, and in the scant moonlight the post-war tract house looked like a child's block left out in the rain. Harry poured himself out the door with a half-wave and a mumble.

I watched for several painful moments as he tried various keys in the lock and then stumbled through the door.

I drove away.

It was nearly midnight when I unlocked the door to my apartment. I could see from the entryway that the answering machine wasn't blinking. I flipped on the light and checked to make sure it was plugged in. It was. I stared at it for a moment with a sense of betrayal, inventing internal maladies. No message on my cell and now nothing on the machine. Kyle should have called. This was a total breach of post-coital etiquette.

I flopped onto the couch and was rewarded with a faint squeak. I scooted over and pulled out Sydney's little purple and green hedgehog. He loved the thing and I didn't know why. I squeezed it a couple times and whistled softly. I needed a sympathetic ear. There was no tick of nails on the floor, no answering woof. Where the hell was he? I whistled louder.

"Sydney, you're slacking off on the job here."

Nothing.

I felt the rib bones over my heart knuckling together like two fists clenching.

I mounted the turret stairs, my eyes on the weak moonlight that filtered through the circle of windows above. I reached for the light switch and was barely able to register dark movement to my left. Something hit me with the impact of a corn-fed linebacker, and I went down into the darkness, my right knee followed by my right elbow as the shadow that had flattened me shot out into the center of the room and made the turn for the roof stairs. Without thinking, I was on my feet following. The figure pounded up the metal stairs in front of me and the roof door banged open. I caught it before it closed and watched him sprint between tea olives trees and geranium pots, heading for the edge of the roof. I grabbed a spade from beside the door and rushed after him, dodging a stack of empty terra cotta pots and hurdling the low brick partition that enclosed one of the flower beds. If he'd hurt my dog, he was going to be sorry.

He paused at the line of the roof and jumped. I ran to the spot, fully expecting to see him flattened on the concrete in the alley, but he was nowhere in sight. While I scanned the ground, he reappeared at the mouth of the alley and disappeared into the street. It wasn't until then that I noticed the nylon rope secured to the ledge with a climbing piton. I had the feeling he wasn't your garden-variety burglar.

My adrenaline ebbed and I felt raw pain radiating from every spot where I'd made contact with the turret floor. It took just a second to register Sydney's bark, and I turned to find him crouched beneath a white, wrought iron bench. I knelt down and he covered the short distance, leaping into my arms. I buried my face in his fur and hid there until my breathing returned to a semblance of normalcy and my heart stopped hammering against the wall of my chest.

I locked and chained the roof door and carried Sydney down the stairs. I had to call Kyle now. I had no choice. I stood for a moment with my hand on the phone, gave up and punched in the number.

~~~

I sat on the couch with a protective arm around Sydney and Kyle sat beside me, Cat uncharacteristically docile on his lap. She'd been in the closet and missed the whole thing. The burglary guys bustled through the rest of the apartment, checking for fingerprints, I supposed.

"You didn't call," I said.

"I know. I was so overwhelmed. I didn't want to call up and say something stupid. I just needed a little time to think."

"That's what they all say. Sure, get the girl in bed and conveniently lose her number."

"I thought it was obvious how I felt about you."

"Kyle, you don't even know me."

"But I want to, Maddie. I really do."

A plainclothes in a faded blue suit from the mid-'80s interrupted before Kyle could make any more lame excuses.

"We're about finished here." He looked at me. "Ma'am, we'll have your statement typed up and you can come by tomorrow and check over it."

Great, another morning downtown. I waited until the two detectives were out the door and turned to Kyle. "Look, I'm sorry. But I expected you to call, and then there's some psycho in my apartment and, well, it hasn't been a great couple of weeks."

"I know. And I was going to call. Honest." Kyle looked at me with those green eyes growing luminous in his tanned face, soft, like pools of a lagoon spreading out to take over more bottomland. I was hooked.

"You want a drink?"

"If you're having one, sure."

I went to the kitchen and grabbed the vodka and two glasses. I considered telling Kyle that Harry had been following Jason, but I wanted to check it out for myself. Harry was a boozehound, maybe trying to make himself seem more important than he was. If the police got involved, Harry would probably just clam up anyway. If I found anything, I could always take it straight to Kyle.

When I re-entered the living room, Kyle was trying to detach from Cat again.

"She likes you," I said as I poured two fingers into each glass. "You should take that as a compliment."

"And you trust her judgment?"

"Sometimes."

He managed to set her on the floor as I slid in beside him. He began stroking my hair. "Why don't I stay here tonight. I'll even sleep on the couch."

"No. That's okay."

"What? Afraid you can't handle the temptation?"

"Believe me, that's the last thing on my mind right now." That was almost the truth. Much as I wanted to give in to his offer, I needed peace and quiet and having him in close proximity was not going to give it to me.

Kyle looked wounded, so I held his hand. "I appreciate your concern, but I want to be alone right now, get some sleep, start over in the morning. Besides, Otto will watch out for me."

"Who's Otto?"

"No one. My guardian angel." Now was not the time to introduce the resident ghost to the boyfriend.

"But we're okay, right. I mean, you and me?"

"Yeah, just as long as you remember to call me next time."

I leaned my head against his shoulder and we sat that way for a while, sipping our drinks in the silence. I pushed off the lethargy that embraced me, then caressed Kyle's head and pulled him toward me, kissing him hard enough that his lips took a moment to part and kiss back.

I broke away. "Okay. Go home now. I'm going to bed."

Kyle inhaled. "You sure?"

"I'm sure."

Kyle checked the perimeter of the apartment one more time before leaving. I thought I was going to have to shove him out the door, but after a longing glance over his shoulder he disappeared into the quiet darkness of the hallway.

Once the glasses were put away and I'd brushed my teeth, I ran out of things to keep my mind off the assault on my home. It could have turned out much worse than a bruised knee and a sore elbow. I could have been killed. Or Sydney, or Cat. My world began shrinking when Irene died and now it closed in on me like a snare, trapping me on a sandbar that was no longer safely above the waterline. Sydney followed me up to the turret and jumped into the centermost window seat. I sat next to him, my bare legs rubbing against the damask cloth, and let my head fall back against the cool window. Sydney climbed onto my lap, puddling my oversized Snoopy T-shirt under his warm belly. I hugged him close against the vast darkness on the other side of the glass.

# CHAPTER TWELVE

The alarm pulled me from vague and unsettling dreams. I'd set it for ten because I had no place important to be and figured that Harry would be sleeping late too.

I was sharing my scrambled egg breakfast with Cat when the phone trilled from the living room. Sydney ran ahead of me, barking all the way. He stopped when I picked up the receiver.

"Sorry I missed you the other day," Erik said. "I was wondering when you could fit me into your schedule."

"Well, actually, I don't have a schedule anymore. I've suddenly found myself jobless."

"I'm so sorry, Maddie. How about dinner tonight? It would give me a chance to discuss that role with you," Erik continued. "We need to move along in pre-production and we're ready to get the casting lined up."

Erik was talking like it was a done deal. And what did I have to lose?

"Okay. That sounds great."

"I'll pick you up at six, if that's okay. And wear something stunning."

"Geez, I don't know if I have anything. You've seen my one stunning dress already."

"Oh, I bet you can make anything look good."

"We'll see."

After I got off the phone with Erik I called Irene's lawyer, who confirmed my partial ownership of the theater. He apologized profusely, explaining there'd been some mix-up and that was why I hadn't been contacted earlier. I figured it was just my rotten luck.

~ ~ ~

Harry's house looked even more pitiful by daylight. Bare patches of dirt outlined long-forgotten flowerbeds, probably those of Mrs. Harry. The small, square porch sagged like a soggy piece of white bread dipped in coffee.

I mounted the three paint-chipped steps and knocked on the screened door. As I waited for Harry to answer, I took a look down the side of the house at a narrow strip of grass gone brown and the chain link fence beyond. Did Harry have a dog? Had there been kids? It was hard to associate any of the splendors of suburban family life with the sad man I'd dropped off last night.

I waited, knocked again. Maybe I was too early and Harry was still snoring peacefully where he'd landed, or I'd waited too long and he was off spending his days however he spent them.

The door opened a few inches, groaning in protest. One eye, half a face, a Salvador Dali greeting. Harry saw it was me, pulled the door open and stood there in a flannel shirt and chinos, feet half covered by black old-man slippers, real leather masquerading as cheap vinyl, creases gone long at the bending points. He looked at me without speaking, leaving me to wonder whether he'd forgotten his invitation.

As I prepared to explain myself he dipped his head and said, "Excuse my manners. Come in, Maddie."

He said my name with an easy familiarity, as if now that I'd seen him at his worst and come back for more I'd passed his litmus test. I stepped through the doorway and the air seemed to change, as if I'd stepped from everyday existence into a snow-dome with dust swirling in the place of winter precipitation, a museum quiet and dark, not available for visitors.

"Coffee?" he said hopefully.

"Sure. Cream if you have it."

Harry disappeared through an archway at the rear of the room, leaving me to interpret the living history on my own. My eyes followed filtered light coming from the slatted wooden blinds, more an afternoon than a morning light, heavy with dust motes as it fell across a sofa, chair and the rug they anchored. The chintz furniture with its yellow background and small pink-and-green flowers brought the quality of light up and cheered the room at the far corners. A plain, dark oak tray table sat before the sofa with its four sides in the upright position, a turtle in its shell warding off the intruder. The wall in front of me and behind the overstuffed chair was covered in all types of clocks: cuckoos with their dusty pine cones hanging from rusted chains, chiming clocks with huge brass gongs sheltered by beveled glass fronts, and smaller more modern examples, none of which bore the correct time. There were forty-two clocks in all, each unique but dark and lonesome looking, their faces no longer luminous with purpose.

I wondered what was keeping Harry. It didn't take that long to make coffee. Maybe he drank it black and only his wife used creamer, so he had to look at the back of a cupboard for the old container, and upon finding it had grown sad about her death all over again.

Obviously the place was having an effect on me.

Turning to face the front windows, I noticed a beautiful old mahogany pedestal table, its red highlights washing onto the faux Oriental rug. The smooth surface was covered in photographs held by ornate metal frames, worn at edges where years of loving fingertip touches had taken their toll. A wedding photo featured a bride in pale satin, a cloche hat holding her curls, the groom wearing a dark suit and an uncertain smile. The same couple a few years later, posed at a table under a paper palm, the man's smile more sure this time. There were more pictures of the woman, formal shots and candids. She was sometimes surprised by the camera, aging before my eyes, shot by shot. A plain brass frame, the outline of Harry's porch giving a matted effect before which stood a young Harry in street beat blue, his arm draped over the shoulder of the nurse beside him.

Every picture centered on Harry and his wife, save for the one in the center: a freckle-faced boy of maybe twelve. A class picture, probably, creased across one corner as if it had befallen some misfortune along the way.

The swish of Harry's slippered feet brought me back from the past.

"Sorry it took so long. I didn't know if you'd had breakfast."

Harry set a plate of orange sweet rolls down on the tray table, the kind that spring from refrigerated dough to a sticky confection in under ten minutes. That's what he'd been up to, making me breakfast. The small fete struck me as awkward, yet touching, the way you feel when someone is pressed into a type of service they are no longer well-versed in.

Harry sat two steaming mugs next to the plate and motioned me toward the chair.

"Thank you," I said. "This looks wonderful. But you really shouldn't have gone to the trouble."

Harry brushed away my sentiments and got right to the point. "So you want to know about Jason."

I gulped too much hot liquid and had to pause a moment to get it down. "Yes, but I thought you--"

"Look, I don't exactly need the money, what I need is someone to help me with this stuff. You'll see what I mean when we go back to the office. My notes are a mess and my record keeping isn't exactly by the book. My wife used to help me with it, but lately...."

I was relieved that Harry'd had a change of heart and I wouldn't have to come up with fifty bucks or a good argument for not paying him at all. "So, I'll help you with some filing and you'll give me what you have on Jason?"

"More or less," he said, taking a huge bite out of his roll.

That last part worried me.

After we finished the rolls and coffee, I followed Harry back through the dimly lit house, past closed doors and bare walls. Harry's office must have once been a bedroom: the walls between the small window and the accordion-doored closet bore the faint outlines where pictures had once hung, visible echoes of some past occupancy. The room was crowded with Elk's

Lodge folding laminate tables piled with boxes and loose sheaves of paper. The dented filing cabinets looked like cast-offs from some government bureau remodel. A single, three-tiered metal bookshelf with arching, gold-toned ends stood watch under the window, only one shelf bearing books.

In a space brushed clear in the middle of one of the tables, an aged Underwood crouched, teeth glinting in what light there was. In front of it a battered swivel chair canted drunkenly, one of its casters gone missing. It was worse than I expected.

I waited for Harry to start, but all I got was an apologetic smile. Finally he said, "I figure if you can help me straighten this up, you can just take whatever you're interested in."

"You mean you don't know where it is?"

"Oh, sure. It's somewhere in here." Harry started picking at a box of file folders.

"Don't you have case files? A system?"

"Not so much." He looked around the room as if he felt the weight of every piece of paper there.

"You mentioned pictures," I prompted.

"I gave Irene the pictures, but I've got the negatives." He lumbered over to a filing cabinet and slid open the top drawer. I looked over his shoulder and saw the strips of negatives, hundreds of them coiled together like a den of shiny snakes.

I was glad I hadn't told Kyle. Whatever useful information was here would have to be found and I didn't know where to start. "Maybe you could just tell me what you found out."

Harry looked out the small rectangle of window to a sun-scorched back yard. "Well, I don't remember details so well as I used to." He turned toward me. "I've got it all written down, though." His face softened, maybe with the hope that those last words had bought him some measure of redemption.

"We could start with what's loose and move on to the boxes," Harry suggested.

My assistance was a fait accompli in Harry's mind and I didn't have the heart to tear the notion away from him right now. But last night's adventure had pushed my ability to cope to the edge and this would push it over. Never mind the fact that all I might uncover were the dissociative ramblings of a lonely old man. I made a show of looking at my watch. "I've got someplace to be in a little while. Could I stop by tomorrow, maybe pick up then?"

"Well, sure. I guess that'd be okay." Harry stood straighter as he walked me out. As I pulled away from his sad little house I wondered if I would be able to break it to him that I wasn't the paper mountain climber he wanted me to be.

~ ~ ~

I let the water pound down on me as I rinsed my hair, surrounded by the scent of Hawaiian white ginger, hula-hoops of foam falling around my feet with each pass of my palms over my head. I heard Sydney barking outside the bathroom door and froze, hands in midair.

I grabbed the silver handle and the water went from hot to cold to non-existent. Now I could hear the faint jingle of the phone, for once a calming sound. I grabbed a towel from the bar and debated letting the machine pick up, but I was already out of the enveloping cocoon of steam.

I yanked up the receiver and gave a breathless hello.

"Maddie, are you okay?" I could hear the concern in Kyle's voice.

"I'm fine. I was in the shower."

"So I guess you're naked then."

"No. I'm wearing my rubber ducky flotation ring, if you must know."

"In the shower? That's more of a tub thing, isn't it?"

"I'm not that coordinated."

"Oh, I wouldn't say that."

"Very funny, Kyle, but I'm dripping on the carpet."

"Okay. Listen, can I stop by tonight? I just found out that I have to go to some lame conference in Chicago, a spur of the moment thing, and I was hoping I could see you before I leave."

I paused for a moment, realizing with a pang that I didn't want him to leave, not even for a few days.

"Maddie?"

"Sorry. I had to move the phone to dry my hair. I'm supposed to go out to dinner with an old friend, but you could drop by later, say ten? That way you can make sure there are no boogeymen hiding under my bed."

I heard muffled conversation behind him, as if he'd put his hand over the mouthpiece. "Okay. Got to go, but I'll see you tonight."

I dried off and drug myself through the motions of getting ready for dinner. I shuffled through my closet for fifteen minutes, finally settling on a black jersey cocktail dress, hoping it didn't look like the $68 dollar knock-off it was. I hadn't worn my hair up since the last time I'd run into Erik, and now I knew why. I cursed the genes that had given me thick, heavy hair that wouldn't stay put and always seemed more comfortable under a baseball cap.

The buzzer pulled me away from the mirror, and I took a moment to glance out the window at the gunmetal grey Mercedes SLK at the curb below before heading downstairs.

Erik was regal in a darker than blue double-breasted suit, and he let out a low whistle as I stepped out of the front door of the building.

"Hi, beautiful," he said, then took my arm. "We've got reservations at La Mer for 6:30, so if you're ready, we'd better go. They have a reputation for not holding a table for anyone."

# CHAPTER THIRTEEN

La Mer certainly looked like a place with a reputation, from the doorman and the snotty maitre d' who had shown us to our ocean view table to the gilt-edged menu with its unpronounceable dishes and conspicuously absent prices. I let Erik order for me, which seemed to be expected, and tried not to look bored as he sampled the wine and nodded almost imperceptibly at the steward.

We engaged in the obligatory small talk, catching up on the years since I'd last seen him. Erik had haunted London for a while as a second unit director and then gone on to various projects as assistant and then lead, making low-budget action flicks in Eastern Europe and little cookie-cutter features in France and Spain before flying back to the nest to try his hand at making a go of it here. My life didn't seem nearly as interesting, but I tried to put a positive spin on it.

Over the endive salad, I called Erik's bluff.

"So what makes you think I'd be right for your movie?"

Erik placed his fork down next to the lemon yellow bowl of greens. "I like a woman who gets right to the point." He leaned back slightly in his chair. "This film, and you'll love this, is a set piece between two women, very emotional, and the writing is fantastic. It's not a flashy film, but it's the kind that will get an actress noticed. I can have the script delivered tomorrow and you can tell me what you think."

I took a breath. Maybe this was the trade-off for all the rotten things that had happened lately. The cosmic scales balancing in my favor for once. "It sounds wonderful, Erik."

At that moment, the waiter materialized, bearing a large

tray covered with steaming plates. He arranged our entrees and accompaniment dishes, offering cracked pepper and freshly grated cheese.

"I think you'll love it," Erik continued. "And I'm really looking forward to finally having some creative control. It's funny, my father started out being able to do anything he wanted and it wasn't until years later than he fell into the rut of making happy little movies with happy endings. I'm going in the opposite direction. I've been so constrained by what other people wanted, and now Evan's giving me the chance to do what I want for a change."

Erik's father, the times I'd met him in social situations, had always seemed a little distant, as if he was breaking any interaction down into his component parts, blocking out everyone's lives for the next scene. I couldn't help but think he only saw the world through a viewfinder. Erik's mother followed dutifully behind him, getting him a fresh drink, finding him an ashtray, while he concentrated on his own brilliance. In retrospect, our upbringings hadn't been that different, only it was my mother who existed on that plane that none of the rest of us could inhabit.

By the time the eclairs and port arrived, the sea had gone flat and black-green like slate tile; the moon reflected off the still water, leaving silver trails like luminous veins of quartz. Erik had charmed me throughout the meal with tales of shoe-string budgets and film crews that spoke no English. I'd found myself gradually relaxing, listening to the cadence of his voice, taking in the warm aromas of the food. He was right, the sea bass had been wonderful, and now that the check had arrived, it was like waking from a comfortable dream.

I glanced down at the sodium green digital readout on the CD player when we got back in the car and felt a momentary start. Kyle would be at my apartment in an hour.

"Would you like to stop somewhere for a nightcap?" Erik asked, as we negotiated our way onto the Seaside Highway.

"I'd love to, but a friend is leaving town and I promised I'd be around tonight to say goodbye."

"You'll have to give me a rain check, then. Maybe we can get together tomorrow night after you've had a chance to read the script."

Erik pushed a button on the CD player and classical music filled the air as we passed through the eclectic blend of architecture that marked the outskirts of my neighborhood, my city within the city.

Otto's castle stood stoic behind the palms, looming over the Mercedes like a waiting father hours after curfew.

"Would you like me to walk you up?"

I could envision Kyle meeting Erik on the way out, the look that would pass between them. "Thanks, but I'll be fine. And thank you for dinner. I can't wait to see the script." I reached for the door handle.

"Let me get that for you." I waited dutifully as Erik walked around the front of the Mercedes and opened my door. I stepped out and onto the grass strip that served as a barrier to the street.

"Until tomorrow," he said.

~~~

By the time I'd stripped out of my dress and traded it for jeans and a t-shirt, Kyle had arrived with a bouquet of daisies and amaryllis in one hand and a six-pack of imported beer in the other. I took the flowers and found a vase while he carried two glasses and a bowl of corn chips to the living room.

"Everything okay?" he asked as I sat down beside him and put my bare feet up on the coffee table.

"Yeah. Better than okay in fact. I might have a job. A director is sending a script over for me in the morning."

"Ooo, and when you're accepting your Academy Award will you still remember the little people?"

"Wait and ask me after I've actually made a movie."

We drank our beer and cuddled on the couch until I caught

Kyle looking at his watch over my shoulder.

"Are you bored, or just seeing how long you can hold your breath?"

"Right. I think you can tell I'm enjoying myself." He kissed me again. "It's just that my plane leaves at six in the morning and I haven't packed yet. I wish I could stay longer, hell, I wish I wasn't going at all. But the detective who was supposed to go had some lousy excuse like his wife going into labor, and I got drafted at the last minute."

"You think I can't amuse myself if you're gone for a few days?"

Kyle laughed. "I'm sure you can. It's just with everything that's happened, I don't like the thought of you being alone."

"I've been alone for ten years and I seemed to have survived it fine."

"That doesn't count. I didn't know you then."

Kyle might not be the designer suit type, but he certainly had a knack for saying the most comforting things just when I needed to hear them.

"Don't worry about me. I'll be fine until you get back."

"Just make sure you are."

He helped me pick up and when I opened the door for him he pushed it shut and turned around to face me. "Promise me you'll take care of yourself."

"I will."

He gave me a long, deep kiss, one that lingered long after I'd locked the door behind him.

# CHAPTER FOURTEEN

I tipped the courier who brought the manuscript and stood there feeling the weight of it, afraid that if I opened the envelope it would be empty, a cruel joke. I sat down on the couch and popped the tape, slid out the handwritten note atop the stark white stack of pages. Erik's strong looping script reminded me to call.

I read the first few pages of *Between Women* with a growing sense of excitement, and began to read faster, forgetting to keep the pages in order, paying no attention as they slipped from the couch and fluttered to the rug. When I finished, I gathered up the pages and placed them back into the box, closed the lid and took a deep breath.

The part of Amanda was compelling, as Erik had said, and nothing like the walk-ons and cheesy low-budget parts I had auditioned for over the last couple of years. More like Farrah Fawcett in *Extremities*, a tour-de-force about a woman confronting the darkness buried inside her. Amanda finds herself spending the weekend with a woman who turns out to be her husband's mistress, decides to kill her, then comes to realize that they aren't that different after all. Erik was right, it could be a breakout role, the kind that makes a name for the actress who can pull it off. I felt as if I'd just listened to some smiling blond bimbo read off the lottery numbers on Channel Four and realized that they were laid out before me in irrefutable ink.

I shut my eyes and opened them again, but the envelope was still there, it hadn't been a mirage. I picked up the phone and held the receiver tightly for a moment, afraid to break the spell, before punching in Erik's number. I waited through five rings and was about to hang up when I heard his hello.

"Erik. It's Maddie. I got the script and I love it. If you want me, I'm all yours."

Erik gave a rich, baritone laugh. "I'll remember you said that. So when would you like to get together?"

I hesitated, afraid I of giving the wrong impression. Besides, I wanted some time alone to bask in my good fortune, to find a way of fitting comfortably into this new aspect of my life. And then there was Harry. The image of him waiting for me with sweet rolls in hand tugged at my conscience.

"Actually, I'd like to have a couple of days. I've only gone through the script once and I'd like to go over the part more thoroughly before we discuss it. And, well, you know the way things have gone for me lately, I feel like I've been caught in the middle of a whirlwind. I hope you don't mind."

"I understand. Take all the time you need. I have a casting call set for Monday so we can find a co-star, and I want you to be there for that. Maybe this weekend?"

"Sure. And thanks again, Erik. I can't tell you how much this means to me."

I hung up, glancing at Burton Willis' card in the frame of the hall mirror, a reminder to get back to him, but I still had no idea what I was going to do with my part of the theater.

All the way over to Harry's, I struggled with conflicting thoughts. I didn't want to disappoint him, and the prospect of finding information that might help solve Irene's murder was tantalizing. But how much time could I devote to a scavenger hunt that might not lead anywhere? The answer was no clearer when I pulled up in front of Harry's house, so I made myself a compromise: if I couldn't find anything useful in the next day or two I'd charm Harry into going to the police himself, explain to him that I was starting a new job on Monday and just didn't have the time to spare. If he still wouldn't cooperate, I'd let Kyle know, and tell him to go easy on the old guy.

Harry had no baked goods, just an expectant smile that reminded me absurdly of a kid on Christmas morning. His cheeks were pink from a fresh shave, his shirt pressed, and I caught a fleeting glimpse of the young man he once had been.

We got straight to the work at hand, sorting through piles of papers masquerading as fact sheets, folders impersonating case files. An hour after we began our assault on the beachhead, Harry stepped into the kitchen to make sandwiches. I heard a glass hit the linoleum and shatter with the sound of cartoon vehicles crashing. Harry didn't answer when I called his name, so I ran down the hallway and found him partially on the floor, hanging onto the counter with his forearm, face ashen and fists clenched.

Harry waved me off as he pulled himself to his feet. "I'm okay. This has happened before. It's no big deal." He pointed to the shelf above the refrigerator. "There's a bottle up there. The one with the red pills. Grab it for me, okay?"

I reached for Harry's medication and filled a glass with tap water. He seemed better almost immediately, standing up straight and re-tucking his shirt.

"Are you sure you're okay?"

"I'm fine. Fine. Nothing to worry about. You go back to the office and I'll finish up in here."

Harry kept pace with me through the early afternoon, although when I stole glances at him he looked a little grey, and once I caught him rubbing the heel of his palm over the center of his chest, as if some stain had blossomed there and he was trying to rub it away. I finally convinced him that a nap was in order, assured him that I could handle the office and would wake him before I headed home.

I returned to my perusal of the files, still amazed at Harry's lack of a system, frustrated by his crabbed scribbles. Apparently he hadn't gone to a school where the Palmer Method was emphasized. Some of the notes, the latest ones I surmised, might as well have been written in Sanskrit. It only made me wonder about the truth of Harry's condition, if there was more to it than just a bout with the bottle or a mild heart condition. Maybe he was in the early stages of senility, or some other malady lurked within him, a dark voyager traveling though the network of nerves and muscles that traversed his body like tiny highways.

I slumped into the chair and glared at the wrinkled pages in my hand, as if I could force them to make sense through sheer will. A cream-colored business card drifted from a crease in a page and when I reached down to retrieve it, I felt a small thrill. Underneath the stylized form of a couple in naked embrace was printed Bravo Productions. The card listed Arthur Pierce and a Van Nuys Boulevard address. Jennifer Chandler worked at Bravo, I saw Jason get into Jennifer's car, and now there was a tenuous connection between Jason and Bravo. Maybe this wasn't a wild goose chase after all. I concentrated on the page the card had been folded into, but Harry's writing blurred like the last line on an eye chart. There was a list of names that would take a while to decipher, so I folded the pages carefully and slid them into my purse, remembering Harry's invitation to take what I needed.

I moved on to the drawer full of negatives and picked up a handful, then pulled a lamp down onto the floor next to me. The first few strips were fuzzy and out of focus; whatever Harry was, he wasn't a photographer.

I glanced at my watch and thought how close it was to quitting time, when one of the black and sepia images caught my eye. I held the strip close to the light bulb until the warmth made the thin skin on the back of my hand tingle. Jason's image stared back at me and I quickly scanned through the rest of the strip. More pictures of Jason. Then the final image, a haunting reversal of positive and negative that looked like a late model Cabriolet.

~~~

Burton Willis called first.

"Ms. Pryce?" he said when I picked up. "We need you to come down to the Orpheus as soon as possible. There's been a break-in."

This is why I generally screen my calls. "When did this happen?"

"Sometime last night. I don't know if anything's missing, but they made quite a mess. I'd like you to fill out a report. Can you come right now?"

Well, I could, but I wasn't about to let him feel that I was at his beck and call. "I have some errands that I can only run this morning," I lied. "I'll be there in a couple of hours."

I don't know if I was angrier with Willis -- who'd taken it upon himself to schedule me whether I was paid or not -- or the dark force that kept invading my territory. By the time I'd showered, dressed and spent my quality time with the kids, I was mad at Willis all over again, treating me like a toady who should jump when he snaps his fingers. That decided it. I would stick around the Orpheus, if only to give Willis some grief.

I dropped Harry's negatives at a one-hour photo shop on my way in. I hadn't been sure what to expect when I pulled up to the theater -- whether I'd recognize my old friend -- but the facade was unchanged, like someone putting on a brave face in a crisis. Inside it was a different story. I couldn't tell where the vandalism left off and the renovation began. The snack bar had been ripped away, leaving a gaping wound where curved chrome had once shined. I saw two workmen lounging near the lobby, swilling coffee from disposable cups while they flicked ashes onto the old carpet. Maybe they hadn't perpetrated the crime I was here to investigate, but they'd brought it on, striking the first blow that signaled for the rest of the vultures to descend.

I followed the sound of Willis' rising voice to Irene's old office, where I found him seated in her chair with his back to me, arguing over the phone. When he spun and caught sight of me, he quickly ended the conversation. Willis had affected a casual look for today in his white polyester zip-up golf shirt, beige Sans-a-belt pants and sockless penny loafers. On him, the all-American Saturday barbecue-grilling outfit looked like a uniform.

He snapped up a stack of incident report forms and handed it to me. No thank-you for coming down, none of the niceties of last week's meeting.

"I need you to make a list of anything missing and any damage you find. Then, on the blank sheet at the back, give me the names, addresses and phone numbers of all the theater employees for the past year. You're welcome to use the office files for that if you need to."

No. I keep the numbers and addresses of everyone I meet in my head, you idiot.

I'm not sure what expression I sent him, but it wasn't the one I felt because he would have blown up on the spot. Did he really think a job here was important enough to anyone to cause them to break in and wreck the place?

"Look, Willis. I'll fill out your reports for you and give you people's names, but I'm not doing it for grins. I'll take the partial salary you offered. When do I pick up my check?"

Willis' face reddened. "I'll meet with the partnership and get back to you."

"I am the partnership. Twelve percent of it, anyway. You'll let me know when the meeting is scheduled?"

He gave a pained grimace. "I'll be in touch. Just leave the information on the desk when you're done."

I wished Irene had been here. She always said I needed to stand up for myself, not be afraid to piss somebody off if they deserved it. Anyway, the fact that the Orpheus needed an advocate now was obvious.

I spent the next hour walking from one area of the building to another, noting cracked mirrors, busted lockers and spray-painted walls, never escaping the serenade of circular saws around me. The screening room itself was untouched, a sacred space still protected by the ghosts of swashbucklers and cowboys. The balcony door hung from one hinge, black boot prints in its paint. It creaked when I pushed it to one side and made my way up the dim stairwell to the wrecked balcony. It looked much different than when I'd ventured up last week. Seat cushions oozed stuffing onto the carpet and gang symbols defaced the curtained walls.

The violation shocked me, but the circumstances were

familiar. I thought again of Jason's clandestine parties up here in high school, when he would invite the popular kids to the old balcony to watch movies and raid his secret stash, getting drunk and high, talking loudly about girls that weren't there and clumsily fondling the ones that were. The parties had been his only contact with the letter-jacketed jocks and designer clothing-clad queens. Jason's moment in the sun had been far away from the light of day, illuminated only by the itinerate flicker of old films.

~~~

Willis must have gone off to either torture someone else or have a heart attack. He was nowhere to be found when I finished the forms and left them on the desk.

On the way home, I picked up the photos, fought back the urge to rifle through them, then stopped at the market for kibbles and cat food. The five-dollar bill I'd gotten in change was screaming to be spent, so I wheeled under the welcoming awning of the Taco Taco, belted my order into the mouth of Pedro the Mexican Clown, and got my festive bag of Mucho Macho tacos, complete with extra hot sauce in little plastic sombreros.

I noticed Mrs. Cullum's door open as I sat down the kids' food and reached for my keys.

"Maddie, dear," she started, just as I got the door open. "I have something for you. It was delivered."

She followed me into my apartment.

"I told the young man I was your mother and he let me sign for them." She swung back and forth on the words like a marionette at a puppet show.

"Quick thinking, Mrs. Cullum."

She scurried off, returning moments later bearing a bouquet of red roses, baby's breath and fern fronds. "Someone has a sweetie," she sang, beaming.

I knew she wanted me to open the tiny envelope and tell

her who'd sent them, but after I thanked her I began filling the food bowls on the kitchen floor. She seemed disappointed that I hadn't rushed to read the card, although I suspected she had. As soon as she left I pulled it out: *Here's to a new direction.*

I put the crystal vase beside Kyle's bouquet, gone brown around the edges and giving off a sickly sweet smell that made me think of cemeteries. Men never understood that I liked my flowers alive and in the ground.

I sat down to my lukewarm tacos and flipped open the photo pouch. I fanned the pictures out across the coffee table, various images of the same person. Jason talking to someone outside the frame, Jason in his car, Jason walking down an unfamiliar street, shoulders hunched in his dirty brown coat. I bit into the first taco, spilling hot sauce on the rug. I dabbed at the spot with a napkin illustrated with Mexican greetings, then got back to the photos. The one image of Jennifer was in profile. She was turned toward Jason, who stood at her driver's side door, her slim left arm draped over the bottom of the square left by the open window, a gold bracelet gracing her wrist. She was pretty in that California girl way, blond hair pulled back from her classic face, the high cheekbones, full mouth and straight nose of an urban princess. Her neck was so thin it seemed translucent in the afternoon light trapped within the photo.

I stared at that picture, that golden girl stuck in time, not knowing if this was the last snapshot anyone would ever take of her. And I wondered how Kyle could stand it, this heavy burden of looking at the missing, looking at the dead.

# CHAPTER FIFTEEN

Harry didn't answer his door, but I could hear a western blaring from the TV in the living room. I called out and got no answer, tried the knob but the door was locked. I walked around the side of the house and let myself through the waist-high chain link gate into the backyard, then took the three steps up to the top of the stoop, where I found the checked-curtained door unlocked.

Harry was laying face-down on the tacky blue and beige linoleum. I rushed over and knelt beside him, listening for breath and feeling for a heartbeat. He didn't respond when I called his name, but his pulse was even as a metronome. I dialed 911 and waited for the ambulance.

I was sitting beside the hospital bed when he woke up.

"You scared me," I said.

"Yeah, scared myself."

"I locked up the house." I pulled his key ring out of my bag. "Should I leave these with the nurse?"

"No. You keep them, keep working. Besides, I like the idea of somebody being around the place."

The attending interrupted, gave Harry a smile and motioned me toward the door. In the hallway he asked, "Are you a member of the family?"

"No, just a friend. Is he going to be okay?"

"For now. He has a form of leukemia exacerbated by a heart condition and the prognosis at this point is uncertain. Do you know how we can get in touch with his family?"

I shook my head.

When I returned to Harry's side, he asked what the doctor

had said. I told him he was going to be fine, which we both knew was a lie.

~~~

Back at Harry's I packed two cardboard boxes with notes and files, picking what looked most promising to take home, saving the stuff that appeared to be older for later. The thought of working in the empty house, every sound a hollow echo, was too much for me today. As I drove home, an idea surfaced, something to fill the nervous emptiness.

I had an afternoon with nothing to do, I didn't want to bother Harry with questions and Kyle wouldn't be back until Sunday. I was an actress. Bravo was a film company. Never mind that I wasn't that kind of actress. I could wear a short skirt and I didn't look like a cop.

After I hauled the boxes up and shoved them into the alcove beneath the turret stairs, I made a trip to the closet. A black leather skirt that I'd bought on a whim and never worn, a sheer white blouse with a plunging neckline and black pumps with not-quite-spiked heels seemed appropriate. I fluffed my hair and applied make-up, blew an air-kiss to the mirror and headed for Van Nuys Boulevard.

The address belonged to a bold yellow office building, three stories of cinder block barely disguised beneath heavily applied paint and '60s latticework. The glass doors opened onto a foyer that hadn't been updated since the *Mod Squad*, the tenants listed on a black tracked board like specials at a sidewalk cafe. Bravo Productions was on the third floor.

The elevator button stayed dark after repeated jabs, so I headed for the stairs that lay behind a brown fire door. I tried to catch my breath and then put my hand against my beating heart as I stood in front of a door with the company name spelled out in gleaming brass. I hadn't put in enough laps at the pool lately.

I opened the door to a rush of chilled air, amazed at the tasteful appointments that greeted me. The carpet was a plush gold and white design, the furniture heavy, real wood as opposed to veneer. The windowless room was lit by brass carriage lamps that jutted from the off-white plaster walls.

"Can I help you?" asked the woman behind the curving, polished secretary that stood in the center of the room. She was elegant, hair swept up to reveal a graceful neck adorned with a gold chain that suspended a single pearl, and her pale blue crepe blouse was demurely buttoned.

I pulled the business card from my purse and flashed it for her as I advanced toward the desk. "I'm here to see Arthur Pierce. A friend suggested that I look him up."

She tilted her head as if sizing me up, then asked for my name. She punched a button on the phone with one perfectly manicured nail and informed Mr. Pierce that Maddie Pryce was here to see him. I realized then that I should have called first, that it was sheer luck that Pierce was here and would see me. Next time I'd plan better.

Within a few minutes, the inner door opened and Arthur Pierce appeared. He was short, no more than 5'6", and handsome. He wore pleated linen pants and a matching jacket over a cream-colored silk shirt open at the throat, and had a deep Cary Grant tan that set off black hair going prematurely silver.

"Ms. Pryce, what can I do for you today?" he said as he ushered me into his office.

I walked through the door ahead of him, realizing that all the lines I'd practiced on the drive over had flown right out of my head. I sat in an ox-blood leather chair across from his desk, crossed my legs and waited for him to settle before I spoke.

"A friend suggested I contact you. About a job."

"And your friend would be...." he asked with a smile.

"Jennifer Chandler." It was the first name that popped into my head. If it meant anything to him, he gave no indication.

"Were you looking for something behind the camera, or in front?"

I fumbled in my purse for my SAG card. At least it would be good for something. He looked it over and handed it back.

"Do you have any experience?"

"Only with more..." What was the word I was looking for? "Traditional roles."

His smile widened and he leaned back, tenting his fingers under his chin.

"You're an attractive woman, Ms. Pryce. Have you seen any of our films?"

"Well, no."

"But your friend suggested that we would be right for you."

"Maybe friend is too strong a word. Jennifer and I only knew each other casually. But when I lost my job, she mentioned that I could make some extra money."

I was flying in the dark here. My one experience with skin flicks involved a boyfriend who suggested we watch one together. I'd ended up laughing so hard at the stilted dialogue and poor production values that he clicked the thing off in embarrassment and never called me again.

Pierce leaned in across the desk and gazed at me intently. "I'll tell you what. Let me make a few calls. I'd prefer that you got a taste of the product before we go any further."

He showed me from his office and closed the door. The receptionist gave me a brief smile as I sank onto a champagne-colored chesterfield sofa, then went back to her computer screen.

Pierce returned within fifteen minutes and held out a mauve piece of stationary. "Stop by this address within the next hour. They'll be expecting you. If you like what you see, give me a call back and we'll go from there."

~~~

From the outside, the warehouse in Venice Beach looked like an airplane hangar. A blond, sunburned man in a muscle shirt and jeans was stationed at the door. He glanced at the paper in my hand and then led me through a warren of false walls and narrow corridors to a cramped sound stage area that contained about a dozen people. My escort left me at the door and walked over to a tall, blond woman dressed in a green leotard, leggings and moccasins, her hair gathered back in a flowing ponytail and a thick sheaf of paper in her hand. She leaned in as he spoke and then looked at me. She was striking from a distance, and as she approached I discovered that she was older than she looked, fine lines snaking out from around her eyes and the corners of her mouth. She extended a hand, her grip firm and businesslike.

"Ms. Pryce. I'm Margo. Arthur wants me to show you around." Her voice was deep and soothing, with just a hint of an accent I couldn't place. "We're breaking right now, but you and I can get to know each other better before the next round of filming."

I followed her back to a square, minimally adorned room dominated by a Danish modern desk, a chaise lounge and a row of wooden filing cabinets. She reached into a mini-fridge and pulled out a carafe of orange juice. When I declined her offer of a drink, she poured a tall glass for herself and flopped into the ergonomically designed chair behind the desk, motioning for me to take the chaise.

"Tell me about yourself," she said.

I gave her the abbreviated version, making sure to mention my short list of actual credits, leaving out everything else I could. I watched her smile grow as I spoke, and I wondered what the joke was. She must have picked up on my bewilderment.

"You'll have to forgive me, but Arthur is a little paranoid. You can't blame him though, these are strange times we live in. He did a little checking, just to make sure you were who you said you were." She took a deep drink of the juice. "To be honest, I agree with Arthur, something about you doesn't seem typical. I think he was afraid you were from NOW, or Citizens for Public Decency, or maybe a delegate to the Baptist Convention. You'd be amazed how much havoc a single person can wreak when there's a tight schedule." She looked at me again, a faint line creasing her forehead. "So you aren't actually familiar with Bravo?"

"Just in passing," I said.

"Well, I'll give you a brief rundown, answer any questions I can, then you can sit in on a shoot. Arthur was afraid you'd get one look and run screaming, I think." She gave a musical laugh. "He worries too much. It's going to kill him one day."

Margo explained how Bravo was "different" from other studios – high production values, striking performers, "specialty" scenarios. After a few minutes, I got the impression that she was working too hard to sell me on it. When her spiel ran down, she re-situated herself on the chair and asked if I had any questions. It was now or never.

"I think Mr. Pierce is fascinating. What can you tell me about him?"

Her eyes narrowed. "Believe me, you're not his type. And I don't think he would be yours."

"Oh, no. I didn't mean that. I just meant that he's not at all what I expected. Maybe I'm naive, but I was expecting someone..."

"Sleazier?"

"Well, that would be one word. Is he the head of the whole outfit?"

"He and a partner."

"And will I be meeting him?"

"Silent partner. This is really Arthur's baby." She glanced at the sports watch circling her wrist. "And we do have a schedule to keep. You're welcome to stick around for a bit, get an idea of what we're looking for." A coolness had entered her voice, as if she'd become bored with me.

Back on the sound stage, props people were putting final touches on the minuscule set, re-creasing red drapes and arranging a plethora of objects I didn't want to guess the uses for. Margo barked orders at the sound and lighting techs, and after further instruction yelled, "Roll."

A topless blond wearing a butterfly-shaped mask and leather panties slunk through the door onto the set, caressed by the dispassionate eyes of the crew. By the time her initiates -- three muscle-bound men wearing harnesses, their faces completely obscured by hoods -- were arranged on the silk-ensconced bed in the center of the room, the woman had chosen a cat-o-nine tails and something that looked like a cattle prod. That was my cue. It took me ten minutes to find my way back out into the sunshine.

~ ~ ~

Harry's condition was serious, but stable. When I called Erik and explained, he gave me his sympathies and told me not to worry about this weekend, just to show up at the studio Monday morning. I'd stopped by the hospital, left flowers and a crossword puzzle book, but Harry was asleep. He still hadn't been released when Kyle returned on Sunday. Kyle and I made plans for the evening, nothing fancy, just a revisitation of our last date.

For a while we just kissed, no talking. When I came up for breath, I fetched two beers from the fridge and plopped back down on the couch next to Kyle, swinging my legs up across his thighs so he could rub my feet. I told him about my role in the movie and waited for his reaction. He just sat there. "Isn't it great?" I said.

"I was just thinking that if you become a big star, I'll have a hard time making anyone believe I ever slept with you."

"Yes, and since you'll only have that one time to tell them about..."

"Gee, and I was hoping to get lucky tonight."

"Aw, you only want me for my evidence. Which reminds me, guess what I did while you were gone."

Kyle raised his eyebrows. "Should I have a few more beers before you tell me?"

"Maybe I should have a few more beers before I tell you."

I started with Harry and how the business card had led me to Bravo, then went through my meeting with Arthur Pierce, finishing up with my brief foray into S & M film making and the little information I had gained from Margo.

For a moment Kyle didn't say anything.

"I could always go back for more information," I said.

"What made you think this was a good idea? And wait...exactly what...I mean, you didn't...."

"You're cute when you sputter."

Kyle pushed my legs to the floor and pressed me back into the couch, then leaned over, kissed me and looked into my eyes. "You can't be left alone you know. Somebody should lock you up where you can't do any damage."

I pushed him back. "Oh, and when I mentioned Jennifer Chandler's name, Pierce seemed to have no idea who she was."

Kyle sat up and I watched the color drain from his face.

"I leave you alone for a week...." He turned toward me. "Look, there's been no harm done, at least I don't think there has, but can you please just leave the cop stuff to the actual cops? This isn't a game, Maddie, really. I'm trying to understand, but...could you just promise me you'll drop it?"

I got up from the couch and went over to the drawer in the foyer table. "I'll do better than that. I'll let you have everything I've got and you can take care of it." I said.

I handed over the pictures of Jason and Jennifer, then went over to the alcove and pulled the boxes out from under the turret stairs. Kyle joined me as I opened a box and extracted a few of the notes. "I went through this stuff yesterday, but I didn't find anything. As you can see, it's a mess. There's some more stuff in Harry's office, but most of it's in worse shape than this. The next time I get over there, I'll take a closer look. You can take this now, maybe have some of your people double check for anything I missed."

Kyle set the pictures inside one of the boxes and closed the lid and shook his head.

"I don't know whether to kiss you or handcuff you."

I put my arms around his neck and drew him down to me. "You could always try both."

Kyle led me back to the bedroom. Actually, first he led me to the hall closet, but after a short process of elimination we found our way to the end of the hall and my bedroom door.

112

# CHAPTER SIXTEEN

The wind tossed palm frond-fulls of rain like scattered shot against my windshield as I drove to the Paragon Studio lot on Monday morning. Cars passed in watercolor blurs, ending up stopped for minutes at a time at intersections where soaked traffic cops worked frantically directing traffic while city workers tried to re-set the lights.

I pulled up to the security booth and the guard diligently crossed my name off a water-spotted list before he waved me through Paragon's wrought iron gates. It was a small lot, nothing on the scale of Paramount, MGM, or Universal, but it was still elegant and regarded with respect. Erik's father helped birth Paragon into the void left by the collapse of the studio system in the late '50s, and had built its reputation film by film, creating a niche between independents and the major players. Nathan Wellman now spent his time wading in the breakers of distant beaches and jetting from one world-famous restaurant to the next in search of the perfect osso bucco. Erik had inherited a figurehead title from his father, much like my minority percentage in the Orpheus, but obviously it hadn't afforded him enough pull to make the kind of movies he wanted without Evan's backing.

Erik's small office was on the second floor in an impressive two-story Mediterranean building book-ended by cavernous sound stages. After his secretary announced me, Erik took my coat and purse and put them in his office, then led me back down the hallway to the brass-framed elevator.

"Damn. Can you hang on a second? I forgot to tell Shirley to run an errand for me." I nodded and he loped back down the

113

hall. He returned a few moments later and pushed the button set within the scrollwork beside the elevator door.

"Sorry to rush you," he said. "But we've got a room full of jumpy actresses who're afraid the rain has melted them beyond recognition and I've left Evan alone with them far too long."

We walked into a room where potted plants filled the corners and cast rounded shadows onto a maroon and olive carpet, a space designed to be comfortable, but that still held the atmosphere of a doctor's waiting room. Two overstuffed burgundy chairs faced a long, heavy table with a scattering of pens and clipboards across its glossy surface.

The door on the opposite side of the room opened and Evan Marks leaned his shaggy blond head in. "It's about time. The bimbos are getting restless."

"Tell them it'll be just a few more minutes and make sure that Mary has their head shots," Erik said.

"Sure thing. Hi, Mads, glad you could make it." Evan gave me an infectious grin and disappeared.

Erik directed me toward one of the tall chairs behind the table and handed me a clipboard. "Take notes on anyone who interests you. I figure we can hash through things this afternoon and set a callback for tomorrow. I want to make sure we have someone you're comfortable with."

"You sure about that?" I asked with a smile. "I don't know anything about casting, other than it never happens to me."

"Nothing to it. And, as I'm sure you've seen, any idiot can do it."

I'm sure he was trying to dismiss my negative past experience, but being relegated to assistant idiot didn't do much for my confidence.

Evan returned and took his place beside me, and the first contestant was kicked into the arena to face the tigers. She was jet-haired and skittish and she flubbed her lines so many times that I began repeating them in my head for her, hoping she would get them right. She left with a muttered thank-you.

The parade continued for a mind-numbing hour, one face

blending with the next. I glanced at Erik's notes to see if he was getting anything more out of this than I was and missed the entrance of the next actress, but when I looked up I noticed something about her, a luminous quality like moonlight on water. She read with confidence, as if she'd gone beyond practicing the words and lived them, her eyes fiery, her hand placement deliberate. I read the list before me, stopping at the name below all those I'd crossed out: Samantha Greer. By the end of the session, I was convinced she was the one.

After the last actress read, an intern dropped off deli lunches and left us to debate the merits of the few women we'd seen who had an ounce of ability. It didn't take long to reach a consensus, and both Evan and Erik agreed that Samantha Greer was the standout.

~~~

Samantha became Sam after splitting an agent over lunch. She'd been appalled that I was currently un-represented, but remedied it over a prawn salad at Vanetta's downtown. I was now the newest client of Mimi Beckwith-Grimes, which was exciting if I ignored the fact that all her other clients were animal acts. The only dark spot during the week was Harry, who had been in and out of intensive care twice and seemed exhausted by even a short visit. I had a sinking feeling that he wouldn't be leaving the hospital.

There was an air of nervous excitement on the Friday after the week's rehearsal, as if we'd all purchased tickets to the carnival and would soon be projectile vomiting onto the crowd below the spinning arms of the Flying Octopus. In honor of the official start of filming, a small set party had been arranged by Erik. There was going to be a bigger shindig at his house tomorrow night, one where grips and gofers wouldn't be in attendance, but today all the little people were joining in the festivities. Maybe Erik had snuck in some team-building seminars in his spare time, or maybe he just wanted an excuse to show his largess to the crew. Whatever the case, caterers were setting up as we broke at noon, white-clad servers piling a table with sushi, fresh fruit, and delicate tarts and pastries. A cooler full of mineral water and Italian sodas stood to the side.

I was trying to decide whether I trusted raw fish that had come across town when Max, the lighting technician, walked up and nudged me with his elbow. "Behold, the bloom of the set romance, so tender and yet so frail. What do you want to bet by the end of the shoot they're throwing things at each other."

I looked over at Sam, Evan's arm around her shoulder, her head thrown back as if he'd just said the funniest thing she'd ever heard. "She's really not that type," I said, as if I knew.

"Oh, honey, they're all that type." Max wandered off to the dessert end of the table.

I decided to skip the fish and stick with the fruit. I loaded my plate with wedges of melon, slices of starfruit, and snuck in one icing-drenched apple roundelet, then turned to look for Erik. He was in heated discussion with a guard, and as I watched, the door behind them opened and Kyle and Ramirez walked through. For a fleeting moment, I held a hope that Kyle had somehow found out where filming was and stopped by to surprise me but the presence of his partner and the badge on the chain around his neck meant it was business.

Kyle froze when he saw me, and Ramirez nearly bumped into him. His look told me he hadn't known I would be here. Our eyes met for only a second before he continued on his path, Ramirez at his heels like a foxhound. I set down my plate and headed after them.

They stopped in front of Evan and Sam, and Kyle spoke without looking back at me. "Evan Marks? I'm Detective Oberman, this is Detective Ramirez. I hate to bother you here, but you haven't returned our calls and your secretary told us where we could find you. We have a few questions for you."

Evan looked shocked. "Excuse me?"

"What I'm saying, Mr. Marks, is that it seems like you've been avoiding us. We just need to clear a few things up, so we can discuss it here or you can come downtown with us."

"Are you arresting me?"

"No, sir. Not yet."

Erik spoke without taking his eyes from Kyle. "Evan, I can take care of things here while you get this straightened out."

I pulled Kyle to the side after Erik followed Evan to collect his briefcase and cell phone. "What the hell do you think you're doing?" I whispered through clenched teeth.

"My job."

"Did you really have to do this now? Here on the set in front of everybody?"

"I am sorry for that, but we need to talk to this guy and this was the only place we could catch up to him. He's done nothing but string us along for the better part of the week, and I'm a little tired of it. Honestly, I had no idea you would be here."

"Would it have changed things if you had?"

"Well, I might have been looking a bit more forward to it, but other than that, no." Kyle crossed his arms over his chest. "Look, it's not personal. We're just working off of the information you gave me. Margo, the director you put us onto at Bravo, finally coughed up the name of the silent partner: Evan Marks. Who, coincidentally, was seen with Jennifer Chandler on the day she disappeared."

"What?"

"Look, I don't have time to discuss it right now, we'll get together later, okay?"

I nodded, still struck off-balance by his revelation.

Kyle gave me a tap on the back of my hand before turning to re-join Ramirez and Evan.

Erik walked over to me. "Correct me if I'm wrong, but wasn't that your escort to the benefit?"

"Yes. But I had no idea he was going to show up here today."

Erik cocked an eyebrow. "Did he say anything to you just now regarding what this is all about?"

Better to let Evan explain the specifics to Erik. Besides, if I started blabbing whatever Kyle told me in confidence, he'd be less likely to tell me anything. "Not really. He just said they wanted to talk to Evan about an open case but Evan made himself unavailable, so they felt the only way they could talk to him was to catch him here."

He cocked an eyebrow at me, and then must have decided to let it go. "Typical of Evan. Instead of inconveniencing himself for a moment to take care of something that's probably completely routine, he just ignores it and hopes it goes away." He shook his head. "I'm sure it's nothing. Why don't we go back to the party? No sense giving anybody more of a whiff of scandal. Once rumors get started it's hard to stop them."

I wasn't really in a social mood, but Erik was right. This get together was supposed to be a bonding experience for cast and crew, the metaphorical breaking of the bottle on the bow of the new ship about to set sail. Time to start throwing some metaphorical confetti.

I put on a brave face, even though Kyle's visit had put me off my feed. It seemed like a bad omen. After forty-five minutes of nibbling fruit and making nice, the little celebration broke up and Sam and I made our escape, deciding that a drink and some real food was in order.

~~~

O'Herlihey's was the standard hangout for people whose names no one stayed in their seat to read at the end of the credits, and it was just a few blocks from the studio. Even in the afternoon it was a veritable hub, populated with extras, gaffers and grips who sat at plain oak tables amid movie memorabilia spanning six decades.

Sam ordered a double dry martini, and had it half drunk by the time my frozen daiquiri arrived. If I had been able to switch a knob and change the scene to black and white, I would've thought Sam to be straight out of a 1940's detective movie, Veronica Lake without Alan Ladd.

She took a last swallow of booze. "So, what's with you and the cop?"

"What do you mean?"

"Well, it was pretty obvious there was something going on there."

"You mean like you and Evan?"

Sam laughed. "Okay, we're even. She picked the olive out of the martini glass and bit into it delicately. "Do you think he's really in trouble? Evan, I mean."

"I don't know."

She tucked her hair back behind her ears and laughed again. "My luck with men. Never could pick a good one."

"Well, there are good guys out there."

"Like your cop?"

While I knew that remained to be seen, I certainly had no evidence to the contrary. "You want to get something to eat?" I picked up two menus and passed one to Sam.

"Oh, I don't think I'm that hungry. You go ahead." She picked up her purse from beside the chair and pointed at her empty glass. "Can you get me a refill? I'm going to run to the ladies' room. Be back in a sec."

I summoned a waiter and ordered a Monte Cristo sandwich, iced tea and another martini for Sam. She returned at the same time the waiter did, and I offered her half of my sandwich, but she refused, saying something about a slow metabolism. I wondered if she subsisted totally on gin-soaked olives.

Sam took a sip of her drink and began to fray the edges of her cocktail napkin. "Did I tell you that when I'm done with filming, Mimi has a pilot lined up for me? I mean, I know that hardly any of them make it through, but you've got to start somewhere. And believe me it's a lot further along than I ever thought I'd be." She glanced around at the vintage costumes, framed posters, and props that hung from the ceiling like extravagant mobiles. "You know, this is what I've always dreamed of. I know every little girl wants to be a movie star, but I never grew out of it. And I just woke up one morning and knew it was the last day I'd spend in Kansas. I haven't been back since."

119

"What about your family?"

"Oh, I have no family. Just ask them, they'll tell you." She laughed. "God, that sounded rough, didn't it? But I've come to the conclusion that to be a good actress you have to have things to draw on. So what if some of them are bad? That just makes you better in the long run. Don't you think?"

I wanted to tell Sam that if unpleasant circumstances contributed to talent, I'd win an Oscar for this picture. Instead I listened to her elaborate on her plans, following her path like the marked steps at the old Fred Astaire dance studios, realizing that I hadn't thought past this film.

Now that bad omen feeling sat on me like a weight. Actors are a superstitious lot anyway, and it seemed like boxcars full of coincidence had derailed right in front of me. I had no defense for my selfishness; I just wanted things to stop going wrong. I wanted it all to have been a mistake, ridiculous happenstance. Right now I felt like a cartoon character sitting under a dark cloud. No matter where I turned, it seemed determined to follow me.

# CHAPTER SEVENTEEN

Dogs are a great judge of mood. Since I got home, Sydney had been hiding in the bathroom, curled on the sisal mat beside the tub. I straightened up books and magazines, searching for some activity to relax my nerves. I dropped onto the couch for a moment, then snapped up to straighten the fringe on the area rugs.

The knock on the door startled me, then I realized Kyle had the code and wouldn't need to buzz up. I looked through the peep-hole anyway to see Kyle all fishy on the other side. I moved with the door as it opened to give him a clear path to charge if he wanted to, but he walked in quietly, hands in his pockets. I waited for him to say what I needed to hear.

"What," Kyle said.

I continued to stare. "You tell me."

"I can keep saying I'm sorry until I'm blue in the face, but like I told you, we really did need to interview Marks."

"I know, it just...startled me I guess. That was about the last thing I expected to happen my first real day at work. And this whole thing about Evan, I just don't..." I couldn't wrap my head around it, let alone articulate it.

"You said you hadn't seen the guy since college, right? I really didn't know you were working with him."

"It just came together the last couple of weeks. I didn't realize I needed to clear it with you." That came out more harshly than I intended, and I immediately regretted it. This intersection of Kyle's job and mine hadn't been something either of us planned. I just hoped it didn't have car crash written all over it.

I took his hand and led him to the couch. "Why don't you

start at the beginning. I still can't make sense of any of this and I don't want it to become some big mess when there's probably nothing to it."

Kyle leaned forward, resting his elbows on his knees. "Well it starts with Margo -- not her real name by the way. She was reluctant to talk to us, but she has some skeletons in her closet, so she eventually gave us what we wanted. She told us Evan Marks was partnered with Arthur Pierce, but that he was trying to break into legitimate films and didn't want his name associated with the Bravo. So that's kind of interesting, but nothing to hang your hat on. At the same time, though, another detective pulls in some of Jason's associates. The one that was most interesting was a loser named Eddie DiFalco. 'Course nobody's going to have to worry about Eddie for long. He has a dangerous habit of opening his mouth. He talked to us for hours just the other day, and he had a few things to say about Marks.

"It seems Jason Shoffit was Evan Mark's drug supplier. Eddie knows this because he was the distribution man one rung up from Jason. Eddie seemed so relieved that we weren't asking him to give up his suppliers that he told us everything we wanted to know about the customers. Jason was also supplying Jennifer Chandler, who was trying to break into acting. She was smart, but maybe not smart enough. So Jason tries to impress her by introducing her to another customer. The only problem was that Jennifer lost all interest in Jason after she met Evan Marks. She and Marks were apparently seeing each other at least casually, and Eddie can place them together on the day she disappeared. And like they say in the commercials, but wait there's more. Jason had something else going, Eddie doesn't know what, but it soured and Jason got scared, scared enough that he took $8,000 of someone else's money and tried to leave town. He didn't make it."

"So, what you're saying is Evan did something to Jennifer, Jason knew about it, and was murdered before he could get away."

"That would be one guess."

"And what did Evan have to say when you talked to him?"

"Oh, he gave us a full confession, what do you think he had to say? He said he was just as surprised by the girl's disappearance as anyone."

"But you don't believe him."

"I get paid for disbelief."

"So, you've let Evan go?"

"For now, with the standard admonition not to leave town."

There was something else nagging at me. "Did Paul Saroyan mention anything about Evan? If he was her boyfriend, you'd think the first thing he'd talk about was some other guy she was seeing."

"It seems that Saroyan was less than honest with us. He made it seem like they were still dating, but in reality she'd broken it off with him some time earlier, and not on the best of terms. A friend of hers said she was 'hiding' from him, whatever that means. Maybe he got overly clingy, maybe it was more than that. Whatever it was, he may not have known about Marks."

"Or he may have known just enough. He didn't strike me as the psycho type, but love does funny things to people. You've got to admit, he seems just a bit unstable. I assume you'll be hauling him back in to clarify that point?"

"Yeah. There's more to that story and this time maybe he'll give us the rest."

Maybe Kyle could have handled it better, but he was doing his job, even though Evan didn't seem like a good suspect to me. Just because you know somebody and something terrible happens to them, doesn't mean you're responsible for it. This was all still circumstantial evidence as far as I was concerned and it didn't explain what happened to Irene. Hopefully Evan could clear it up, provide the cops with an alibi. I didn't want to think about the other possibility, the possibility that I was wrong.

"I'll just be glad once all this is sorted out. The roller coaster is starting to make me a little sick."

Kyle put a hand on my thigh. "Are you sure this is a job you need right now?"

"Oh, I hope you're joking. This is the first..." I looked up to the ceiling for composure. "How about if I ask you if this is a job YOU need right now? I don't think you have any idea how long I've been waiting for a break like this. Look, I know you don't mean to, but..." I gathered my fists against my lips for a moment then looked at him. "Kyle, this is who I am. This is the part of me that runs away every time I take my finger off it just long enough. It's a big deal. I don't want you to be dismissive of it, even if you were joking. It's too important to me."

He stared back at me, and then looked down. "I'm sorry."

"I just want to lay some ground rules here. I don't want you thinking that what you do is a real job, and what I do doesn't matter. It matters to me."

"I don't think that. I would never think that. It's just that my job shows me some things that I'd rather you didn't know about. Seeing you there today, it startled me as much as it did you. Maybe I'm trying to keep you safe before there's any reason to. Just be careful. That's all I meant."

I got up off the couch, feeling the pins and needles of legs crossed too long, and Kyle followed me to the door.

"So, we okay?" He looked for a moment the same way Sydney does when I catch him in the trash, asking to be forgiven for something that was in his nature. Boys.

"We're okay. Just trust me to handle myself."

"I promise I'll try." He leaned down and kissed the corner of my mouth, less a kiss than an convergence of two things hoping to maintain contact. Maybe he was afraid I'd bite, and not in the good way. I closed the door behind him.

Sydney poked his head out of the bathroom door, as if surprised by the sudden quiet.

I broke the vodka out if its prison in the freezer and took it and a glass up to the roof, with Sydney trotting after me. I decided on a bench under the arms of an ornamental fig, and once I was settled with my drink Sydney came over and jumped up beside me, gently licking my hand.

Damn Kyle. Just when things were going to so well, he had to go and act like a guy on me. As far as I could tell, men fell into two categories: the ineffectual but pleasant, like my father, or the kind that always had to be in control. The former were easier to deal with in the long run. Maybe there was a third kind out there, a man who accepted you as you were, listened when you needed him to and left you alone when you didn't need him at all.

There was no middle ground here. If Kyle was going to be dismissive of my career, this was never going to work. And then there was the whole thing with Evan. I found it hard squaring what he'd implied about with the easygoing guy I'd known in college. He was the guy who'd crack a joke to relieve the tension, be the first to walk away from a confrontation. I tried to think of him summoning up the anger necessary to stab or shoot or strangle, but I couldn't. Of course drugs could change a personality, but I still couldn't imagine Evan as a killer, no matter how many permutations I tried. Maybe it was just something I couldn't get my mind around, the possibility that some horrible act could be ascribed to someone I knew, someone I painted stage sets with, someone whose kid sister I took to Disneyland one summer.

I finished my drink and decided against another. Today had been a bad day, but morning was going to sneak up on me and I couldn't afford the lost sleep. I left the roof and went to bed.

# CHAPTER EIGHTEEN

Erik's house was lit and garlanded, polished and filled with the scent of expensive finger foods and fresh flowers. I'd bought a new dress for tonight, even though it was just a "get-together" according to Erik. As usual, I'd worried over my appearance, wanting to hit just the right note, but it wouldn't have mattered: the mix of people was an eclectic blend of show biz strata, from studio people to indie actors, willowy models to deliberately scruffy musicians, serious looking "creatives" to flavor-of-the-day TV personalities. I stood near an ornate newel post at the foot of the sweeping stairs, watching people converse in a foyer big enough to have an echo. If someone would have made a bet, I could probably accurately pick sides for an imaginary scrimmage: Erik's guest list versus Evan's. Classic Ego versus Id. Anybody who looked like they were ready to do business probably belonged on Erik's team and anybody ready to party would be on Evan's. Years ago affairs like this would have attracted society columnists and polite cameramen would have taken down my name, being sure to get the spelling right, but now, with the circle expanded and the fame a 15-minute deal, it was just another Hollywood party.

Since I'd arrived, I'd seen people I recognized but no one I actually knew. Finally I saw Evan and Sam framed by the arched entrance to the living room. Sam gave a little wave and Evan leaned over to whisper something into her ear before breaking off and heading toward me.

"Hi, Mads."

I greeted him and glanced around, wondering where Erik was.

"It's okay, you can ask."

"And what am I supposed to be asking?"

"What happened with the cops. Everything's cool. I know you and the detective are, well, friendly with each other. I hope he hasn't convinced you I'm some kind of lunatic."

"He's met you once, and I've known you for years. I think I'm the better judge of your character."

Evan slid an arm around my shoulders. "That's my girl. And it's nothing really, just coincidence. They'll clear it up sooner or later, after they finish stumbling over each other's feet. No offense intended."

"None taken," I said.

Erik walked up and held out a glass of champagne. "Evan finally found you. I think he was a little worried that you'd be wearing a strand of garlic or carrying a silver cross."

"That's me," Evan said. "Count Dracula. And I see a neck I need to bite. I'll catch you later." He walked off toward Sam, who was backed up against the wall talking to a grey-haired man in an ill-fitting tux.

"Sorry I didn't greet you," Erik said as he led me back toward the center of the house. "I'd forgotten I invited half these people. A party always sounds like such a good idea, and then you remember all the boring friends you have. I hope you're not having an awful time."

"Not at all," I lied. "It's kind of fun to play dress-up every once in a while." At least that part was true.

Erik laughed. " Hey, it's been years since you've seen the place. After the parents jaunted off and never came back, I made a few changes around the old homestead. Come on."

He grabbed my hand and we twisted our way between knots of conversation to the rear of the house, where the kitchen opened up onto ornamental gardens and tennis courts. The room was totally revamped. Where I could remember dark oak and wrought iron -- the Mediterranean look that had been the rage twenty-five years ago -- there was blond wood and gleaming tile. The back wall had been torn out and replaced by an open garden room full of greenery, with a raised hot tub in the center. Currently, the room was abuzz with caterers and wait staff hoisting trays dripping with fruits, canapes, and assorted drinks.

"Isn't it a little bizarre to have a Jacuzzi in the kitchen?" I asked.

"What? You cook, you eat, you take a little dip. Combines all my favorite things."

Erik opened one door of the stainless steel double refrigerator and poked around, then excused himself between workers as he walked over to the wine rack against the wall and ran his fingers over the half-exposed labels of the bottles.

"Can't find what you're looking for?"

"Hmm. I was trying to find a good bottle. I mean a really good bottle. What would you pick?"

I didn't want to tell him that I rarely drank wine and had no idea what a good one was. "Whatever you think."

"Okay, one more trip then."

We left the kitchen for the back hallway. But before we could get any further, a short woman in a black jacket and pants came up to Erik and cleared her throat, then whispered something I didn't catch. Erik turned his attention back to me. "I'm sorry, Maddie, but there's a minor catastrophe with the food. I'll be right back."

I looked around for Sam, but she could have been anywhere. I began to thread my way through the grand rooms on the first floor, but there was no sign of Sam or Evan. Hell, I was going to have to start making conversation soon. It wouldn't do to be the wallflower at the school dance, looking on as all the cool kids mingled. I'd made my way back to the bottom of the stairs, when I heard a faint thud from above me, like a door being slammed, followed by a faint, tinkling crash. A few people near me looked up towards the second floor momentarily, but the music from the drawing room and the burble of conversation had masked the sounds to everyone else. While I was debating whether I should go investigate, another thump came from upstairs. A moment later, a young woman in a lilac tulle skirt and a leather jacket came hurrying down the stairs. She passed by closely enough that I caught the scent of her perfume and could see the tears on her cheeks, the streaks of eyeliner from her ruined makeup. Her honey-colored hair was artfully mussed, and I couldn't tell if there'd been a struggle or it was supposed to look that way.

She stumbled through the foyer as guests parted around her and wrenched the door open and ran out into the night. For a moment everyone stopped, and then as if it had been only a minor commercial interruption, restarted their conversations. I started up the stairs. What had Kyle said about curiosity? Well, he wasn't here. The upper hallway was empty, the doors closed, and the portraits on the walls weren't talking. I continued down the hall to another intersection, still no sign of anyone. When I neared the back stairs, I could make out Evan's voice from below. As quietly as I could, I crept down to the landing, still out of sight around a corner, feeling like a one of Charlie's Angels, dressed to the nines, but still determined to solve the mystery.

"You certainly could have handled that better," Erik said. His voice was clipped and harsh.

I peeked around the corner, but I could only see Evan's shoulder. This place needed better set decoration.

"Hey, I didn't invite her here. I just wanted to get rid of her as quickly as possible. It's hardly my fault she's crazy."

"You seem to attract the crazy types," Erik replied.

"It's my irresistible charm. It comes with the territory, Erik. You know that."

"Doesn't matter. You need to start comporting yourself with a little more decorum."

Evan laughed harshly. "Sure thing, professor. You're one to talk. I seem to remember helping you out with some girl problems once upon a time."

They shifted position, and I could see a slice of Erik's profile. He looked genuinely angry. "That's ancient history, and at least I learned my lesson. I mean it, Evan. Stop acting like nothing you do matters. I would have thought the police showing up would have been a wake-up call, but maybe you really can't change your spots. You need to grow up."

"Or what?" Evan challenged. "You'll call my parents? Jesus, Erik, you need to stop being such a tight-ass. Daddy's not watching your every move anymore. Daddy doesn't care. Maybe he never did."

Even from my rotten vantage point, I could see Erik tensing up, his shoulders rising.

"Shut up, Evan."

"Stay out of my business."

Crap. This was going to end like every schoolyard confrontation in the history of time, it was just a matter of who was going to throw the first punch. Instead, Erik took a step back, and I could no longer see his face. When he spoke again, his voice was more measured.

"I'm just trying to make something here, Evan. And I need you to do it, much as that sometimes pains me. You could be really good at this, and not just because you've got money, but because you've got that charm. You can do a hell of a lot when you put your mind to it. Don't you want to make a name for yourself, have people admire what you can do instead of what you inherited?"

"Hey, that's your shtick," Evan replied, but he sounded less hostile.

Erik sighed audibly. "I'm just trying to help you out here. Think of it as payback. I really hate to see people waste their lives. If you're given a talent, you should use it."

Evan laughed again, but this time with genuine humor. "You could say it was my 'talents' that got me into this mess. Maybe instead of directing, you should go on the road as a motivational speaker. I bet you could pack a house."

"Isn't that half the job anyway? Coaxing the best out of people?"

"Or keeping the cattle in line."

Erik moved back into view, and I could see the smile curving his lips. "Oh, they're not all cattle. What was it Hitchcock said, 'I never said all actors are cattle; what I said was all actors should be treated like cattle.'"

"Don't let Maddie hear you say that, she's liable to sock you."

"Oh, Maddie's different. She works hard. She cares about what she's doing."

"If I didn't know you better, I'd say you were sweet on her."

"Strictly professional," Erik replied. "You should try it. It'd do wonders for your reputation. And speaking of your reputation, you'd better get back out there before people start making unpleasant connections. But remember what I said, just cool it a little with all the bad boy shenanigans. The last thing we need is the police hauling you back in."

They moved from earshot, and I sat down for a moment on the steps. I was still bothered by the crying girl in lilac, so easily dismissed. Maybe I'd been wrong about Evan, and he was a jerk who had a problem with women, but I still couldn't see him as a killer. He certainly hadn't sounded guilty, just defensive. All in all, I'd much rather the melodrama stayed in front of the camera, rather than behind it.

I retraced my steps through the upstairs hall and back down to the floor. Sam tapped me on the shoulder at the bottom of the steps and I turned, sure she could read the emotion on my face.

"Maddie. I'm so glad I found you. I just wanted to tell you I was leaving. I'm getting a massive headache."

"You okay?"

"Yeah, except for the headache. Why?" The skin around her eyes tightened into pale creases. "Did you see Evan?"

I tried to formulate an answer.

"It's not what you think, Maddie." Sam said. "Some little tramp he used to date showed up. He thought she might make a scene so he went to talk to her. He's going to meet me at the car in a little bit. It's really no big deal."

"If you say so."

"I say so. Don't worry about it. I'm not." She kissed my cheek. "I'll see you on Monday, okay?"

As Sam headed off in one direction, Erik approached from another. He seemed no worse for wear from his tet-a-tet with Evan.

"Sorry it took me so long, but I think I've got everything purring along again. Ready for the expedition?"

I considered trying to work the word "cattle" into my reply, but thought better of it. "Sure," I said. "Lead on."

We made our way to the back towards the kitchen then down a flight of stairs that opened onto another hallway with five closed doors. Erik paused and tapped one of the doors. "Remember this? For years I thought the old man lived down here. Of course the nice thing about having your own screening rooms is that there's never a line for tickets."

He headed for the last door on the left, opened it onto the damp smell of old stone and flicked on the light. I followed him down another set of steps, placing my feet carefully on the narrow steps so I wouldn't trip on my dress and land on top of him. This room looked like a true wine cellar, the kind you might find in a European castle, with rough-hewn walls and dark flagstone floors, vaulted arches and a barrel ceiling. The recesses were dark pools that the light didn't touch.

"Very atmospheric," I said. "I don't remember ever being down here."

"Oh, my father loved this even more than he loved the screening room. Said that it maintained the perfect temperature and humidity. If he could have packed the thing up and taken it with him to Europe, he would have." He wound his way through racks that reached to the ceiling, and picked up a bottle.

"So," I said. "You have the inventory memorized?"

"Just the very best bottles. Chateau Lafitte Rothschild 1970. Wonderful Bordeaux. Hints of black currents, violet and oak."

He sounded like he was reading from a brochure. "I'll take your word for it."

"Not a wine enthusiast?"

"Afraid I'm more of the queen of beers. I can pick out a great India pale ale or a nice oatmeal stout, but grapes always seem like grapes. I'm always afraid I'll choose the wrong one."

"Well, I was going to try to impress you with a glass of this," he said, gesturing with the bottle. "But I'm sure we can find you a bottle of something dark and grainy upstairs."

"That would be swell."

I turned to head back up the stairs, but despite all my caution the heel of my shoe caught in the uneven slate of floor and I felt myself pitching forward. I had the immediate image of crashing wine racks and the shattered debris of bottles worth more than a month's salary, but Erik caught me, managing to maintain his hold on the Bordeaux while halting my fall.

I tried to find my footing again in his embrace, his breath against my cheek. I could feel the accelerated beat of his heart under my palm, and I wondered if it was the unexpected intimacy or the residual image of me destroying half his inventory. Whether it was temporary shock or something else, his hand lingered on my side and his lips brushed my neck as we managed to right ourselves without bumping into anything.

"Close call," I said lamely.

Erik let out a shaky laugh. "No harm done. You sure your okay?"

"I would do a little dance to show you, but I think that could be dangerous down here."

"I think you're right. Let's go topside and I'll find you that beer."

We made our way back up, the sounds of laughter and music growing stronger with each step. Before we reached the top of the last flight of stairs, Erik turned to me. "In case I forgot to tell you, I'm glad you're here tonight, Maddie. It's been nice having you back. Thanks for coming."

It was awkward, but sweet, as if Erik had suddenly dropped the sophisticated pretense he wore so comfortably and we were kids again, separated by a few years, but still relegated to background while the adults talked over our heads and we snuck into kitchens to raid the canapé trays. We hadn't been particularly close, but we'd ended up conspirators more than once by circumstance, extras there to add a little family touch. And now here we were, the grown-ups, following in our parent's professions, playing out the same scenes they had against the same backdrops. I flashed back on Evan's mention of me in the overhead conversation, and the way Erik had brushed the suggested attraction off. I certainly didn't need that entanglement. I hoped that nostalgia was all that was fueling Erik's sentiments. I was willing to chalk it all up to the overwrought Gothic atmosphere of the wine cellar.

Erik did find me that beer before making the rounds of conversation necessary to good hosting, and I managed to nurse it, though I really wanted to knock it back with wild abandon. I walked the perimeter of the thinning crowd, but saw no familiar faces. I hadn't seen Evan leave, but I assumed that he had met Sam at the car and all was well or would be when she got something for her headache.

I stayed a little less that a half hour more, made sure to find Erik, and thanked him for the evening. We parted with a respectful peck on the cheek.

When I got home, I pressed the play button on the answering machine with some trepidation, but there were no message from Kyle. Instead, a canned voice, speaking too loudly and too closely to the receiver, crackled from its hollow home. "Ms. Pryce, this is Dr. Denison. I'm sorry to tell you that Harry Gaines passed away this evening. We've informed his son, who'll be handling the arrangements." I listened as the doctor left his voicemail number and gave his sympathies again.

Poor Harry, finally through that long, lonely stint without his wife. I thought of his rotting backyard and had the sudden impulse to go over there and cut the grass, pull the weeds, some last act of remembrance. I hadn't said goodbye when I'd visited the day before.

# CHAPTER NINETEEN

Harry's funeral was even smaller than Irene's had been, and involved no more than a handful of strangers under a dingy green tent in a treeless Catholic cemetery. I'd never inquired about his religion because he seemed a man who had none. The sun felt wrong on my bare shoulders and the grass smelled too sweet, putting me in mind of picnics and ballparks, anything but the solemn occasion that was taking place. The man next to me was tall, thin and red-haired, and if I squinted hard I could see his face superimposed over the child's photograph on Harry's table. I caught no hint of remorse over years lost between a son and father; he had the body language of someone suffering a minor annoyance, like having to take a detour on his way home.

After the service I watched as Harry's coffin was lowered into the ground, then turned with the thought of offering condolences to his son. He was already gone.

~~~

After the funeral I was stuck with the dilemma of returning his keys. I couldn't just keep them, but repeated tries to contact his son had met with no success. I wished it had occurred to me to take them to the funeral, to hand them over then, but it hadn't. I decided that the best course of action would be to stop by and leave them at the house where whoever was taking care of the estate would find them.

I stripped the bed and took a load of sheets, pillowcases and towels down to the washer so they could run through a cycle while I was gone, then headed over to the house.

I let myself in the front door and met a wall of silence, as if the house had been stuffed with cotton. The clocks were gone from the wall in the living room, the pale echoes of their shapes a mute testament to the years they'd hung there, keeping time until it ran out. The furniture and appliances were also missing, except for a few pieces that apparently hadn't been worth selling or sending to another destination. Boxes bound shut with masking tape lined the hallway, the word *Goodwill* scrawled across them in magic marker. It hadn't taken long to pack up Harry's existence.

I re-locked the front door and checked the back door to make sure I wouldn't need the keys to secure it, then searched for someplace to leave them, finally deciding on a kitchen counter. I stopped with my hand on the doorknob. I didn't know if anyone had bothered to collect the rest of Harry's notes, if anyone had stopped to consider that he spent his days doing anything other than drinking bourbon. I'd made a contract with Harry to go through his files, and if they were still there, I would. I made my way back to the office, which was unchanged except for the absence of the old Underwood. Whoever had begun the systematic plundering hadn't gotten that far or had taken one look at the disarray and left it for later.

I couldn't find any more boxes, so I hunted through the house until I discovered a white trash bag under the sink in the kitchen. That would work.

I gathered up all the stray pieces of paper and stacked them as neatly as I could. Some were ragged and coffee-stained, some were faded and obviously years old. I stood there in the silence with the half-full trash bag hanging from my hand, feeling like a burglar, wondering what I would say if someone came in. I still didn't know exactly why I was doing this. Except for the few snippets of information I'd already found, there hadn't been anything that shed light on what happened with Irene and with Jason. But I needed a sense of completion and it would only take another few hours to go through the sad collection so that I could feel I'd tried everything, looked under every rock.

I scooped up the last few scraps of paper and twisted the bag shut. I let myself out the back door and stood in the forlorn yard, saying my last goodbye to Harry.

I didn't bother to go up to the apartment once I got home, just carried the trash bag down to the basement so I could check on the progress of the laundry. It was cool and dim, quiet enough that I could sit down and just be. I moved the wet sheets and towels to the dryer and pulled over one of the cast-off chairs, then settled down to page through the last of Harry's scribbles.

Harry's obsessive lists went into one pile, receipts into another, and I sorted all the torn-out pages from notebooks and legal pads into a third. I'd considered trying to transcribe the mess, or at least take notes, but as I scanned through page after page of Harry's cramped handwriting, I realized that most of this had nothing to do with anything; all the names I saw meant nothing to me.

I began to place the neat stacks back into the bag, a lot of work for something I would probably just end up throwing away. The dryer clicked off and I was about to call it quits when I heard a furtive sound behind me, back in the dark reaches of the cellar. The sound came again, the scrape of something against wood, and a hundred thoughts went through my mind, most of them having to do with me ending up dead down here in the dark. I looked around for something, anything that might work as a weapon. There was a tennis racket weeping strings leaning against a corner and I picked it up and hefted it. Why couldn't we have any weekend softball players in the building? A bat would have been much more reassuring. The scratching stopped, and I had begun to convince myself that it was just a mouse when something crashed from the next room, back where the boiler was. I shot toward the stairs with thoughts of finding Lyle Lambert, or anybody, but my foot tangled in Harry's trash bag and I sprawled onto the stone floor amid the few scattered papers I had yet to replace. A muffled meow came from behind me, and I almost laughed in relief. I got to my feet and walked over to the massive wooden door at the back of the room, then opened it slowly.

Chauncey slid out from the opening and began to twine around my ankles, looking up as if to ask what took me so long.

"How'd you get down here?"

Chauncey didn't answer, just continued his figure-eights around my feet, accompanied by his motor-boat purr.

I picked him up and he increased the volume. I leaned over with him cradled in my arms and shoved the rest of the papers into the trash bag, then slid it over beside the washer. I'd figure out what to do with it later.

When I deposited Chauncey back at Sharon's apartment, she was thrilled to see him. Apparently he'd darted out the door and been gone overnight and she'd entertained all kinds of ideas about speeding cars and cruel teenagers. She had no idea how he'd gotten into the basement.

# CHAPTER TWENTY

My lazy Sunday afternoon was interrupted by a knock, and the view through the peephole treated me to the top of Kyle's head.

When opened the door, he was staring down at his hands, and when he finally looked up I could see white lines of tension drawing down the corners of his mouth. He looked like the cop who had come to the door following my parents' accident, like cops who came to doors everyday in L.A., who couldn't quite make eye contact as they mechanically reeled off bits of horror and sorrow.

"I need you to come with me." No pleasantries, no nervous banter, just a cold edge under his voice like a knife waiting to cut.

"Kyle. What's wrong?"

He brushed past me into the small foyer, turned and ran one hand over his short blond hair, as if trying to dislodge an unexpected spider web.

"You want to know what's wrong? I'll tell you what's wrong. Kids who shoot other kids over sneakers. Homeboys who take out four-year-olds on playgrounds in drive-bys. Parents who starve their children because they traded their food stamps for crack, and when the kids cry they shake them so hard their brains hemorrhage. And when you look at them, there's nothing there. No remorse, no idea, like a fucking empty box. Kids who get off the bus and in a week they're giving themselves away for a hamburger. Disposable lives. This city is a fucking cesspool."

I could see the electricity in his eyes building toward release, the kind of look that men get just before they punch a wall. "Just come with me," he said.

"Kyle..." I began.

"Just thirty minutes of your time. Is that so much to ask?"

I felt a tingle of fear. A friend in an acting class had once off-handedly warned me never to date a cop. She said that they were all psychotics who needed a badge to excuse themselves when they crossed the line. Kyle had never frightened me, but how well did I really know him? Sleeping with someone a few times, sharing a few beers, didn't prepare you for the point when the monsters crawled out of the basement and showed their claws. What if the last few weeks had given him time to open his own cellar door and become acquainted with what was down there? I'd forgotten to hand out the dating questionnaire that asked if he'd ever hacked up a previous girlfriend. Right now he looked like ball lightning trapped in a jar and I didn't want to open it.

"I'm not sure I'm comfortable with that, Kyle."

He looked away and clenched his fists as comprehension dawned on him.

"Christ, Maddie. You think I'm going to hurt you? You think this is some sick revenge thing because we hit a little rough spot? Give me some fucking credit." He shook his head. "I'm sorry I just barged in like this, but it's been a long, bad day. Don't you dare think I would do this if it wasn't important."

I hesitated again, but there was something in his face, below the white edge of anger and the despair in his eyes. Did I trust Kyle? I guess I did.

"Let me get my jacket."

Kyle was silent on the ride across town, and I watched his knuckles whiten as he gripped the steering wheel. I tried to think my way inside his head but he kept himself apart from me, as if the inches separating us in the front seat were a gulf neither of us could hope to cross. As we drove up Mulholland, I stole glances at him, the shadows from the trees along the road shifting across his profile. He never looked at me.

Up ahead, I saw yellow police tape flashing through the brush and I could smell the misty scent of incipient rain drifting through my half-open window. Police vehicles lined the sides of the road, and as we pulled up behind a dark sedan, Ramirez glanced up like a startled deer. She looked for a moment as if she didn't know where she was. Or maybe she knew, and really just didn't want to be there.

Kyle turned to me as he opened his door. "Stay with me. I'm not exactly in bounds bringing you here, so if anybody asks anything let me do the talking."

He was out of the door before I could object, leaving me no choice but to follow him as he trudged off toward a small trail that led up the canyon side. Ramirez intercepted him before he could reach the two uniformed cops posted at the trailhead like temple guards. She blew air through her teeth and turned her head from side to side as if someone might be sneaking up on her.

"What the hell do you think you're doing?"

"I want you to keep her here, Angie."

Ramirez looked at me then cut her gaze back to Kyle. "Why did you bring her to a crime scene?"

"She needs to know, Angie. She needs to realize what we're into here before she goes and gets herself mixed up in it too."

Ramirez stared at him for a few beats, then shrugged. "If anybody asks me who brought her, I'm not going to lie."

"I'm not asking you to. Just keep her down here while I go up, okay."

"Fine. It's your funeral." She turned away, but not before I caught the wounded look in her eyes.

Kyle took off again, past the cops and up the grade. I saw the hillside scrub grab at his jacket and try to pull him off-course. Then a small rock came down the path toward us. It lodged against a clump of grasses before reaching the bottom.

"So what exactly is..."

"I'll babysit you but I won't teach. Let him bother if he thinks you're worth it." She never looked at me, just kept her focus on the hillside, on whatever it was that was about to happen or had happened up there.

There was a ring of people at the top of the ridge, which

sloped away from us, obscuring all but the people closest to our position. There were a few pines and spindly stands of chaparral, lonely looking dust bowl plants, but not what you'd call a tree line. I could just make out Kyle as he approached a bearded man. He shook his head and Kyle said something emphatic, accompanied by hand gestures.

I tried to make sense of the scene around me. Uniforms, plainclothes and technicians swarmed the hillside, a colony of ants with some joint purpose I couldn't fathom; snatches of conversation made no sense. The stretcher was surrounded by people and I didn't see it at first. When they began to carry it down the hillside like you see in those search and rescue stories on the news, I could clearly make out the black bag that lay upon it. It looked deflated, like a balloon from a party that was long over. There wasn't going to be any rescue here today.

"Some college student, grad school entomologist or something up here looking for bugs. He found the first one," Ramirez said.

"The first one," I repeated.

"He was smart enough, or panicked enough, not to touch anything. Just called the cops. The press doesn't have a bead on it yet, but that won't last." Late sun broke through the clouds on the horizon, and Ramirez glanced back toward the sprawl of L.A. to the west. "You wouldn't think you could hide something very well in an area of twelve million people, but the oldest one they've found so far has probably been here a year. Hopefully the M.E.'ll be better able to narrow that down."

"What the...."

"The missing girls," Ramirez said in a low voice. "They aren't missing any more."

The cop came back by with a fresh stretcher.

"How many?" Ramirez called.

"Four so far, as near as we can tell."

There was a shout from the hillside.

"Make that five."

I felt the urge to run. "Do you mind if I just go sit by the car?"

Ramirez looked at me with something almost approaching empathy. "Go on. Get out of here."

I was going to sit on the hood of Kyle's car, but when I touched it and felt the sting I ruled that out. I knew the inside would be unbearable in this humidity, so I crouched down on the dirt in the small amount of shade afforded by the passenger side. This was one of those times I wished I smoked, or carried a bottle of vodka on my person at all times. But in reality, this was one of those times for which no amount of planning would help, nor be appropriate. I wanted to be mad at Kyle and I was, a little. More incensed, if I was honest with myself. Mostly I just felt a tearless sadness for these poor strangers. I didn't dare let my mind wander to what circumstance might have brought them here, what heinous acts had been perpetrated upon them. And I thought about Paul Saroyan and Jennifer Chandler. I thought about Bravo and Evan. And I thought about my dead: Irene, Jason, now Harry. I turned my thoughts to the rest of the world around me. I tried to listen for any rush of wind that might come, any birdsong that might distract me from the activity going on behind me; I waited for something to bring the sweetness of nature back to this place. I sat there so long that my calves began to go numb, when what I really needed numbed was my brain. I couldn't even pretend anymore that this was just something you watched from the safety of your living room, some feature where they'd edited out all the really bad stuff.

I heard footsteps in the gravelly dirt and put a hand on the hot car to steady myself to a standing position. It was Kyle. It didn't look like him, but I knew that it was. And what I could read in his eyes was nowhere near what he'd just witnessed, but it was brutal enough to make me want to cry.

"Why did you bring me here?"

"Maddie." He cleared his throat and tried again. "Maddie, I see this stuff all the time, but it's part of my job. It may be familiar, but it's never usual. It always hurts and makes you mad at the same time. I didn't want you to just hear this from me on the phone or at my desk. I needed for you to understand that this is real."

"But I don't see why…"

He put up his hand. "I just felt like…" He looked down at the dirt then back up at me. "When I got this call, the first thing I thought was that I wouldn't know what to do if I ever… If there's any chance that you're close to any of this, please get out now."

"Was Jennifer Chandler…"

"The coroner will have to make a determination, but I don't have any doubt."

I knew I should say something. I should cuss him out for bringing me here. Or I should give him a "your heart was in the right place" speech. Nothing would come out of the blender of emotions in my head. I just looked at him, quietly, trying to affect no particular expression until I could figure out which one, if any, was the right one.

After an immensely long silence I did manage something. "Can we go now?"

"Yeah," he said under his breath, fumbling in his pants pocket for the keys.

I got into the car and didn't look at him. I guess it must've been his turn to watch me now. All I wanted was to go back in time to this afternoon in my apartment where the biggest crisis to deal with was what to thaw for dinner. How selfish a thought was that? But if I had it to do over again, I wouldn't open the door, I'd hide inside the safety of my world until Kyle's knocking ceased and he went back down the stairs and into the light of day alone.

More cops had poured into the road at the bottom of the hill, and there were news vans pulled up at odd angles. The bearded man from the ridge was here now and was yelling at a woman in a red suit, who I recognized from Channel Five. Her cameraman was shooting their live shot for tonight's newscast. As we drove past and made our way back down Mulholland, I made a promise to myself to skip the news, for tonight anyway. There would be more details soon enough. For now, I'd seen and heard all that I needed to know.

# CHAPTER
# TWENTY-ONE

The next two days went by like a half-remembered dream punctuated by the pulse and patter of normal life. Memory came in flashes when I wasn't looking, then floated away like a child's balloon in the last hours of a carnival. Words the anchorwoman said, the wafted scent of Erik's cologne and the sharp point of his Italian shoes, the light brown of Kyle's watchband and the glint of his hair in the sun, Ramirez' dangling pink-gold earrings just tugging apart the pierce of her lobes, the melting orange Creamsicle I ate that reminded me of summer, the books I dropped in the resounding drum of the metal repository in the library parking lot. I filled my head with all the stingless words and images I could gather, filled it to the point that I could no longer remember my lines. They would come and not stay, unlike the details I was afraid might come and never leave.

The TV changed from scene to scene, light bouncing off the walls like flashbulbs for still photographs as slices of decay and death were sandwiched between mini-van ads and toothpaste commercials. At a glance kids filling the ground then spilling from opened vehicle doors, teeth being studied for identification then gleamed for shine.

Only one name had been released so far. Jennifer Chandler had been buried in a shallow grave amid the underbrush off Mulholland Drive. Now it was real, had gone out to thousands of eyes and ears, was part of human record and could not be revoked. Her picture, a black and white high school annual shot, pointed her toward the outside of the TV screen rather than the inside, not an acceptable format on my college newspaper, but probably all they had to work with. I wondered about her parents' grief, having heard the death of a child is the hardest to bear. And I thought too about the grievers connected to the yet to be identified, the people out there waiting to hear the worst news they would likely ever know.

On the set I tunneled inside my character so completely that the world beyond the soot-black sound stage doors did not exist. Should someone slip in or out, I justified the presence of a slant of light as a shiny sword brandished by an actor not associated with our drama, practicing his swashbuckling scene. The smooth flow of rehearsal that had prevailed to this point seemed to be straining at the seams, the personality conflicts that severed every workplace surfacing. After all, now Evan was no longer just a person of interest in the disappearance of a possible runaway, he was the main suspect in a serial murder case. It would have seemed absurd if it wasn't too goddamned awful. How do you deal with that? There are no instruction manuals.

Sam would disappear for a half hour at a time, alternating petulance with an almost embarrassing desire to please. Erik seemed unhappy with either extreme, and more than once I saw Sam glance around for rescue as he pulled her to the side and hissed instructions through clenched teeth. I steered clear of the skirmishes and only nodded when Erik snapped direction.

The storm that had been brewing erupted Wednesday afternoon halfway through a scene where I was to confront Sam's character for the first time. She'd been erratic during the morning, mumbling her lines then working a scene like a diva in the spell of a breathless aria. She started out as if she were on fire, volleying dialogue back and forth with me, each of us feeding on the other's emotion. Then she seemed to drift and the focus of the argument was lost.

Erik rushed to the center of the set and moved between me and Sam, and I heard her gasp as he grabbed her arm.

"What the hell's the matter with you!" Erik's voice held all the wrath of an Old Testament god. "You're this close to blowing the biggest chance you'll ever have."

I placed my hand between the tensed muscles in his back. "Erik."

He turned toward me and Sam massaged the red coil left by his fingers. Erik exhaled slowly. "Jesus. I'm sorry, Sam. I know we're all under pressure, but I just want everything to be perfect. Look, everyone, why don't we take a break and start up again in an hour."

The crew scattered, and I headed back to my dressing room for a few moments of quiet. The door opened before I could acknowledge the knock. Erik stepped inside, subdued, as if he'd caught and re-caged whatever personal demon had escaped earlier.

"Let me apologize again for what happened. There's no excuse for that. It's just...." He rubbed his temple.

"There's something else, isn't there." I said. "What is it?"

Erik pulled up a chair and sat down across from me, taking my hand in his. "I don't want to worry you."

Sheesh. "Look, I'm already worried, so why don't you just tell me."

"Okay. We may have a problem. This whole...mess is really taking a toll on Evan's psyche. They've been leaning on him pretty heavily and apparently they're not liking the answers he's giving. He's talking about just pulling the plug on the film. Or at least halting production until this is sorted. If only..."

"If only what?"

Erik shook his head. "If only a lot of things. But I can't force him to fund the picture. Even it I tried to, a legal battle is about the last thing he needs right now."

"And there's no way you could make up any shortfall yourself? Find financing elsewhere?" I inwardly winced at my selfishness, but I still wanted this to go forward. It was the only thing keeping me sane right now.

I watched unreadable emotions cross Erik's face. "I wish I

could, Maddie. I really wish I could. But everything about this is temporarily radioactive. I think I'd have a hell of a time finding backers. I just want to keep everything on an even keel for as long as possible. My concern right now is Samantha. If she seems unstable, that could be the thing that forces him over the edge. I can't have her fall apart right now. I think she just needs guidance from someone who's more level-headed, someone she can relate to. I'm obviously not the right one to do it, as you just witnessed."

"But you think I am."

"Just give it a try, Maddie. I was thinking we could take a dinner cruise, just the four of us, mend some fences. I'll try to calm Evan down and you can have a little heart-to-heart with Samantha. Try to salvage this thing."

My first instinct was to beg off. I felt drained and out of sorts. I hadn't been sleeping. The thought of attempting to shoulder someone else's burden, of putting myself out there as some steadying force, was almost too much. But Sam was radiating distress like a beacon, and Erik was right, I could feel things on the set spiraling out of control.

"What the hell", I said, "Just don't expect any miracles."

~~~

The Beverly Hills Marina was filled with unfurling white sails, and boats lined the horizon like debutantes who'd just come out. I made my way past glossy hulks nodding at their reflections to the slip at the end of the pier, where Erik's boat rose from the water like an amber-glassed glacier. The word Lorelei danced in script across the bow.

I was trying to figure out how to board when Erik popped onto the deck in a mint green pullover, faded jeans and deck shoes. He helped me climb the polished ladder as Evan poked his head out of the cabin door. "Can we get going now that the princess has arrived? I'm starving."

Erik turned to me. "How about it. Are you ready to set sail?"

"As long as you know how to steer this thing."

We sailed into the coming dusk and anchored far enough away that the lights of the shore became stars, afloat on a slice of deepening blue trapped between the moon and the water. Inside the spacious cabin, Erik put out a meal of cold herbed chicken and pasta while we sipped expensive Chablis and made innocuous small talk, as if everyone was afraid of saying the wrong thing. From the outside the four of us must have looked like an advertisement for the good life. After the meal was finished, Sam excused herself and made her way to the head, dragging her slim, black purse behind her.

Erik seemed to be trying to telegraph something with his eyebrows. I blinked my best semaphore back at him. There was a short awkward silence until Sam returned, her eyes artificially bright. Erik delivered his line.

"Sam, why don't you and Maddie go enjoy the air while Evan and I clean up?"

I grabbed my wine and Sam followed. We leaned on the night-chilled railing, staring into the black glass of the ocean.

"You must have drawn the short straw," she said.

"That obvious, huh?" I turned and reached my hand toward her forearm. "I'm sorry, it's just--"

She pulled away, waving off my concern. "Hey, it's okay. Don't worry about it. I've just been waiting for the other shoe to drop. And I want you to know that I blame myself for what happened today. I had it coming."

"No. Erik was totally out of line. But he knows that. We're just all under a lot of stress."

Sam was silent as she turned her eyes back to the sea.

What the hell was I going to say to her? "Don't take this wrong, but you need to get control of your life."

"Tell me about it."

I took a deep breath and said something that had been on mind since the night of Erik's party. "You know, I've known Evan for years, but maybe he's not the best thing for you right now. At least until filming's over. Then you can step back and reassess this." I wasn't sure that was exactly what Erik had in mind when he'd pulled me into this assignment, I wasn't sure what complications would ensue from a breakup of whatever relationship the two of them had going, but I had no doubt Evan was not healthy for her.

Sam gave no response, so I moved on.

"And you and I should get together, do some things outside of work. Hang out, go shopping."

Sam gave a harsh laugh. "I don't need you to babysit me. That's the one thing I don't need, anybody's pity."

"It's not like that."

She whipped around to face me. "What's it like then? Suddenly you want to be my BFF? Would you even be out here if Erik hadn't asked you? You're more like them than you think," she said, nodding toward the lighted cabin. "You've have this safe, happy little life, and when it gets messy, you pick a spot and scrub and scrub until it comes clean. Until everything's perfect again. I really don't think you can scrub me clean."

I tried to think of something that wouldn't sound like she was right, that I wasn't on a mercenary mission to pull her back together so the show could go on. "You want the truth, Sam? I don't have many friends. For whatever reason, I find it easiest to just keep to myself. The less you depend on people, the less chance there is for them to disappoint you, or be disappointed in you. I think we're probably alike that way."

"And, yeah, Erik asked me to talk to you. I can't vouch for his motives, I can only vouch for mine. I know we don't know each other very well yet, but I like you. Maybe I see something in you that I see in myself. Whatever it is, it's worth saving, worth caring about. And if the production closed down tomorrow, I'd still feel the same way."

Sam cocked her head at me. "You seem so sincere." The sarcasm was there, but there was something underneath it. Maybe she wanted to believe me after all.

"What would you like?" I said. "Got a safety pin? We can prick our fingers and become blood sisters, like it's fifth grade all over

150

again. Or how about I walk the plank? Erik probably has a plank around here somewhere."

Sam's laugh this time seemed a tiny bit genuine. Maybe I was wearing her down. "Mutiny. No reason they shouldn't be walking the plank. We can raid the fridge and then sail to Tahiti."

"I think Hawaii's closer, but I was never very good at geography." I glanced back at the lighted windows of the cabin. "We should probably go back in. But I meant what I said. Maybe we could both use a friend. And if I bore you to tears, you can always run the other way."

"Maybe a little boring wouldn't be so bad."

"Tell me about it."

Inside the cabin, Erik looked more relaxed and the vibe had changed. Maybe he was right, and everybody just need to slow down and take a breath.

The four of us finished the bottle of wine and then moved out onto the deck, listening to the distant noise of other parties on other boats as it was blown to us on the wet, warm breezes of the night air. Around ten we headed back for the shore, pinpricks of light redefining themselves, marking boats, houses and street lights. Sam gave me a brief peck on the cheek before she followed Evan onto the pier.

I hung behind and after we watched them disappear into the darkness, I turned to Erik. "I take it things went okay with Evan?"

"I think so. If I can just get him to remain calm and listen to reason, I'm sure this will all blow over. Samantha seemed much more relaxed after your little intervention."

"I wouldn't really call it an intervention. I suggested we go shopping."

Erik laughed. "Well, if you can just exert your calming influence on her a while, I think she'll be fine. Sometimes girls like that just act out, and once you call them on it, they straighten up. You see it a lot with actresses."

"Do you now?"

Erik couldn't miss my tone. He dipped his head and then

sat down on one of the padded benches outside the cabin, motioning for me to join him. I couldn't think of an excuse not to. "I didn't mean that the way it sounded, Maddie. And certainly not about you." He paused. "You work hard, you care about the art. You always have. You were always a serious kid, you know."

I didn't remember it that way. I always thought of myself as a lonely kid. I'd been lucky enough to live a life of privilege, but didn't have anybody to share it with. Nobody except the people on the screen. I could say none of those things without sounding like I was feeling sorry for myself. And he wasn't giving Sam enough credit. Despite her erratic behavior, when she was on point, she was amazing.

"I just want so badly for this to go well," I said. "This role couldn't have come along at a better time. To tell you the truth, I was kind of toying with the idea of looking for another line of work."

Erik reached over and took my hand, held it between his. I couldn't decide if that was a fatherly gesture or something more. The moonlight and the slow rock of the boat, on top of a few glasses of wine, was making me sleepy.

"Oh, that would be a terrible mistake, Maddie," Erik said. "I never said it, but I always thought there was something special about you. Samantha's sort of flashy and high maintenance. If she were a sports car, she'd be a Jaguar. Sure they look great and go around the track fast, but after a few laps, they start running hot and before you know it they're a smoking mess. And good luck finding a mechanic to get it back into shape.

"You, on the other hand, you're more BMW. Elegant, but with hidden depths. I've always wanted to see what you had under the hood."

Wow, that ranked up there with the worst lines I'd ever heard in any club, bar, or even a high school kegger. Maybe I hadn't read him wrong at the party the other night. I slowly pulled my hand back from Erik's wondering how to best deflect this without embarrassing him.

What to say? He was like the older brother I'd never had?

Ugh. "Oh, Erik, I never thought of you, us, like that."

Erik froze for a second, then turned to look at me, a line creasing his forehead. Then he laughed, a low chuckle that seemed to spread upward.

"Oh, Maddie, you thought.... I'm sorry. That wasn't what I meant at all. Oh, my." He stood up and reached for my hand. "Come with me a minute. I want to show you something."

Erik led me through the galley to a recessed door that opened onto three compact steps.

"Now, don't think I'm making a move here, I just want to show you something." We entered a gleaming stateroom with a polished wood floor and brass knobs fitted to built-in cabinets. The room was dominated by a raised bed with a square of moonlight shining down on it. Erik walked over to the built-in cabinet, flipped on the reading light and reached inside the top drawer.

He withdrew a small leather photo album. The front was embossed with entwined stylized gold hearts. He held it out for me. I opened it up to a photograph of Erik on a bright ski slope, goggles pushed up across his high forehead, his arm around a rather stunning woman in a fur-lined parka. She was as tall as he was and smiling at the camera ferociously. I flipped through. Another picture of the same woman, her mane of honey-colored hair cascading down her bare back as she stood on a beach, looking over her shoulder. The woman sitting at a small table at an outdoor cafe with her head on Erik's shoulder.

"Her name is Avika," Eric said. "And despite her demure looks, she has a remarkable temper and is a tad possessive."

Demure, sure. "She looks rather formidable," I said.

"Quite. Right now she's off doing a photo shoot in -- what day is it? Well, it hardly matters. She's always doing a photo shoot somewhere. Having a long distance relationship is great, because if you only see someone every couple of months, it's always fresh and exciting. You never get bored. Of course, the downside is that while she's on some beach with an unpronounceable name being ogled by photographers, I'm here waiting."

I felt like an idiot. Maybe idiot was too tame. I handed back the album.

"Erik, I'm sorry, I didn't..."

He laughed again. "Don't be sorry. Totally my fault. You're in this business long enough you fall prey to the disease of being overly glib. Even when you're sincere, you end up sounding like some sad Lothario." He slid the album back into the drawer. "You wear a mask long enough, you forget you're wearing it. Blame the whole thing on my tortured metaphor."

It was my turn to laugh. "That was pretty atrocious. I have a suggestion for you, never compare a woman to a car, or a big-screen TV, or a nice bottle of wine, for that matter. We like to be seen as people, not expensive possessions."

"Duly noted. I promise never to speak about your tantalizing bouquet, or the number of pixels you can fit onto a screen." He walked around the bed and put his arm around my shoulders. This time it felt more familial and less creepy. "But despite my inartful metaphor, I was being sincere. Thank you for what you've done to keep this whole situation together." He did not ruffle my hair to make my humiliation complete.

I drove home with the top down, feeling the bizarre dislocation of living in two worlds, one where directors on yachts told you about their supermodel girlfriends and another where bodies were unearthed from a crumbling hillside. Unspoken tonight had been any words about that second world and the fact that Evan was walking around under a cloud of suspicion. I'd certainly tied those thoughts up and pushed them into a closet and locked them up for the time being. Of course they didn't go away, not really, and that big, fat question mark was still there, floating around and causing trouble. Hopefully it would be answered sooner rather than later, at least as far as Evan's guilt or innocence was concerned.

# CHAPTER TWENTY-TWO

A week later and there were still no answers, just a tense purgatory. Evan was absent and Erik was distracted. Sam was being a good girl, and I was holding my breath. The bad news came right before lunch and I knew what it was before Erik opened his mouth to speak. He promised the crew it was a temporary setback, probably no more than two weeks. I wondered if he had pulled that time frame out of thin air. I retreated to my dressing room to contemplate what I was going to do now, checked my phone and found a message from Kyle.

I punched in the number and he answered on the second ring.

"I'm returning your call," I said.

"I'd like to talk to you--"

"So, talk."

"I mean I'd like to talk to you in person. I promised I'd keep you up to date, and that's what I'm trying to do. It would also be helpful if you could go over what happened the night of Jason's death again. We have some more information, and maybe there's something you didn't remember."

"And when did you need this?"

"As soon as possible. There's also someone here you might find interesting."

"What you think is interesting and what I think is interesting are two totally different things."

Kyle exhaled into the receiver. "Maddie, please."

I looked up to see Erik framed within the open door.

"Okay. I'll stop by as soon as I can." I switched off the phone without waiting for Kyle's reply.

Erik walked in and threw himself into the chair.

"What happened?" I said.

Erik ran a hand through his hair and then slowly massaged his temples.

"Evan's punked out. I thought he was going to hold steady, but he says there's no way he can go forward with this right now. Just like that, as if nobody else is depending on it, as if it's all just about him." Erik was angrier than I'd ever heard him.

"Maybe he's just a little freaked out, maybe if you --"

Erik slammed his palm down on the dressing table. "All I've done the past few weeks is hold his hand. Hell, I told him to just stay home, out of sight, and I'll take care of everything. But the press has got wind of it now, and he's got some insane idea that this is all tainted. So he's just going to drop it like he drops anything when it loses its shine, when it becomes too hard. He's always had it so easy, because there's never been any consequences for him. He doesn't understand working for something, creating something. Everything in his world has always been separated into fun and not fun. I guess this was all just a distraction to him after all, and he's decided it's not fun anymore. Damnit." Erik paused and then looked up at me. "Unless..."

"Unless what?"

He shook his head. "Nothing." But Erik's face wasn't saying "nothing," it was saying something rather loudly.

I crossed my arms across my chest and waited for him to finish whatever inner struggle he was participating in. He stared at me a moment, and then finally blinked.

"Unless there's something to the accusations." There. Finally somebody said it. I was absurdly glad it hadn't been me.

"You've spent more time with Evan than anybody else," I said. "Do you believe that's possible?"

"No," Erik said quickly. "I don't. I mean, Evan can be a cad and a dilettante. He thought it was cool to date porn stars for the shock value. He seems to like to set fire to wads of cash just to watch it burn, because he's got a bottomless stash of anything he wants. He's never cared about appearances because he's never had to. He's bought himself out of every mistake. He likes to walk on the edge of things as long as he knows he's got a safety net. But I've never seriously entertained the idea that...." He shook his head. "Until someone brings me incontrovertible proof, I don't believe it. But I'm just so incredibly pissed off at him." He stood up and smiled, although I could see the muscles working in his jaw as he gritted his teeth. "But I shouldn't take that out on you. I'm sorry. I'll get over it."

Erik walked to the door. "Who knows, maybe something can be salvaged. I'll just have to see what I can do... What about you, do you have any plans for your now gloriously empty afternoon?"

Sure, I had plans, problem was they weren't mine.

~~~

Kyle was waiting for me when I checked in, his tie pulled to the side under the chain that suspended his badge in the center of his chest. He asked how I was, but didn't wait for my answer before taking my arm and propelling me through the building. I didn't like the sense of ownership that implied, so I planted my feet and glared at him.

"Wait a minute. I was kind enough to come down here like you asked, and I am fully capable of walking without your assistance. Why don't you just stop and explain what's going on."

He gave an exaggerated sigh, which got me mad all over again. "I'm about at the end of my rope, Oberman. If you brought me down here to treat me like a criminal, I can walk right back out the door."

"Okay, okay. I'm sorry." He looked suddenly lost. "I just don't quite know what to say to you anymore, so I act like a jerk." He pulled me to the side, out of the traffic in the hallway.

"We pulled in Eddie DiFalco again and decided to pick what was left of his brain. Seems he's remembered some details he neglected to mention the first time around. We've got him in now, going over his story again. I thought...well, I thought that you might remember something that Jason said in a different light."

"And that's the only reason you called me down, to impress me with you interrogation skills?"

"No. Like I said, I promised I'd keep you updated. And I wanted to see how you were."

"Well, I'm just peachy. Oh, and you'll be happy to hear that filming has been halted thanks to the investigation. And don't you think there was an easier way to find out how I was than dragging me down here again?"

"If I could have thought of one, I would have used it. So, you want to see DiFalco or not?"

"Sure, why the hell not. I bought the ticket, I might as well see the whole show."

Kyle stationed me in front of a two-way mirror that looked onto a barren interrogation room, then left my side. The room was occupied by a heavy-set black man I'd seen around before, a thin, older man with an ax-blade face and grey hair slick against his skull and, at the table between them, a pale, skinny guy in dirty clothes that seemed to swallow his frame. His black hair swayed as he ripped an unlit cigarette to shreds before him, his head bobbing to the beat of his sneakers on the floor.

I saw the door inside the room open, and watched as Kyle leaned in and said something to the grey-haired detective. Kyle returned to my side and flipped a switch on the wall which allowed me to hear the slow, deliberate words of the black detective, who sat with his fingers tented in front of him.

"That's Parker and McLemore," Kyle whispered, nodding toward the glass. "And that waste of skin is Eddie DiFalco."

I listened to Parker's voice rise above the nervous tap of Eddie's sneakers.

"You gotta work with us, Eddie. The Feds don't care about you. They're going to grind you into chum, throw you out and see what they catch. So let's start over again."

Eddie rocked back against his chair, mumbling. "I already told you everything. I didn't have nothing to do with it. Jason was the one that knew, and they killed him, didn't they." Eddie started to rock faster, the legs of the chair whacking on the floor. "Look, you gotta let me outta here. The people I deal with, they won't take it so good, me bein' in here so long. I can't be in here much longer, okay? You keep me, you might as well go ahead and shoot me."

"You really think you're that important to anybody, Eddie?"

Eddie stared at him dully, still rocking back and forth in his chair.

"You keep coming up with a little something more. So, one more time. What did Jason have?"

"I dunno, man. I told you. He had this sweet blackmail deal, said it was foolproof. But there wasn't no way he was gonna let me in on it. I thought he was just yankin' my chain, talkin' like he always does."

"Who was he blackmailing?"

"Some guy, I dunno, some big-time guy. Jason hung around the movie types, that's what he thought was cool, dealing to the stars. So it was somebody like that. He took something from him and wasn't gonna give it back until he got paid. And that's all I know."

"You sure, Eddie?"

"I ain't talking to you no more." Without warning, Eddie jumped up, flipping the table. Parker caught it before it could smack his thighs and McLemore banged on the door with a fist. He grabbed Eddie's hands and yanked them behind his back, and Eddie began to dance like a man at the end of a hangman's noose, trying to kick McLemore's shins.

Uniforms came in and removed the struggling informant. Parker looked toward the two-way glass and shrugged.

"Well," I said. "That was fun."

"Oh, it always is. So can you think of anything Jason said that might indicate he had blackmail material?"

"I told you everything he told me, and it was much fresher then than it is now."

"I'm sorry, Maddie. But we've got to make sure we run down every lead over and over again to make sure we haven't missed anything. The people at the top of the food chain want this solved."

"So do I, in case you don't remember."

"How 'bout we get a cup of coffee, and I'll tell you what I've come up with?"

"As long as you're buying."

We took paper cups outside into the sunshine, and sat along the low, concrete wall near the sidewalk.

"So, spill it," I said.

"Well, I think you can pretty well put most of it together with what you know. We've got five dead women. The Chandler girl and the four others they found up in the hills. They've identified two more of them. One was a working girl, and the other was an adult film actress from the low end of the totem pole."

"Which leads you to Bravo again."

"Yep. And we've got Jason tied to Evan Marks and to Jennifer Chandler, and Marks tied to Bravo. And if you believe DiFalco, Jason was blackmailing somebody. Put it all together and it could be coincidence, but I'm not a big believer in coincidence."

"And what about Irene?"

"What would be your best guess?"

"That whoever Jason was blackmailing--possibly about the murders--somehow felt Irene was a threat, or knew something, and killed her."

"Maddie Pryce, girl detective." Kyle's face turned serious. "Which also leads me to worry about you."

"And why is that?"

"Because you knew Irene, you knew Jason. Then a pro breaks into your apartment but doesn't take anything, and the next night someone breaks into the theater."

160

"Which could just have been random vandalism."

"Maybe. But it doesn't make me worry any less. Nothing else, I don't know, odd has happened lately?"

"Nope, except for the fact that I seem to have lost another job."

Kyle stared down into his half-full cup. "I am sorry about that, whether you believe it or not. I would never wish anything bad for you."

"Well, maybe Erik can get things back on track. He's hoping this is just a bump in the road that will flatten itself out once Evan is cleared." If he's is cleared. "How seriously are you taking Evan as a suspect?"

"Seriously."

That wasn't what I'd hoped to hear. I felt immediately selfish again, as if the shoving match over Evan's guilt or innocence meant no more than a film credit. But still, I wanted Kyle to show me everything they had, so I could pick it apart and prove it was all circumstantial. I knew that wasn't going to happen, but waiting for him to do his job was driving me crazy. "What about Paul Saroyan? Did you ever check out his alibi for the night Jason was killed?"

"Yeah. Not the greatest. He was staying with a college buddy, but they both said he turned in early. He could have snuck out, and nobody can physically account for him at the time of the murder."

"And the fact he didn't know about Evan?" It was my turn to grasp at straws.

"It seems that Jennifer Chandler had moved on, and Saroyan just couldn't admit it. Once she got heavier into whatever she was into, she broke it off with him and became pretty good at giving him the slip. Not that he didn't keep trying, but their relationship became a lot more one-sided than he implied."

"So does that make him more or less attractive for her murder?"

Kyle sighed. "I know what you're thinking."

"Oh, do you."

"You're hoping that there's somebody out there who's a lot better suspect than your friend."

I looked down at my hands. My nails had made little half moons in the side of the cup.

"That's true. I don't want Evan to have done something so horrible, so...." I didn't have the words to match the images in my head. "But I also want to find out who killed Irene. Who killed poor Jennifer and the rest of those girls. I want that more than anything. If it's true, and Evan is somehow the one responsible for all this, prove it and put him away forever." I looked up into Kyle's green eyes. "I just want it to be over."

"Fair enough," Kyle said. "I didn't mean..."

I set the coffee cup on the grass and scooted closer. I could smell the faint scent of the soap he used, something woodsy and clean. "I know."

"To tell you the truth, Maddie, if it was just Jennifer we'd found, I'd be happy to move Saroyan to the top of the list. Overprotective boyfriend gets shoved aside while his girlfriend is out partying it up, yeah, I can see that. I just don't see Saroyan methodically killing women and burying them. Not that he's in the clear by any means. He could still be involved in some way I can't see yet, hell, he could be the guy. We're going after him as hard as anybody else. But my gut tells me it's not him."

The silence stretched between us, and even though we were almost touching, there was a jagged little barrier between us, built shard by shard by tragic circumstance and our clumsy efforts to have a normal relationship under extraordinary pressure. I pushed away the sudden thought that it had been doomed from the start.

Kyle laced his fingers in mine and squeezed my hand. "I'm sorry."

"Me too."

"Things are going to get better. I can't promise you when, but trust me, this won't last forever. And I'm sorry about the movie, too. But I'm sure in no time your career's going to be back on track. I just don't want your job to become as 'fun' as mine, okay?"

"My job's only fun if you don't do it right. Artist's angst, and all that. And I pride myself in laboring in a constant low-level state of good, serious misery."

"I guess there's something to be said for angst, so long as it doesn't give you wrinkles."

"That, sweetie, is why god gave us botox."

That at least gave us a chuckle, a nervous, waiting-room sort of a laugh to be sure, but something better to leave between us that we'd had in a while.

~~~

When I got home, there was a handwritten note under my door. Lyle and Christie Lambert were giving a barbecue on Sunday and the invitation exhorted me to *Bring A Friend!* I hate exclamation points. They usually indicate an enthusiasm that no one actually feels. Still, it would be nice to do something with normal people, or as normal as the people in my building get. I mentally ran through a list of "friends" as I let Sydney out onto the roof. I briefly considered inviting Kyle, but that thought made my stomach flutter. I had to admit to myself that I'd be walking on pins and needles the whole time. What we needed right now was space. What the heck, I could ask Sam to drop by. Time to make good on my offer from that night on the boat. She was probably even more at a loss than I was.

# CHAPTER TWENTY-THREE

Sam showed up early in the afternoon on Sunday, her blond hair pulled back from a face devoid of make-up, as if she had shed the persona she'd been hiding behind the last few weeks. She looked eighteen and innocent, carrying a cooler filled with organic juices, wearing cut-offs and sandals.

She flopped down on the couch and immediately began making baby talk to Sydney. He hates being talked down to, and when he trotted off, Sam looked around the apartment.

"This is a great place. How in the world do you afford it?"

"My parents left me enough money. Not a fortune, but I've been able to live comfortably enough since they died."

"Must be nice. All my parents ever gave me was a bus ticket to California."

"You never talk about your family, or where you came from."

Sam shifted on the sofa and grabbed one of the juice bottles from the cooler. "Not much worth telling, well, not that you haven't already heard. Some people just shouldn't be allowed to have children." Sam twisted off the cap and tossed it onto the crushed ice before slamming the lid shut. "The only person who ever cared about me was my Aunt Becky. She has a place in Wyoming, and I used to go there summers when I was little. She wasn't much older than my mom, but she was the only one who ever seemed like a grown-up. I still call her every Christmas." Sam bit her lip, as if trying to decide whether to go on. "I've been thinking about that since the other night, and maybe, if

Erik can't get filming started back up again, I was thinking about taking a vacation. Maybe you can't go home again or you don't want to, but maybe there are other places you can go that are close enough. I might go see Aunt Becky for a while."

"That could be just what you need," I said. "Sometimes I wish I had somewhere to escape to, some happy place from my past, but I've always been here."

I brought the potato salad from the kitchen and Sam picked up her mini-cooler. Music from the back garden greeted us as we made our way down the stairs, the Counting Crows singing about daylight fading just before it's gone. The smoky, spicy scent of marinated chicken wafted up from a black-domed barbecue that looked like a 1950s movie spaceship, and ice chests dotted the landscape as if they were rations dropped from a C-130.

Lyle and Christie Lambert held sway over the festivities. They'd done a remarkable job of mowing and clipping, hung paper lanterns from the yew trees and set up a croquet game on the uneven lawn beneath the broken obelisk. No one was whacking the color-ringed balls, although Mr. Alexander was using the stick end of a mallet to do battle with a child I didn't recognize.

Christie approached me with a frozen margarita, which she exchanged for the potato salad. "I'm so glad you could come. Would you like to introduce me to your...friend?"

After a gentle attempt to convince Christie that Sam and I were fellow actresses and not life partners, we made the rounds and staked our claim to an area around a punch bowl filled with salsa.

"I made that, you know," a voice over my shoulder said. I turned to see Mrs. Cullum blinking at me with her bright little bird eyes. I was about to say how wonderful that was in what would probably be a very patronizing way when she lit off after another victim.

A sparkling water later, Sharon walked up to us with a beer in her hand, gushing about how exciting acting must be. I made polite conversation and didn't even notice that Sam had wandered off. I excused myself and went after her.

When I caught up with Sam again, she was surveying the beer selection in one of the coolers, her fingertips running over the cubes of ice.

"Are you okay?"

She nodded. "I'm fine. It's just everything that's been going on. And Evan's coming over tonight. I thought about what you said. I'd really like to break if off with him."

"Do you want to talk about it?"

Sam looked around and I let my eyes trace the same pattern: Mrs. Cullum laughing with Lyle at the grill, Mr. Alexander terrorizing the three-year-old, Christie handing Sharon a drink. When I looked back at Sam's eyes, they didn't seem to belong in her face, much less at this party, in this world where not a lot happens but everyone winds up the day relatively pleased.

"Can we go to my place, or would that be bad form?" she asked.

"No, that's fine. Let me just say goodbye to the Lamberts. I'll be right back."

Sam's apartment was twenty minutes away, to the south and west of Hollywood proper. The building was cheap, pink, sun-baked stucco, two stories and a flat roof, wrought iron railings fencing a narrow walkway from which opened pastel doors with paint-chipped numbers, giving the appearance of a tacky motel you wouldn't want to stay in more than one night. A courtyard cut into the building, forming a block-shaped letter C as if someone had taken the heart out and left concrete arms, outstretched to nothing. What could grow on its own ran wild and what couldn't survive without help died, leaving behind a patchwork of gravel and crumbling earth.

I followed Sam up the iron stairs to the flaking turquoise door of Apartment 2B. A strip of living room just wide enough for a brown, three-legged corduroy couch opened onto a galley kitchen lined with cabinets the same chocolate brown as the carpet. There was nothing to tell you who lived there, or that

166

anyone lived there at all. I couldn't imagine Sam coming home to this every night, the tiger losing her luster away from the big top lights, returning to a cold and dirty cage after the crowds have gone.

After depositing the cooler and her keys on the kitchen counter, Sam cranked open the window next to the front door and a desultory breeze stirred the sheer yellow curtains. "It's not that bad," she said. "It's only temporary."

Sam pulled open the refrigerator as I stood in the middle of the room wondering if I should trust the stack of paperbacks holding up the fourth corner of the couch or take the red vinyl beanbag chair that slumped beside a black lacquer table. Sam decided for me by waving me toward the sofa. I scanned the environment for something to attach conversation to. I'd been taught it was polite upon first entering someone's home to make a favorable comment even if one didn't readily present itself. But I couldn't very well remark on how easy it is to disguise stains on brown carpet or that the paperbacks keeping me from tumbling to the floor must make great reading. Sam handed me a sangria served in a fast-food franchise tumbler, the etching bearing the semblance of some cartoon character I did not recognize.

Sam settled onto the other end of the sofa and pulled her tanned legs up under her amid the creak of unwilling springs. "I really don't spend much time here. Evan absolutely hates it." Sam took a sip of the cheap wine. "But people like Evan, even people like you, don't understand how much better even a pit like this is than where I came from. At least I can lock the door and be alone here and pretend that things worked out the way I saw them in my head when I got on that bus a year ago."

"Things are getting better, though, right?" I said. "Erik believes in your talent, and if he's right, it'll just be a few weeks before filming gets started again. It's a great opportunity. You just need to cut out the drugs, and maybe cut out Evan too."

Sam's laugh was a harsh bark. "It's not that easy. There are games that I don't even know the rules to. And do you think that if I dump him, he won't find some way to get back at me? You piss men off, they make sure you pay for it."

"You think Evan would hurt you?"

"There's lots of things about Evan you don't know. Lots of things he wouldn't want you to know. He seemed like a nice enough guy at first, but with some of them, that's just a show they put on until they get you alone, until they have some kind of control over you, then they make you do whatever it is they want you to do. If you want to know the truth, that's when I started using heavy. I mean a little bit here and there, everyone does it, right? But after..." She trailed off with a barely perceptible tremor.

"After what?"

"After he changed." Sam drained her drink and placed the cup on the floor, then let her arm drop beside her as if it had gone numb. "Look, I'm going to go put something else on. Get another glass of wine, help yourself to whatever's in the fridge. I'll only be a couple minutes." She bounced up from the couch and I watched her disappear through the bedroom door, listened to it close behind her with a hollow thunk. Just one more stone in the monument that was slowly being built to Evan's guilt. Maybe I could get Sam to go to the police, although in her current state I didn't know if she'd go, or if they would take her seriously.

I waited for more than ten minutes, but there wasn't a sound from the bedroom. I went over and rapped on the door, but there was no answer. I twisted the handle and looked through as I called Sam's name. She was standing on a chair in front of a recessed closet, its curtain drawn to the side to expose a huge assortment of clothes and shoe boxes. What money didn't go to drugs obviously went to her wardrobe. Sam turned at the sound of my voice, nearly losing her balance, one hand still arched up inside the closet opening. She looked at me for just a second before turning her back, and I could hear the faint, hollow click as she maneuvered something into place.

"I suppose I should've waited until you left."

I hated Sam for putting me in this position, but then again, she didn't seem to have anybody else. I took a deep breath. "Let me get you some help."

Sam stepped down from the chair. "Not today. Tomorrow I'll go anywhere you want, but I have to get through tonight first. I'll break it off with Evan tonight, the hell with it, and once that's done I'll be able to handle all the other stuff."

"You don't really want to do that. You can't confront him alone. What if he hurts you, and there's nobody here to stop him?"

"It won't come to that."

"How can you be so sure?"

Sam laughed again, with the high, tight sound of a frightened horse. "You think he's going to hit me?"

"Or worse."

"You don't get it. Evan's only into mind games. I don't think he would have the guts to raise a hand to anybody. Hitting someone isn't the only way to hurt them."

"Then why have you let him do this to you? I don't understand."

"Yeah, you don't understand. You'll never understand."

Sam climbed back up on the chair and reached into the space hidden above the arched top of the closet entrance. After fumbling around, she pulled down a paper bag. She walked over and shoved it at me. "Here. My whole stash. You take it and do whatever you want with it, throw it away for all I care. I won't be needing it."

"Okay. That's all well and good, but you shouldn't confront Evan alone."

"Look, Maddie, I know you're trying to help, but to be perfectly honest with you, I can handle it. If you hang around it'll just screw things up. I'll call you tomorrow and it will all be over, me and Evan, the drugs, everything. Tomorrow it'll all be okay."

"And what if I won't go?"

"I haven't needed a mother since I was twelve and I sure as hell don't need one now. This is really none of your business," she spat.

I could see the muscles in her face and neck tightening. The window of lucidity had come and gone, and I didn't know what else I could do. Once I was in the car, I dialed Erik's number and explained the situation to him.

"Why does she think Evan would hurt her?" Erik asked.

"She doesn't, but I do."

"Maybe Sam's exaggerating the situation. It could just be the drugs talking."

"I'd rather not take that chance. Just get here before Evan does." I glanced down at the crumpled paper bag next to me on the seat. "Shit."

"What now?"

"Sam gave me her stash. Told me to get rid of it. But I'm sure as hell not driving around with this in my car."

There was silence on the other end of the phone.

"Erik?"

"I'm thinking. Is there someplace there you could hide them? I'll pick them up and dispose of them when I get there."

"Are you sure you want to do that?"

"Do we have any other choice?"

I glanced around the courtyard, and finally decided on a battered metal trashcan chained to the corner of the building.

"Okay, there's a trashcan at the northwest corner of the complex. I'll put the bag there and cover it up. Just hurry."

"Don't worry, I'll take care of everything."

Even as I was pulling away from the desolate courtyard I had second thoughts. I hated the way it made me feel to run away from the problem, but Erik could handle it better than I could. And then maybe, just like Sam said, tomorrow everything would be okay.

# CHAPTER TWENTY-FOUR

I woke to find Cat seated squarely on my chest, her little feet curled into balls, her eyes half shut against a light that shouldn't be on. I wondered where I was for a moment. This was my bedroom, but I didn't leave the light on. Otto?

But it wasn't the presence of light that awakened me. I closed my eyes and tried to grasp the fleeting thought that had sunk back through the depths of sleep. It was like chasing something down an ever-lengthening corridor, something I could barely glimpse as it moved farther away. The harder I concentrated, the more elusive it became.

I opened my eyes again and Cat stared at me as if she held every secret to the Universe and I was just too stupid to understand. Night still pressed against the windows and as I glanced at the bedside table, the clock blinked 12:00. Could a power surge, or a short somewhere, have caused the light to go on and the clock to go off?

I fumbled for my watch on the table. It was a little after two o'clock. I shoved Cat from my chest and slid out from under the covers, listening for any sound, any other indication that something wasn't right. I swung my feet to the floor and stifled a shriek as Sydney licked my bare toes.

That did it. I was fully awake now and all the doubts and problems that had crowded my mind before I fell asleep came flapping back like a flock of carrion crows.

I got up and stalked from the bedroom, flicking on lights as

I moved to the kitchen with the animals at my heels. I pulled a coke from the fridge and popped the top as I leaned back against the counter, Syd and Cat staring at me as if they were waiting for me to get the joke.

"What?" I felt like everything and everyone in my life was conspiring to drive me crazy, and now I was wide awake in the middle of the night with my animals trying out ESP on me. Perhaps Otto wanted some company, maybe he had been responsible for the wake-up call. I padded up to the loft, catching the spicy scent that was almost like pipe tobacco but not quite. If I could blame the light on Otto, at least I could push the thought of burglars, rapists, and serial killers to the back of my mind for the moment. I sat down on the window seat with my back to the night, trying to think of something to fill the time until the rest of the world would wake. It would be unreasonable to call Erik now, but I still felt the tug of guilt from having left Sam there alone. Erik had assured me he would take care of it, and I'm sure he would have called if it had gone badly.

I shut my eyes, trying to find a quiet, dark place that would lead me back to sleep. But I kept seeing Sam standing on that rickety chair, the look on her face a mix of shame, anger, and some strange hint of hope that now she could pass her secret burden on to someone else. No sense sitting here and going over the same scene over and over again. Maybe a hot shower and back to bed.

I stood, and a wave of dizziness hit me, as palpable as a giant hand shoving me back off my feet.

I thought again of Sam on the chair, reaching for her stash, and my memory slipped like a needle on a scratched phonograph record, back to Jason in his secret balcony, atop a stepladder that he kept behind the faded velvet curtain, reaching up for his cache of pot, the drugs that were his only hope of being popular or at least tolerated, his one shot at belonging somewhere, anywhere.

If Jason, arrested in adolescence as we was, wanted to put something where no one would find it, where better than his old hiding place among the vents and filters? Nobody would remember it, nobody who mattered anyway.

I pulled on jeans and a T-shirt, then slid my feet into battered tennis shoes and pulled my hair back into a ponytail. I picked up the phone and put it back down, assailed by the vision of getting Kyle out of bed for a wild goose chase. I could call him just as easily in an hour, if there was any need to.

I hunted in the kitchen junk drawer until I came up with a pocket flashlight. When I slid the switch, a weak beam flowed from the bulb. I grabbed a bent screwdriver and shoved it into my back pocket. Good enough. I felt my heart rate jump a notch as I snuck down the stairs and out into the darkness.

The Orpheus rose black against a blacker sky as I passed the Now Showing: Renovation sign and pulled into the alleyway. I hurried to the side door, keys jingling an echo against brick. It was silent inside, and I picked my way around renovation debris with the help of the dim flashlight. The door to the balcony had been replaced, and as the beam bobbed over the new doorknob like a will-o-the-wisp, I realized that I wouldn't have a key to open it. I needn't have worried, when I touched the smooth new finish, the door stuttered open an inch. Most likely it had just been left open. No need to lock the interior door in a building undergoing what amounted to an internal razing.

I made my way up the darkened stairway. I'd felt for the light switch and found it dangling from disconnected wires like a blinded eye protruding from its socket. When I stepped onto the balcony carpet, I swept the light across the seats and was greeted with a gap-toothed shark's smile; the haphazard removal indicated that some of them had been reluctant to leave their moorings.

I played the fading light over the swags of red velvet draped around the upper edges of the three walls. I had a sudden fear that I'd be stuck up here alone in the blackness, or worse, that once the light went out I wouldn't be alone at all. I walked around the perimeter of the room, shining the light behind curtains until I caught the silvery glint of an air-conditioning duct. I struggled with one of the uprooted seats, trying my best to wedge it against the wall. The light winked out, then came on again. I was running out of time. I climbed on the seat and felt it shift under my weight, so I gingerly placed one foot on each arm, trying to balance myself. I had just touched the grate, realizing that I would need to find a ladder to access all the screws, when it fell forward and just past me to the floor. I ran my fingers over the lip of the opening and inside, the sudden vision of some black, hairy spider dropping onto my bare skin almost causing me to draw back. But there was nothing above or below my reaching hand. Then I felt my fingertips brush against something cool and metallic. I reached in farther, precariously balanced on my toes, and tried to gain enough purchase with my fingers to drag the object out. It slid forward. I pulled it over the edge and stepped back into empty space. I missed the seat of the chair completely, my knee banging against something hard as I went down, the floor meeting my back and knocking the air out of my lungs. I saw stars against the utter blackness that engulfed me, the flashlight lost. I lay there for a moment, gasping for breath.

When I thought I could move again, I felt around me for whatever had tumbled from the vent. It lay less than a foot from where I had fallen. I sat up and explored the edges as if it was some relic of indeterminate origin, then picked it up and held it to my chest. A film canister. I pried off the top and felt the slickness of the celluloid inside. Maybe crazy Eddie DiFalco should have believed Jason about the blackmail scheme.

I felt my way to a wall, followed it around to the door, and managed to make it down the stairs without killing myself. I stood there, letting my eyes adjust to the filtered light that came through the dusty glass doors at the front of the building. I was standing in a theater, holding a film. The temptation was too great.

The light was working in the projectionist's booth, and after a few attempts, I managed to loop the film along the right path and feed it into the machine. I flipped the cold metal switch to illuminate the film and prayed that the screen was still up, or at least I'd find a wall bare enough to view it on. I turned to find the screen intact, the hairy blips and empty frames, then perched on the stool to view whatever this was.

The first shot was featureless white, out of focus. The camera panned upward, over tanned, bare feet bound together with black cord. The shot lingered there a moment and then moved upward slowly, caressing the subject as it was revealed.

The woman was sitting in a chair, her wrists tied to the ornate arms with the same black cording which also criss-crossed her torso. The white bra was a stark contrast to her tawny skin and a triangle of white panties showed at the juncture between her closed thighs. Her head was covered by a black hood. The camera pulled back and became stationary, framing her against an off-white background that hung like a painter's drop cloth and continued across the floor underneath the chair. The light source was not in the shot, but I got the impression of candles flickering somewhere nearby, brushing bare skin with an amber glow. In a moment, another figure entered the frame, obviously male, dressed completely in black including skin-tight gloves and a mask that obscured his features. I strained for any hint, any indication that I knew this man, but he stayed in the shadows, keeping the woman the center of attention, blending into the background as much as possible.

He stood behind her and whipped the hood from her head with a flourish. The sheer panic in her eyes took my breath away and recognition stabbed through me. There was no mistaking poor, doomed Jennifer Chandler, whose body was so recently zipped into a black bag on that lonely, shrub-covered hillside off Mulholland Drive.

Her chest rose and fell rapidly, straining against her bindings as the black figure moved around her and reached into the darkness behind the chair. Silver flashed in the light and she began to scream as he tilted the blade in front of her face, letting her watch her own distorted reflection. Soon, he began to cut.

I watched as Jenny Chandler bled out in Technicolor. It was slow and it was ugly, but I watched until it faded to black, until the film spun out and flapped against itself with the whap, whap, whap of a playing card stuck in the slow revolution of a child's bicycle wheel.

I shut the projector off.

# CHAPTER
# TWENTY-FIVE

I sat back down and stared into the darkened theater, unwilling to accept what I had witnessed, that final scream bouncing around in my head like a trapped animal trying to find a way out. This thing I had wondered about and strained to understand for weeks was now coming clear and all I wanted was to run from it. Now I had an idea why Jackie Kennedy had climbed as far away from her dying husband as she could that awful day in Dallas. Sometimes you just get more than you can handle, no matter what your idea of the grace of The Divine.

The film was slick and cool as snakeskin against my fingers as I removed the reel and coiled it back in the canister. I replaced the lid as if I could re-close Pandora's Box before all the evil slipped out to caper madly through my previously sane world.

I couldn't bear to turn off the light and let darkness follow me down the stairs, so I left it on as I made my way back to the lobby. I tried the phone in the office, but received a dry click instead of a dial tone. I'd left the cell phone locked in the car. I passed through the massive lobby, pushed open the side door and turned to lock it, then took the few steps to my car.

I never saw him, just felt the fist slam into my abdomen and the crook of an elbow hold the gasp inside my straining throat. I was being dragged toward the dark mouth of the alley, trying to find a foothold on the asphalt. Lights flashed against the darkness as my brain worked on using the last of my oxygen. There wasn't any more coming. I beat and scratched at the arms that held me, but my nails were ineffectual against the leather of his jacket.

My vision went grey around the edges as we entered the narrow aperture, and I felt muscles cramping as lactose built up from my failed fight or flight response. The screwdriver was still in my back pocket, but there was no way I could reach it.

I took in one burning breath as the pressure on my trachea eased. My attacker spun me so that I was facing him and slammed me against the brick of the alley wall. He shoved his arm back under my chin, grinding the back of my skull into the rough surface.

"You just couldn't leave it alone, could you?" He spat the words into my face, his breath washing over me in a hot wave that smelled of overcooked meat. His eyes were flat and black as a snake's, and not in proportion to the large bones that seemed to jut from under the skin that stretched to contain them. An untidy scruff of beard sprouted around his chin and spread to his ears like out of control ground cover in a neglected garden.

"What?" I managed to gasp.

He shoved me again and I could feel the darkness reaching up to claim me.

"Don't fuck with me. You should've kept your damned nose out of our business, but at least you finally turned up our property."

It wasn't until that moment that I realized I wasn't holding the canister anymore. It must have fallen when he jumped me. I tried to mentally retrace my motion back to the point of origin of the ghastly dance he'd imposed upon me, but I needed air. Right now I'd trade the film and everything it meant for one more breath. I brought my knee up toward his groin, but he anticipated the move and stopped the knee with one arm while pressing harder on my windpipe with the other.

"You gave us almost as much trouble as that stupid kid. But it's all over now." He reached behind him with his free hand and pulled up a matte black automatic. It was probably no impressive piece, but at a distance of three inches from my brow it looked like a cannon.

What little light there was seemed to coalesce and concentrate on the smile that split his face. My life had compressed itself into these final few moments and all I could see were his little square teeth in the moonlight.

The flash, when it came, was without heat, and I closed my eyes against it, waiting for the pain or the shock or whatever would come. Instead, there was a shout from the mouth of the alley and I opened my eyes to an incandescent glow that created supernovas when I blinked.

Despite the shouted order to the contrary, the man with the gun to my head didn't drop it, he just spun in slow motion like an outlaw in a spaghetti western and faced toward the light. The gun went off with a small pop, like a soda can being opened, and the light shifted but didn't go out.

Some feral thing inside my head realized this was my last chance, and I ripped the screwdriver out of my back pocket. As I launched myself at the man, I caught the glint of his earring in the deflected light that washed down the brick. The swift realization that this guy had been in my home was just one more piece of kindling for the blast furnace that had opened in my brain.

I hit him with all the force I had, trying to keep the screwdriver straight in front of me. I felt resistance and then a sink, like a straw successfully plunged through the tough plastic lid of a fountain drink. The man grunted and tried to push me back, but I clung to him, not wanting to give him enough space to throw a punch. I kicked as hard as I could and tried to re-grip the slick handle of the screwdriver. He slammed something hard into my back -- a fist or the butt of the gun -- but that just drove the tool deeper into his abdomen. He jerked back, with nowhere to go. His right elbow cracked against the wall and I heard the clatter as the gun fell to the pavement. Both of us stopped, staring at the gun three feet away. I moved first and kicked it with the outward bone of my right foot, and it skidded to a point beyond the fractured light.

He stared at me, his mouth a round, dark O of surprise, as if he couldn't comprehend how things had gone so wrong so fast. He hissed through his teeth and took off down the alley toward the light, clutching his injured side. I heard another sound beyond the glow that streaked across the bricks. It sounded like my name.

Kyle lay close to his police-issue flashlight, his head turned away from me, a dark stain spreading across his sweatshirt. I dropped to my knees beside him and took his hand while he tried to move his lips.

"Don't talk," I said, trying to remember anything I'd ever seen about gunshot wounds on TV emergency shows. I peeled his shirt away from the wound and removed mine, wadding it up and pressing it as hard as I could against the hole in his chest.

"Lucky shot," he mumbled.

"What the hell are you doing here? No, don't answer that, don't talk."

He struggled against me as if trying to rise, then one bloody hand came up with a radio. He shoved it toward me, and I pushed and clicked until I was rewarded with a burst of static and an indistinct female voice.

"Officer down," I blurted and gave the address of the Orpheus.

Kyle was muttering, and I leaned down to tell him again to shut up, to hold on, that help was coming.

"I was just looking out for you...." He tried to smile, but it turned into a grimace, and I could feel tacky blood soaking through the T-shirt and onto my hands.

He closed his eyes and I sat there holding the bloody clump of material to his chest as the sirens wailed ever closer.

# CHAPTER TWENTY-SIX

The waiting room was stocked with tubular chrome connecting chairs and several side tables and counter tops of varying heights. It was not a comfortable space, and even the air seemed to take on a shade of Coke-bottle green from the passing scrub-suited doctors. Although there were many mauve touches, no doubt the idea of some hospital consulting firm, the overall effect of too much white could not be warmed. Every surface of the room looked like something you would slide off of rather than sink into.

A sympathetic nurse had dug up a scrub top to replace the blanket the paramedics dressed me in, and I'd washed the blood off my hands and arms, but there were still dime-sized maroon spatters on my jeans and tennis shoes. I stared at them as if some pattern would emerge, my own connect-the-dots. At some point during the ordeal I'd ripped one fingernail down to the quick and now it throbbed in time to my heartbeat, reminding me I was alive.

They'd let me ride in the ambulance with Kyle, probably because I'd threatened violence if they didn't. The officer who showed up at the hospital after they brought us in told me they'd found the gun and would try to trace it. The film was gone.

Angela Ramirez came around the corner cradling a paper cup in both hands.

"Anything?" I asked as she slid into the seat next to me.

"He's still in surgery." She looked straight ahead as she spoke, focusing on a seascape that seemed to seep into the wall. She wore jeans and no make-up, her short, dark hair tucked behind her ears, and right now she could have passed for a grad student rather than a homicide detective. She sipped from the cup and leaned forward so that her elbows were on her knees, still staring at the wall.

"He's been following you, you know. Any time he's not working, he's checking on you. It's an obsession with him." She glanced over at me, as if she wanted to make sure I was still there, her eyes hard and unforgiving. "I told him he was acting like a jerk, that he was going to get himself in trouble, but Kyle never listens to what anybody says, just goes ahead and does whatever he wants. I swear there's some music playing in his head that no one else can hear."

The fact that Kyle had been stalking me -- regardless of his intentions, regardless of the fact he'd kept me from getting shot in the head -- was one more unsettling facet to a world where all the rules I thought existed had somehow ceased to apply.

"I didn't know," I said.

"Why didn't you just call the cops instead of going over there?"

"I don't know, Ramirez. You're surrounded by people who do stupid things for no reason."

Ramirez set the cup on the table beside her chair, leaned back and ran both hands through her hair, then clasped them in her lap. "About a year and a half ago, in fact it was the first case we worked as a team, there was this kid. Well, he wasn't a kid really, probably in his early twenties, but he was retarded or schizophrenic or god knows what. He was a witness in a robbery that went bad, some T-shirt vendor on the strip who got popped. Not that the kid could tell us anything, he was too far gone for that. But there was something about him, something that Kyle just couldn't let be." Ramirez focused on the seascape again.

"The kid had been doing some work for the vendor, unpacking boxes or something, and now he was back to wandering the street, talking to himself, scrounging in dumpsters for food. For some reason, Kyle couldn't get it out of his head. He took to looking for the kid, bringing him food or clothes he picked up at thrift stores, like he was some kind of fucking big brother or something. Tried to get him work, but people like that, there's just no fixing them, you know? Like slapping a Band-aid on an amputation. And Kyle warned him away from places, I mean, East L.A.'s like fucking Baghdad sometimes, and this kid's just like a puppy, thinking everyone'll be his friend.

"So, one night we get this call, some John Doe behind a liquor store. The kid with his head bashed in." Ramirez rubbed her hands absentmindedly. "And Kyle still didn't get it. It doesn't matter what you do, it's like throwing yourself in the middle of a river to try and stop the flow. You've got to just wait for the shooting to stop, then pick up the pieces before it starts again. And if you don't accept that, then you're just standing in the middle of the highway waiting for the lights to catch up with you." She let out a deep breath and slumped in the chair.

It occurred to me then that Ramirez was in love with Kyle, maybe not in an idealized romantic way, but that she saw in him the kind of person she thought she would never have the courage to be.

When the doctor came out, he seemed uncertain who to officially give the information to. He didn't ask, just divided his attention between us and said that Kyle was out of surgery and in ICU recovery, that he was stable but it was too early for promises, that he would keep us updated.

I let Ramirez go in first, and watched through the glass partition as she brushed her fingertips across his forehead as one would a sleeping child's. As she took his hand, I tried to sort through my conflicting emotions. Maybe neither Ramirez or I would be the last girl Kyle ever dated, and if there was someone out there waiting for him and I didn't want to be responsible for his never showing up.

~~~

I rode with Ramirez as her sedan nosed through early morning traffic, headed downtown to go over my story again and page through mug books. She left me to thumb through picture after picture, the faces blurring together in a collage of scars and scowls. It took me forty-five minutes to meet up with Alphonse Creider again. This time he glared from the black and white confines of a mug shot, minus the scruff of beard and a few years. But it wasn't easy to forget somebody who so recently was destined to be the last person I ever saw. I touched my finger to his name and heard it echo inside my head.

"Are you sure?" Ramirez asked when I roused her from her paperwork.

"Like I could forget."

She returned with his arrest jacket and summarized his brief, violent life for me. Creider had started his career enforcing for local distributors, but he didn't want to be under the thumb of any undereducated punk in gold chains, so he branched out to burglary, assault, and armed robbery and somewhere along the way fell off the face of the earth. His record stopped three years ago when he'd either left his life of crime or gotten smart enough not to get caught.

"So, what happens now?" I asked.

Ramirez closed the folder in front of her. "We put out an APB, try and find the bastard."

"And what about the film. What about Evan Marks?"

She fixed me with her gaze for a moment then looked away, back down at the table, at the flyers tacked to the wall, anywhere but me.

"Are you really sure about what you saw? I mean, most of these things are hoaxes. As far as the experts believe, snuff-films are just urban legend. No one has actually seen one."

"I saw one. And Jennifer Chandler is dead."

Ramirez glared at me. "And so are four other women. You don't have to remind me."

"Well, are you going to do anything about it? You can at least

184

bring Evan in again."

"We don't have the film. And we don't have any other new evidence, except the stuff on Creider, which could take a while to run down. We can't just go hauling Marks in every day. It makes his bullpen of lawyers cranky. Can you positively identify Evan Marks as the man you saw on the film?"

"No. But it makes sense. Evan and Bravo, Evan and Jason, Evan and Jennifer...." Evan and Sam. "Is there a phone I can use?"

Sam didn't answer when I called her apartment. I even called again, just to make sure I'd dialed the number right, and waited through eleven rings. Nothing. I punched in Erik's cell phone number, and when he answered I didn't stop to explain what had happened last night, just blurted out, "Have you seen Sam?"

"No. And I tried to call you this morning but there was no answer. I didn't call last night because I got in late and didn't want to wake you. Are you all right?"

"I'm fine. But I need to know what happened last night."

"I got there and got rid of the stuff. But Sam was already gone."

"What do you mean, she was already gone?"

"Calm down. Sam wasn't there when I went to her apartment. I waited around for a while, talked to the manager, but she didn't know anything. I tried to find Evan, but it took me a while. He finally showed up at a club on Santa Monica where he hangs out, but he swore he hadn't seen her, said she'd called and begged off." He paused. "Maybe she's playing some kind of game with you."

"For heavens sake, why?"

"I don't know. Who knows why people do things. But it probably has something to do with the drugs. Maybe she panicked when she started coming down and realized she'd given you all her stuff, so she took off to find some more."

"I don't believe that."

"Then what do you think happened?"

"I don't know. But I'm going over there."

"Do you want me to come with you?"

"No. I'll call you when I find something out."

I filled Ramirez in on the drive over.

~~~

The apartment complex seemed even more forlorn than it had the day before. Ramirez and I tried the door, and when I convinced her that there really was a reason for concern, she went to find the manager for a master key.

It was stuffy and silent inside, and the rooms looked much as they had yesterday, except now the bedroom floor was littered with hangers, skeletons without their fabric skins. Ramirez poked around, opening drawers, wandering through the four rooms. I sat on the couch, trying to come up with an explanation that would calm the nervous flutter in my stomach.

"Did your friend say anything about leaving?" Ramirez asked when she'd finished her cursory examination.

"No." Well, that wasn't strictly true, but I didn't want Ramirez to back off. "This is all too convenient, don't you think? The night she's ready to break up with Evan she just disappears?"

"Stranger things have happened. And there's no sign of a struggle, nothing to show she didn't leave under her own power." Ramirez sat down next to me on the couch. "Suppose it went something like this: she's having a rough time, show biz isn't exactly what she'd imagined. She starts doing drugs, gets into a bad relationship, does more drugs, and the walls start closing in. You said yourself that nobody knows when filming's going to start up again, if it ever will. So maybe she decides it's not worth it, decides on a change of scenery."

"She had other things lined up."

"Do you know that for a fact? Or is that just something she told you?"

"Damnit, Ramirez. No, I don't know it for a fact, but can't you see this just doesn't seem right? This is all too...." I couldn't think of a word that would properly express my growing dread. "Evan is the best suspect you've got, and his most recent girlfriend turns up missing. Can't you make the connection? I'm sure that if I happened to be in the wrong place at the wrong time you'd sure as hell bring me in for less."

Ramirez put her hand up, a gesture that reminded me so much of Kyle that I felt a little hitch in my chest.

"I'm not saying I don't believe you," she said. "What I'm saying is that it's not enough. People run away every day in L.A. And I'm not talking about kids. Old people, young people, mothers, guys with families. People with a lot more to hold them in one place than your friend had. We'll get a team over here, just in case, and I'll see what I can do about a missing persons report. But this just isn't enough."

"What is it you need? Another body?"

Ramirez stood up. "Look, I'm trying to help. What you need is to go home. I'll call you the minute we turn up anything."

~~~

Everything I had hurt. As long as I stood under the cascade of water, I could almost ignore the aches that had settled in, the bruises blooming like hothouse flowers over the landscape of my body. I reluctantly turned off the tap and limped from the shower. The bathrobe felt heavy against tender skin, but I was too exhausted to find something else.

I pulled up the covers on the bed and lay down on top of them next to Sydney, mentally examining the small traceries of pain, waiting for the aspirin to work. After Ramirez had taken me back to pick up my car and I'd driven home, I called Erik and told him about Sam, about Kyle, about Creider. He'd been upset that I hadn't said anything, wanted to rush over, but I convinced him I needed some rest. I'd assumed that once I was still, everything would shut down, but there was too much to think about, too many kaleidoscope images wheeling through my brain.

No matter what, it still came back to Evan, but by the time the police put it all together, it might be too late. It might be too late already. I jerked into a sitting position and Sydney cocked his head at me. I threw on sweats and sandals, grabbed my keys and headed down to the basement.

Harry's trash bag was still wedged beside the washer. I pulled it out and began to plow back through the drift of paper, piece by piece.

There it was, among all the deteriorated writing, hidden within the barely legible script of a lost language for which there was no Rosetta Stone, a tiny string of letters in a sea of scrawl. Creider. I knew I'd seen the name before.

I read the page again, struggling with each word, making my way over loops and squiggles like picking through grains of sand and trying to count them all. Alphonse Creider had injected himself into the picture, and Harry was still on the ball enough to identify him. A few lines after the name first appeared there was a notation: *E.M. Payroll?*

That was enough for me, enough to solidify the suspicions that had been slowly growing since Kyle first pulled Evan in for questioning.

I found Ramirez' card, called and left a message. She was probably doing what I couldn't, either sleeping or sitting watch at Kyle's bedside. What I had wasn't much, but it was a start. I needed someone to help me fill in the blanks.

Erik answered the phone before I'd even formulated what I was going to say.

# CHAPTER TWENTY-SEVEN

By the time I'd dressed and fed the animals, the sun was going down.

Erik was on his way to the boat when I called, so I told him I'd meet him there. He was waiting for me on deck, the sun setting over his shoulder, throwing its golden glow across the water.

"You okay?" he asked as I climbed aboard.

"It's just been a long, damn day."

"I know it has. Come in and sit down, have a drink. I'll find a quiet spot to anchor and we'll sort this out. We'll figure out what to do." I let him lead me into the galley, where he pulled a bottle of vodka from the refrigerator. I settled onto the padded bench and took the drink, the long blue sweep of the Pacific stretching out behind me.

The hum of the engine and the movement of the boat lulled me and I must have slept, because it was dark outside the cabin windows when I opened my eyes again.

"Feeling better?"

I stretched and felt the immediate return of every bruise and scratch I'd collected in the last twenty-four hours. "Not really. What time is it?"

"Only a little after eight. Don't worry, I didn't let you sleep long, but I didn't want to wake you."

"As soon as I get this all settled, I'll sleep for a week. I promise."

I retold last night's story in more detail, picking up speed, rushing through my description of the film as if I could talk about it without actually focusing on it, let it out of my head and never have it there again. I ended with my identification of Creider from the mug shot.

"You're sure it's him?"

Why did everybody keep asking me if I was sure? You'd think I was an idiot child who couldn't be trusted to repeat her own name.

"I'm sure. But the police have their doubts about what I actually saw on the film, and since it's gone, well, they only have my word for what happened, which should be good enough, but somehow isn't." I turned to face Erik. "Evan's the perfect suspect. It has to be somebody with just enough film experience, someone who could charm some poor girl and convince her he'll make her a star. And now Sam disappears the same night she's going to break it off with him. I just can't help but see her, tied up somewhere while he...."

Erik squeezed my hand. "Don't, okay. Thinking about that right now isn't going to do anybody any good. So if you're convinced of Evan's guilt, how come the police don't believe it?"

"It's not that they don't believe it, but Ramirez said they need more evidence. There might have been something on the film, but Creider got it."

"And you're absolutely sure it was Evan on the film?"

Ramirez had asked the same question, and I'd thought about it over and over, but I'd watched the footage in a state of shock. The man had been approximately the right size and build to be Evan, but there was nothing to give me easy reference in the film, and he'd never spoken, never revealed an inch of skin.

"No, I can't be sure. But it makes sense. Can't you see that?"

"Maddie, I've known Evan for years, and so have you. Do you really think he could do that?"

"Somebody did it. Somebody who's walking around like he's actually human. Somebody who doesn't look like a monster on the outside."

"Okay, if you're sure, I'll guess I'll have to keep an open mind.

So what can we do about it right now? Do they have any leads on Creider?"

"I don't know. I left a message for Ramirez and but she hasn't called me back yet. But when I went home, I started going through Harry's notes, and that's when I found it."

I pulled the creased pages from my purse. "This links Evan to Creider. I thought maybe you'd know something else, something you didn't think you knew. After all, you've been around Evan a lot more than I have. And if we can put enough information together, we'll have something more substantial to hand over."

I got up and walked to the galley table, then spread the notes out under the light. Erik leaned over the table next to me. I underlined Creider's name with my finger and pointed to the initials below. "See, that's not my imagination. Creider said 'we' when he was talking about the film, and Harry thought Evan hired Creider."

Erik stared down at the crumpled pages, then picked them up, a frown creasing his forehead. As he did, another of Harry's scrawled lists unstuck itself from the back of one of the pages and floated down to the tabletop. Poor Harry, he'd made the lists obsessively, as if they could keep his deteriorating life in order. Hamburger buns and light bulbs, pickles and peanut butter, bread and toilet paper. All the mundane things that filled a lonely existence. I was about to fold up the paper when I focused on the final line of the list, underlined twice in a shaking hand. Match batteries. What the hell were match batteries?

"What did you say Creider looked like again?" Erik said.

I shoved the list into the pocket of my jeans and described Creider again, in as much detail as I could remember. "Does he sound familiar at all?"

Erik shook his head. "I don't know. Evan knows a lot of people who, well, you wouldn't invite to dinner. Maybe if I saw a picture it would ring some bells." He handed the notes back to me. "We'll go to the police together, take a look at this Creider guy and see if we can get something going, okay?"

"At least that's a start. I just feel like this is all buzzing around inside my head."

Erik poured more vodka into his glass and knocked it back. All of the sudden he looked as tired as I felt. "I really wish things hadn't turned out like this. You plan so carefully, you try to do everything right. But I guess people are going to be how they're going to be. You try to steer them the right way, but they're stubborn or they're careless. They give in. And then you've got to clean up the mess they leave behind." He stared into the empty glass.

"It's not your fault."

He looked up at me, unfocused for a moment, as if he'd forgotten I was there. I had the uncharitable thought that he might be more upset that his pet project had been sunk than the fact that his old friend was a psycho. All I could think about was Sam.

"We really need to get back, Erik. Sam's out there somewhere."

He took my hand and held it between his. "I know. But before we go back, I just want to tell you how sorry I am, Maddie. If I could have seen how this would all turn out, if I could roll back time to some juncture where it would have been different, I'd do it."

"Like you said, if only."

"Yeah, if only." He gave me a sad little smile before standing up. "No help for it now. Why don't you lie down while I head the boat back in, try to take another cat nap. We're not going to accomplish anything if you're dead on your feet. I'll wake you up when we dock."

Erik left me in the stateroom, and I tried to relax. At least I was finally getting somewhere, and if things went they way I hoped, Evan would be in custody tonight. The thought should have been a comfort, but it wasn't, and I lay there in the glow of the single light Erik had left on listening to the muted chug of the motor. I tried to make my mind go blank, but there were so many disjointed thoughts crowding me that I began to feel claustrophobic. I glanced at my watch, wondering how long it would take to get back. Then I looked back down at the little round dial again, mesmerized by the second hand ticking off the tiny increments of time. An impossible thought opened like a flower inside my head and I pulled the list from my pocket and smoothed it out against my knee. Match batteries. *Watch batteries.* And then it hit me, like looking at one of those magic eye pictures where you stare so hard that you finally see the cowboy or the dinosaur staring back at you from amid the geometric soup. Even after hours of wading through Harry's notes, I hadn't picked up all the nuances, all the individual ways of shaping lines until they became letters. I had never picked up on the small fact that Harry made his capital W so that at first glance it looked just like an M.

Everything I'd said to Erik came back to me in a rush, all the little twists of logic I'd thrown out to prove Evan's guilt, all the facts that could so easily point to someone else: Erik. But that was ridiculous, it had to be.

I opened the door of the stateroom and walked back into the main cabin. My purse was still on the floor next to the bench that hugged the bottom of one window. I sat down and pulled the papers out and found the reference to Creider again, looked at it until it blurred. My purse slid off the bench and upended on the floor, and I began to pick up lipsticks and pens, pieces of paper, all the detritus that finds its way into my bag. It wasn't until I sat up and closed the purse again that I realized the cell phone wasn't there.

It wasn't on the floor either. Maybe it had fallen out in the car. I was in such a rush to explain the situation to Erik, that I might not have noticed. But I didn't really believe that. The view out the window featured only a few distant lights, not the familiar shoreline I expected, no indication that we were headed back in. When I looked out the window on the cabin door, I could see Erik facing the back of the boat, leaning against the railing and looking out to sea. He certainly wasn't steering the boat anywhere. As I watched he reached into his pocket and retrieved something, and I saw a wink of green light before he dropped it over the side.

So much for my paranoia. And so much for the cell phone.

He turned, and there was no time to duck, to hide. He strode back across the deck and let himself into the cabin.

"You're still up?"

"I've got a headache. I thought I'd try to find some aspirin, but I didn't have any luck."

He fumbled in one of the cabinets and came up with a clear bottle full of white pills, then grabbed a bottle of water out of the fridge. "You really should lie back down, Maddie. You don't look well at all."

I palmed the tablets he handed me. "How long is it going to be? I'm kind of anxious to get this over with."

"Not much longer. Can I get you anything else?"

"No. This is fine."

I imagined his eyes following me as I let myself back in the stateroom door. I locked it behind me and sat down on the bed, examining my options, which seemed to be rapidly dwindling. Erik obviously hadn't had the reading comprehension problem I'd had when looking at Harry's notes. He had to know that it would only be a matter of time before I realized my mistake. Now I was in a little box on a big ocean, nobody knew where I was, and Erik had no intention of returning to the marina, at least not yet. What I really needed was to get off the fucking boat. The cell phone was gone and I couldn't very well ask Erik where the radio was or how to use it. Excuse me, I just need to call the Coast Guard and let them know I'm stuck on a yacht with a serial killer. I couldn't physically overpower him, and I had serious doubts he'd take the chance of letting me get back to shore. Whatever would happen would happen here. Which left me with one option, not a good one, but the only one I had.

I took my tennis shoes off and stood on the bed. I could just reach the hatch, and it opened a fraction of an inch when I tested it with my fingertips. Score one for my side. I pushed it open as quietly as I could, fit my fingers around the edges and pulled. I'd never been any good at pull-ups, and I felt every muscle in my back, chest, and arms protesting. I tried again, pushing off the soft surface of the bed with the balls of my feet. The extra five inches I needed might as well have been a mile. I looked around, but every piece of furniture was a built-in, there was nothing to breach the distance. I tried the drawers that lined one wall, hoping that Erik kept extra linens on board. I hit the jackpot on the last drawer: sheets, blankets, what looked like a handmade quilt. I pulled everything out, then stopped cold. Underneath the linens lay a small box, made of some elaborately carved dark wood and tied with a red grosgrain ribbon. Something about the box drew me in, and I untied the ribbon and lifted the lid to expose a tangle of jewelry. I lifted the bracelets and necklaces out, letting them drip from my fingers to the floor. At the bottom of the box was a stack of photographs, each one nearly the same, except that a different woman sat against the same pale background. The last in the stack was Jennifer Chandler. I thought of Erik laying here at night, under the gaze of an indifferent moon, trailing his fingers over the adornments of dead woman, masturbating to the movie that must constantly play behind his closed lids. I returned everything to the box and placed it in the drawer. Any doubts about my course of action were erased.

I stripped the bed and folded everything into squares, placing the pillows on top, then climbed up and reached for the lip of the hatch. I tensed the muscles in my calves, counted to three, and pushed off, twisting my hands outward so they would land palms down on the deck, pushing as hard as I could with my arms. For one breathless moment I thought it wasn't going to work, but my elbow hit the deck and I leaned into it, my lower body dangling from the opening. I struggled and got one knee up. Piece of cake. I rolled into a crouch on the deck and listened, but there was just the lap of water over the hum of the engine. I closed the hatch behind me and crawled to the edge of the deck, gazing out at the lights, like the stars, so very far away.

Ever since my headlong dive at that first swimming lesson, my parents had called me their water baby, and that had served me well through varsity team in high school and on the compulsive laps that kept me in shape through years of auditioning. I debated for a second about warmth versus drag, then slipped off my jeans. I was going for speed and I'd worry about hypothermia later.

Clad only in panties, bra and a T-shirt, I crawled under the railing and lowered myself over the side.

Without another thought, I slid into the water.

# CHAPTER TWENTY-EIGHT

The water was colder than I could have imagined, the shock running through my body like an electric current. For a split second the task ahead seemed impossible, then I began to adjust, finding the symbiosis that would allow me to work with the water rather than against it. I dog paddled away from the boat with only my head above water, afraid that every sound would be magnified and alert Erik to the fact I'd jumped ship. This was worse that the game I'd played when I was learning to sprint. I'd imagine a horrible beast chasing me, gaining on me, and that would propel me forward, to the point of my endurance. But now I couldn't use that fear for speed, I had to steal away from this beast slowly, grin and bow and draw away bit by tiny bit.

I pulled myself through the water, counting until I reached one hundred, then looked back at the dark hulk rising from the water, the starboard light an uncaring eye. How long would it take Erik to realize I was gone? I tread water, trying to make out any movement, then broke into a breast stroke, my arms slicing through the chill air and hitting the resistance of the water.

I kept my focus on the shoreline, the strip of lights like a runner in a movie theater aisle pointing the way to the exit. I hit the first stumbling block, that peak before muscles are warmed up and ready to work, and blazed through it, swimming harder in order to get into a rhythm, find a place where fear wasn't projected with every reach of my arms. The jack-o-lantern smile of the half moon shimmered on the water around me and I wondered if it penetrated through the depths far enough to touch the prismatic scales of the night fish gliding through their dark kingdoms below me.

The vastness of the universe opened above me as if my form had lost its definition and become adrift in a wet, featureless space with nothing to push off or against. I couldn't see the boat behind me now, but the lights before me had not grown any closer. If I couldn't make the shore, maybe I could find safety in the hollowness in between. A passing boat, a buoy, something.

The cold was a knife that invaded my core and my breathing became ragged and harsh. The sting of salt in my eyes blurred everything into a seamless world where there might as well be stars in the water and fish in the sky. The spray that hit my face smelled faintly of fish and reminded me of a day two weeks past my twelfth birthday, one of the occasions when my father had taken me to do kid stuff. The carnival had been set up near Venice Beach and the air was redolent with the odor of decaying creatures left stranded by low tide. I wound my way through rides and games until I was alone, my father somewhere in my sawdust wake, and found myself staring at the sleek man who paced like a panther in front of a gathering crowd. He produced from the pocket of his purple and gold striped vest a fan of orange tickets and waved them before onlookers like pages from a book of arcane and forbidden knowledge. The silver curtain behind him shimmered, splitting the faces of anyone before it as he parted the metallic strands to let the ticket buyers inside to see the freaks and the fire-eaters. He winked at me as he gave his pitch and I can remember the hot flush that crept across my cheeks. I didn't have the words to explain it in my twelve-year-old brain, but the way he looked at me, the oily way his words rolled through the still summer air, made me feel contaminated, as if he already knew all the secrets I would never share with a soul. I never saw the freaks because my father came and drug me away for the more appropriate world of fun house mirrors and cotton candy.

My stroke faltered and my head dipped below the surface of

the water, jerking me back from that summer day fifteen years ago. I don't know how long I'd been in the water, but I realized I couldn't feel my toes and a pins-and-needles sensation was creeping across my body, filling in spots that weren't already numb. My head dipped again and I came up spitting seawater, feeling the burn through my nostrils. I searched for my second wind, for the easy stroke that had carried me this far. I picked a spot on the dark glass of ocean between the waves, a place only a few yards ahead where I could draw an imaginary line to cross.

The cramp, when it came, was a hot wire shoved through the muscle of my calf. The pain exploded upward until my only thought was how to make it stop. I grabbed at it, my shoulder and head rolling into the water, giving me a mouthful of brine.

When the agony began to dissipate I rolled onto my back to catch my breath. I thought how easy it would be to just let go and drift, as long as I could stay this still, even if it meant floating down until the sea took my breath and held me in its eternal arms. I backstroked erratically, borne by the tide like a figurehead from some ship dashed on the shoals. The whisper of the waves separated into words and called my name. I opened my eyes and the moon came on. No, it wasn't the moon, it was too round and too bright and painted the water that lapped toward me with a pale yellow luminescence. Erik was coming.

I jerked up, kicking furiously beneath the water and ignoring the pain that reasserted itself into the muscles of my leg. The spotlight swept past me again, and it didn't matter if I drowned out here, I wasn't going back on that boat. I feinted to the left and right in an attempt to escape the searching light, flashing back on bad *Hogan's Heroes* episodes and Sydney bucking and dodging the rinse water after a bath. All my focus was on keeping my body out of the paint flow, as if I would be marked and identifiable if it touched my skin.

"Come on, Maddie. Aren't you cold? Aren't you tired?"

I could hear the hum of the motor now. I don't know how I had missed it before, how I'd ever thought I could get away in the first place. The light hit my face, blinding me, destroying any defense. It came closer until it was a thousand suns burning through my retinas and searing into my brain. I heard a splash but could see nothing, nothing but the light that held me captive. I had gone from being lost in the vastness of the ocean to being lost in this tiny, yellow, roofless room, and now the house was about to crumble.

A shape cut the light and I felt hands on my shoulders before I went under. I tried to push him away put I couldn't feel my arms.

"You're not as good an actress as I thought," Erik said, before forcing me under again.

I fought for the surface, for the air that could only be inches away, but his hands were steel hooks cutting into my skin. I opened my mouth to a rush of seawater, the fireworks behind my eyelids fading until everything went black.

~~~

The world was an abstract painting, where blobs of color are supposed to represent everyday, recognizable objects but somehow don't. Reality flickered around me, half-glimpsed.

My first conscious thought was that I was breathing. I blinked against the dull ache radiating from behind my eyes and tracked the diffuse light to a sconce on the wall. I felt a tickle that rode the wave of suffering swelling in my head, and with each expelled breath, a strand of hair danced across my brow, just dipping down to my right eye. When I tried to sweep the hair away, my hand wouldn't rise to my command and I realized my arms were bound behind my back. As I explored my range of movement, I found I could barely brush my fingertips against each other, and a constriction around my neck threatened to cut off my air supply. My ankles were likewise bound to the front legs of the simple wooden chair in which I was trapped. My clothes had been replaced by a black lace teddy with spaghetti straps, the material silky against my skin.

I recognized the flagstone floor beneath me, and the

realization of what kind of trouble I was in came rushing back in a flood of images. I had fallen through a dark looking glass onto the plains of hell. There was a furtive rustle behind me.

"Pay no attention to the man behind the curtain." Erik's voice echoed off the stone walls like the last voice in an empty house awaiting new tenants. His footsteps grew closer until he appeared in front of me wearing a grim smile. The mask had finally slipped away, his eyes slits of dark fire, his slowly parting lips transforming his face into something I no longer recognized. What I had taken for genuine sadness, human regret, out there on the boat was gone, if it had ever been there at all.

"I could have watched you swim all night, but I didn't think you would last much longer. No sense letting all your talent go to waste out there where no one would see it."

I searched for a strain of reason, words to form a defense, some beginning to the web I could weave to climb out of here. "You can't get away with this, Erik. The police will be looking for me...looking for you. It's all over, Erik. Why kill me when it's all over?"

Erik's laughter sent a chill through me. "Maddie. You were convinced it was Evan, and with a little encouragement the police will be to. And if Evan isn't around to refute any of it... Well, you'd be surprised how common it is to come across bad drugs in L.A. You live a careless life, it's bound to catch up with you eventually."

"You set Evan up all along, then."

Erik walked around the chair, and I focused my gaze on the floor in front of me instead of trying to follow him with my eyes. "Not at the beginning. At the beginning he was just a convenience. He knew women who...didn't use the best judgment. And he was always so busy chasing a piece of ass or trying to score drugs. Let's just say he set himself up."

"The police will figure it out."

"You have too much confidence in the wrong people."

"But you've gotten sloppy, Erik. You let Jason get a hold of the film, and they'll find Creider, he shot a cop. You ought to quit while you're ahead."

Erik's voice came from behind me, and I could hear the rustle of the curtain. "Jason was a stupid mistake."

Erik approached again, this time carrying a makeup box, the kind you find on any set for touchups between takes. "And you can blame Jason for Creider tailing you. It seems Jason had some kind of a grudge against you, and he convinced Creider that you knew where the film was. Of course by then it was too late for Jason, he became an annoyance that had to be dealt with." Erik stepped in front of me, a compact in his hand. "I knew you didn't have the film. You would have said something, wouldn't you?"

"I didn't know where the film was until last night."

"Well, it's a good thing that Creider is a loyal little bulldog, then. When he gets an idea in his head, it's hard to dispossess him of it."

"He worked for you all along. He killed Jason." I paused. "He killed Irene. Why?"

Erik loomed over me. When he reached down to brush my the hair out my eyes, I flinched. Erik sighed and stroked my cheek.

"Happenstance. The old woman came out while they were retrieving Jason's car, started an argument. Creider had decided Jason had to go, just as soon as he'd returned what he'd taken. Dumb as he was, Jason probably saw it coming. He took the opportunity to run, and he didn't look back. Creider doesn't like loose ends."

I sat there with a lump in my chest, remembering Irene so small behind the desk, her determination that she wasn't going to bail Jason out again. Happenstance. What an innocuous word for all the paths chosen or not, the everyday decisions that lead to dominoes falling, the tiny delays like lost keys or unexpected telephone calls that put us in the wrong place at the wrong moment.

"What's to stop Creider from talking now? He obviously knows what you are, what you've done. What's to stop him from making a deal?"

Erik knelt down beside me and began to apply makeup to the cuts and bruises on my legs.

"As I said, Creider's a bulldog, a loyal bulldog. A useful little psychopath."

I managed not to say anything about pots and kettles and glass houses. Erik continued his ministrations, as if I was a piece of furniture that needed a good polishing.

"I hired him because of that loyalty, and his many talents. Also the fact that he could keep his mouth shut. He's very good at taking care of what needs to be taken care of." He glanced up at me, and then went back to dabbing. "Funny, for all his Neanderthal qualities, he's a good businessman. Once he became aware of the true nature of my...work, he was the one who realized the potential for the art I could provide."

Erik began to hum as he rustled through the box, through the pots of flesh tones and little sponges and brushes. My mind had stopped ticking, stalled trying to wrap itself around what he'd just said. I flashed back on the film, the splashes of red against the canvas behind. A commodity.

"There are men far more powerful, far more ruthless than you imagine me to be. Creider is clever enough to realize if he ever starts talking, it won't be for long. After tonight, I imagine he'll find a way to absent himself. Loyalty has its rewards."

I sat there, limp against the bonds. It was all too much, this sick ecosystem where insane people did what they wanted and got away with it.

Erik leaned back to admire his handiwork. When he spoke, he didn't look at me. "No more questions, Maddie? Isn't this the part of the film where the villain just keeps talking and talking, explaining all his plans in exquisite detail, giving just enough time for the hero to ride to the rescue? The part where I say, 'Go ahead and scream, no one will hear you'?" He glanced around the room. "Well, that part is true."

He replaced the makeup in the box and closed the lid.

"It'll all be over soon. Cold comfort, I know." He still wouldn't look at my face.

He had seemed genuinely sad on the boat, genuinely sorry in his apology to me.

"Erik, look at me."

He walked out of my view, carrying the makeup kit.

"Erik!" I shouted after him.

I heard his footsteps returning, could feel him behind me. "Don't make this harder than it is, Maddie. I told you I never wanted this to happen. I didn't want you to be here. If I could take it back, I would. But it's too late."

"Why is it too late? We were friends, Erik. Why do this to me?"

He finally moved into view. His hair had fallen down over his forehead, making him look younger, more like the teenager I'd known. He must have been crazy even then, but I could bring up no memory that would have served as a warning sign.

"Because you know, Maddie. Because you've seen me. Because you'll never look at me the same again."

"I don't understand," I said, and I didn't. I couldn't fathom what had happened, if he'd just been born wrong or if something had happened along the way that had twisted him to what he'd become. "Make me understand!"

He took two rapid steps toward the chair and I rocked back, choking against the rope around my neck.

"You're not like them," he said, sweeping his arm to the side as if the ghosts of those girls had joined us down there in the cellar, watching. "So much beauty, so much talent. And they never knew. So many empty pretty little things, just filling themselves up with drugs so that they never felt anything. Do you know hard it is to make them feel something?"

He dropped his arm to his side and paced in front of the chair. "Such a waste. They were just going to throw their lives away anyway. But I gave them meaning. Art tells the truth. It shows us what we are. Art is forever. What I did made them more than what they were."

He finally stopped pacing and looked at me. His face

softened. "Do you remember that time we snuck downstairs and watched *Duck Soup*? Nobody even noticed we were gone. They were busy being important." He took a step forward. "You loved the Marx Brothers. That's what I remember about you, you sitting there laughing, hysterical. You must have been all of fourteen, but you got it. You turned to me and said, 'That's what I want to do.' I never forgot that."

He opened his mouth as if to say something else, but a faint moan came from somewhere behind me.

Sam. I'd forgotten about Sam.

"What did you do to Sam?"

Erik's face sagged and he closed his eyes. "I'm sorry, Maddie. If only."

He walked behind my chair and grasped the back, tilting it up slightly, then started dragging it backwards. I tried to say his name again, but it was all I could do to keep breathing as the cord tightened across my throat. He finally stopped and set me upright, and I could turn far enough just to see Sam, her head slumped against her shoulder, tied to the same chair I'd seen in the film.

"She'll be awake soon," Erik said quietly. He walked past me without looking back.

I shouted his name, but he kept walking. I kept shouting until I heard the wine cellar door slam with the hollow sound of a nail being driven into wood.

I was still for a moment, catching my breath. I glanced back at Sam, but she was completely out of it. I tested my bonds again, but there was so little give that every time I moved more than an inch, the noose tightened around my neck, and lights danced behind my eyes. But I refused to sit here like a stupid cow, waiting for the sledgehammer to come and blot out my existence.

The chair that held me was not as massive as the one Sam was tied to. Erik must have had to make do with one of the antiques from upstairs. It was solid enough, though, barely creaking as I rocked back and forth to the extent the cords would allow. I rocked harder, ignoring the burn where rope bit skin. I caught my breath as the chair tipped backwards, teetering on the back legs before falling forward with a crack. The rope felt looser, but maybe that was the mirage in the desert just before you died of thirst. I shifted my shoulders and tried to bring my hands together behind my back. The rope was looser, just a bit, and as I brushed the fingertips of one hand against the palm of the other, I could feel a jagged piece of wood against the tender inside of my arm. One of the cross-pieces had given way to age and pressure.

I felt the wood cut into my skin as I pressed against it with as much leverage as my position allowed. I got nothing in return but a slow, sticky trickle of blood that ran down onto my hand. The walls that defined my prison were harsh red stone, uneven and coarse-grained. They seemed solid enough to withstand anything from the fires of hell to an atomic blast, and the chair might as well be made of that same red rock. *But it wasn't.* I gauged the distance to the closest wall, but the five or so feet seemed a never-ending span.

I rose up on the balls of my feet and twisted the front of the chair toward the wall, pushing with my ankles until it shifted. I couldn't swing my head, so there was little momentum, and the tiny lurches were accomplished almost exclusively with the use of my feet, hips and ankles. The exertion and burning agony was worse than that I'd felt in the water and the wall still seemed as far away as those distant shore lights had been. But the thought of Erik's skeletal smile kept me moving, inch by inch like some demented slug across the rock floor.

I don't know how long it took me, but by the time I was a few inches away, sweat ran down from my hairline in wet ropes and I gasped for breath. I worked to position the chair so that the back was at an oblique angle to the stone, then shoved off with my left foot, slamming the corner of the chair back into the wall. The chair bounced back to the floor with a whack. I repeated the process over and over, praying to the gods of decrepit joints and aging wood, wondering which would give out first, me or the chair. After more than a dozen tries I forgot to pull my elbow in, the same elbow I slammed into the hatch framing on the boat, and I heard the dry snap of bone before a rush of red agony tore everything else away. I could only have been out a few minutes, and when I opened my eyes again, the room remained the same, no reprieve from the nightmare.

I fought down nausea and wiggled against the back of the chair. It creaked in protest, but there was no mistake, it was giving out. I took a deep breath as bursts of black and white exploded behind my eyes, and rammed the chair once more into the wall. The crack was much louder than the sound of the bone in my upper arm giving way. The bottom half of the chair went downward while the upper half wedged against the wall, the rope tightening around my neck. I launched myself backward with my toes and landed on my broken arm, trying to breathe as waves of pain flooded over me. I twisted onto my left side and slid my bad arm over the jagged edge where the arm of the chair splintered, biting the inside of my lip until it bled, ignoring the pain that seemed like it would never end. At least the tension around my throat had eased and I could breathe. I felt for the knot at my bound wrist with the fingers of the other hand, but it seemed to be a solid ball with no beginning or end, so I picked at it with my nails, trying to find an edge to grab onto. The silken cord began to unravel into fine strands like doll's hair. I lay against the cool of the stone, picking at new strands, waiting to hear the footsteps that would tell me it was too late.

When I felt the cord loosen, I freed my good arm and pulled the broken one halfway up my back to remove the cord from my neck. A scream I could not contain bounced back at me from the walls. I let the throbbing arm drape to my side as I untied my ankles.

I stood and felt the tingle as circulation returned, then ran to Sam. As I felt for her pulse, her eyelids fluttered and she mumbled something unintelligible. I thought about taking her with me, but Erik could be back any time, and there was no way I could haul her around with my broken arm. Better to find a phone and call the police.

I ducked behind the curtain at the back of the room and found an ornate table holding an array of instruments that winked in the light, grabbed the largest knife and headed for the door. I hesitated with my hand on the doorknob. If it was locked, all this was for nothing. I held the knife between my teeth, turned the brass knob and the door creaked open.

In the light that streamed over my shoulder I could see the glint of wine bottles in rack upon rack. I knew now that I had to go up at least one story to find a phone. I crept through the racks like a child caught in a box hedge maze until I could make out the hump of stairs leading upward. At the top I stopped and listened, but I could hear nothing beyond my own steady heartbeat.

I opened the door onto the hallway that contained Nathan Wellman's screening rooms. I darted down to the steps at the far end and headed up to the main living floor, trying to remember the layout of the rest of the house. I knew there was a phone in the foyer, could visualize it sitting on the square table next to the coat closet.

The main floor of the house was dark, and I was uncertain where the switches were. I rushed down another hall, through an arch and into the foyer, where the moon shown bright enough through the expansive windows that I could see my goal. I placed the knife on the table in front of me and picked up the receiver. I punched in 9-1-1 and after one ring was rewarded with a canned voice that intoned, "All circuits are busy, please hold the line." I listened to the message repeat, over and over. No wonder people die everyday in this city. You call fucking 911 and get put on hold. I hung up and cast around for a directory -- which turned up in the drawer under the phone -- and picked up the receiver again.

A bored voice answered.

There was no way I could explain this to him in a way that would get them here quickly enough. "Get me Detective Angela Ramirez, now!" I yelled.

"What's this in regard to?"

"It's in regard to a fucking emergency, that's what its in regard to."

"Calm down."

"I will not calm down. Listen, you need to tell her this is Maddie Pryce and I was wrong. It's Erik Wellman. Get someone out to Erik Wellman, no, Nathan Wellman's house."

"Which is it?"

"Nathan Wellman. I don't know the address. Ramirez will know, just get her."

There was a deep sigh on the other end of the line. "Hang on a minute."

I was still waiting for her to come on the line when the phone went dead. I clicked the reset button several times but got no dial tone. A whisper of sound behind me caused me to turn, and there, his face full of moonlight, stood Alphonse Creider.

# CHAPTER TWENTY-NINE

"I already called the police."

Creider cocked his head to the side like an inquisitive dog. I faltered, unable to set aside the image of whoever had answered the phone crumpling my message in his hand. "They're on their way. Get out while you can."

"Maybe they are, and maybe they aren't," Creider said, his voice like a footstep on gravel. "But we've still got time to get to know each other better." He decreased the gap between us by a step.

I tried to feel for the knife behind me on the slick table top. "Give it up, Creider." He flinched. "That's right, they know who you are."

"Think you got it wrapped up, do you? We'll see about that." He took another step toward me, but his hand went instinctively to his side. Good, at least the screwdriver had done some damage. Give me half a chance and I'd finish the job.

Unable to find the knife, I backed up against the gilded edge of the table, fingers scrabbling over the polished wood. Finally, I brushed across it and grabbed the handle. "You're as crazy as Erik if you think you'll get away with it."

He smiled and kept coming, angling his trajectory so that he was between me and the front door. I went the other way, past the table and against the wall, kicking it into his path. He tripped over a protruding leg and went down with a grunt of pain. I had to buy some time. I ran for the staircase and pounded up the stairs, the knife slick in my hand. I threw my shoulder into doors as I passed them, and a few pushed open. Let him play hide and seek for a while.

Once I came to the juncture of hallways, I slowed down, trying to control my breathing, and crept down the back staircase. I couldn't hear Creider behind me. I could make another run at the front door, but he might be waiting, biding his time and figuring I'd try to get out of the house. Better not to take the chance. I didn't know where he was, but I knew where he wasn't. I moved under the arch toward the stairs that went down to the screening room floor. I ducked into the last room on the right, pulling the door shut behind me until I heard a click. I felt my way around a row of seats until I found the back wall with my outstretched hand, then followed it until I came to the door of the projection closet. Once I was inside, I pulled that door shut too, then got to the floor and scooted until my back was to the corner. How long until Ramirez got my message, if she got it? Nothing to do now but wait.

I understood why solitary was so effective, no way to tell the passage of time, no sound but your own heartbeat. It might have been fifteen minutes or twice as long, but I finally heard doors thwacking open down my hallway. Creider must be good and pissed off by now. The door to my screening room opened and light flooded through the aperture in the door, the opposite of how it should be. Creider's footsteps were muted by the thick carpet, but I heard his approach, heard him stop in front of my hiding place. I crouched, every muscle tense, and when the door opened I sprang forward before he could move into the space, thrusting upward with the knife and following through with my shoulder. He stuttered back and I sprinted past him, unsure if I'd stabbed him or not. I flew up the stairs and back toward the foyer, Creider gaining behind me, and when I turned to look I saw the glint of the knife in his hand.

I yanked the front door open and came face to face with Ramirez in a sweatshirt and jeans, a gun in her hand.

"Duck," she yelled.

I hit the floor, and the explosion over my head reverberated into the night.

~~~

I was reluctant to go with the paramedics until I knew that Sam was out of the house. They fussed at me until I made it clear I wasn't going anywhere just yet. I stood on the emerald expanse of lawn as the sun came up and the cops mopped Alphonse Creider's brains off the marble floor of Erik's foyer, shivering beneath a leather jacket Ramirez had dug up somewhere and draped over my shoulders. She'd also pulled an old pair of tennis shoes from her trunk. Her feet were much larger than mine.

Ramirez didn't look much better than I felt. She kept running her hands through her hair, and now it stuck out like straw from the slack face of a scarecrow. She'd handed over her gun after shooting Creider and I could tell she felt lost without it. I watched her flutter about, a moth in the psychedelic spray of light from the emergency vehicles, talking to uniforms and the same grey-haired man who'd been at the body dump site. She ended back up with me.

"C'mon. You need to have that arm looked at."

I stared at the house, watching lights go on in windows as a cadre of officers searched the mansion. Ramirez put an arm around my shoulders and tried to nudge me toward the driveway. "No sign of him yet. I'm pretty sure we spooked him off."

I couldn't take my eyes from the house, as if it were a puzzle box I couldn't quite open.

"Maddie. Come on. There's no point to this. You're going to drop like a rock any minute now."

I looked at her, unable to think of a single thing to say. All rational thought had been vacuumed out of my skull and I was left with a rushing emptiness.

"We'll find him," Ramirez said as I closed my eyes.

The next thing I was aware of was a stabbing pain that

seemed to travel from my fingers straight to my brain. I opened my eyes to bright lights and the pock-marked, earnest face of one of the paramedics. His hair was light and cut short, and for a second he reminded me of Kyle. I felt laughter bubbling up despite the pain, thinking how pissed off Kyle was going to be when he heard about this. Good thing he was already in the hospital, he was going to have a stroke. The paramedic -- Stryker, his little gold badge read -- pushed me back against the gurney and pulled the door closed.

"Nice outfit," he said. "I especially like the shoes."

I passed out before I could start laughing again.

The ride to the hospital occurred without me, and I vaguely remember being wheeled inside, the doors to the emergency department opening in a way that reminded me of the entrance to the headquarters in *Get Smart*. I imagine I said something quite witty in reference to this, because the nurse on my left gave me the most bizarre look. The rest was a swirl of white and beige, fuzzy like a dream sequence. A doctor, at least I assume he was a doctor -- he had the polished look of someone who spent a lot of time being very serious and throwing out words normal people couldn't pronounce -- held up a clipboard and a pen. I scrawled my name with my left hand and let all that whiteness overtake me.

When I woke up, the pain was distant, as if it had retreated to the farthest corner of my body to await the next round. I was conscious of a great thirst, as if I'd been crawling in the desert for days, and swallowed a whole lot of sand along the way.

Ramirez sat in a metal chair beside the bed, and she looked up from the notebook in her lap as I mumbled.

"Water," I managed on the third try.

She left, returned with a plastic cup of ice, and I let her place a few chips on my tongue. Heaven. After I'd dispensed with half the cup, I felt I could manage speech, although my tongue felt swollen and unfamiliar.

"How's Sam?"

Ramirez scooted the chair closer. "They say she's going to be okay. They're waiting for the tox screen to come back so they can find out what's in her system, but other than that she's just dehydrated. No injuries."

At least not on the outside.

Ramirez continued. "There's no sign of Wellman. We can't figure out which car he took, if he took one at all. The airports are staked out and we've confiscated the boat." She hesitated. "And we've got some people at your apartment building."

My apartment. "I need to go home."

"Well, I don't know when they'll release you. And going to your apartment might not be the best idea in the world."

I sat up to a wave of dizziness and the realization that my right arm was a lot heavier that it should be. I gazed at the cast in wonder, having no recollection how it got there.

"You have a fracture," Ramirez said.

Obviously. That didn't change the fact that I'd been gone too long and Sydney was going to have fits. "I have a dog and a cat. They need to be fed. Sydney needs to be walked." I looked down at the papery hospital gown. "And I need some clothes." For some reason, it was the thought of my missing clothes that brought the tears. Strange how something that simple, after all I'd been through, was the thing that made me come undone.

"I can do that," Ramirez said, and the hard lines on her face softened. "I'll have a locksmith let me in and change the locks. I'll take care of your animals and pick up what you need."

After all the animosity that had passed between us, I didn't know what to say.

Ramirez smiled. "I'm out of the loop anyway. Standard procedure when you blow somebody all to hell. I really don't have much else to do."

I didn't bother to tell her she looked like she could use a week's worth of sleep. No sense looking a gift horse in its tired mouth. I gave her the entry code to the building, explained what the kids ate and where the leash was. Even though her offer eased my anxiety, I still ached to be in my own place, surrounded by my own things.

"Look," I said. "You've got the place staked out. Once you check it out for yourself, I'd be just as safe there as anywhere." I looked around the austere and antiseptic hospital room. "I really don't want to stay here any longer than I have to."

"I don't have to tell you how dangerous Wellman is. From what you said, he's decompensating now."

"And that means?"

"Even organized serial killers, which is what Wellman would be classified as -- control freaks, highly ritualized killers -- they get to a point when they get sloppy, when they become totally unpredictable. That's what usually gets them caught. The more internal pressure they feel, the more mistakes they're likely to make. You'd think somebody with Wellman's resources and connections would just get out of town, but there's no way to predict what he'll do. Taking you was a stupid thing but, in his mind, he thought he could get away with it. And he might be fixated on you as his ideal victim, which means he'll try again."

"But I'll be surrounded by cops."

"Well, surrounded might not be the best word. And I really don't want to get anyone else killed."

I thought about that for a moment. "Is there any way you can stop me from going home?"

"Short of arresting you? No."

"Then just surround my building and wait for him to show up."

Ramirez sighed. "Now I know what Kyle saw in you. You're completely impossible. For some reason, men seem to find that attractive." She stood and tucked the notebook under her arm. "I'll go to your place. When I get back, we'll talk about it."

She stopped at the edge of the room. "By the way, Kyle's much better. He'll be out by the end of the week. " She slammed the door behind her. The old Ramirez was back.

~~~

After convincing a doctor that I felt much better and didn't need the IV, I got a nurse to wheel me to Kyle's room.

It was filled with flowers, bright spots of color amid planes of green that gave me the impression I was trapped inside a hothouse. Kyle was sitting up in bed, staring out the window.

"Hey," I said, as the nurse deposited me beside the bed.

Kyle turned and his eyes widened.

"What the hell happened to you?"

They hadn't filled him in. I didn't know if that was a good thing or a bad thing. "Nothing much."

The shocked look didn't leave his face. "Geez, Maddie. You look like hell. Are you okay?"

"You always did know how to sweet talk a girl."

Might as well get it over with. I told Kyle everything that happened. Well almost everything. I tried to gloss over the parts that made me seem particularly reckless. When the explanation wound down, Kyle looked away again, out at the sunlit expanse of parking lot. A stubbly growth of beard hugged the line of his jaw, and I noticed how pale he looked in the wash of light.

"I guess I just wanted to thank you for saving my life," I said, the tears threatening again.

He took my hand, but didn't look at me. "I'm just glad you're okay," he whispered.

We sat there, holding hands like high school sweethearts, unwilling or unable to say more.

When the silence became uncomfortable, I spoke. "I've convinced them to let me out this evening. But I'll come back and visit. And once you're out of here...." I didn't know what would happen when Kyle was released, didn't know if what we had was irretrievably broken, or changed in a way that made it impossible for us to even be friends.

"Yeah," Kyle said.

I kissed his cheek, then rested my head against his shoulder. "You just get better."

Ramirez was waiting after I ran the gauntlet back to my room. She'd picked up panties and a bra, socks, moccasins, a pair of sweatpants and an oversized T-shirt.

"So, you've convinced them you're ready to leave," she said.

"Hey, you know these medical types. I just told them I wouldn't pay for a night in the hospital."

I had no choice but to let her help me get dressed. She told me everything seemed fine at my place and that she'd gotten someone over to change the locks. "Your dog's a psycho, though. Little creature acted like he'd never see a leash before."

"He's just fussy that way. Don't take it personally." I slid my feet into the moccasins and stood up. "I want to tell you that I appreciate everything you've done. You didn't have to. And I just, well, really appreciate it."

"Maybe Kyle's rubbing off on me. Patron Saint of Lost Causes." She headed out the door.

It was after five when Ramirez pulled up in front of my building. She walked me to my door, handed me the new keys, then insisted on going through the apartment once more, Sydney at her heels. When she was satisfied no one lurked beneath the bed, her duty seemed finished.

"We've interviewed everyone in the building. Let them know what to look for."

"Whee. Now I'm a celebrity in my own home."

She ignored that. "We have unmarked cars in front and out back, just in case Wellman shows. Whatever move he makes, we'll get him. But if you notice anything, anything weird or suspicious at all, you call...or scream. They'll hear you."

I thanked her again and locked the door behind her, then sank into the couch. I was just glad to be home. I could forget the fact that I was again an unemployed actress with a dwindling bank account and no prospects, the fact that my last employer was a psychopath still roaming the streets of L.A., probably looking for me.

I debated mixing vodka with the painkillers they'd issued, and settled on a glass of water and toast. After dinner I stood in the shower with my cast hanging out of the curtains until the water ran cold. I still didn't feel clean.

The last round of pills was taking effect by the time I let

Sydney out, and the world seemed to sway around me. At the foot of the turret stairs, he stopped and barked so furiously you'd have thought the phone was ringing.

"Tonight is not the night, Otto," I said. "Go to bed."

Sydney gave up and followed me to my room. I fell into a fitful sleep as soon as I closed my eyes.

# CHAPTER THIRTY

I dreamt of Kyle. We were in a passionate embrace, together in a way that bridged the gulf between us. I awoke as he called my name, a faint, spicy scent wafting over me.

It wasn't Kyle's fingertips on my skin, and it wasn't Otto floating around the room. .

"Don't scream," Erik said.

I did a remarkable job of not screaming, considering I could feel a point of cool metal dimpling the tender skin under the point of my jaw.

"What are you doing here, Erik?" I whispered.

"I didn't have any place else to go." He said it matter-of-factly, like it made all the sense in the world. He sat beside me on the bed, leaning close enough that I could feel the heat coming off his skin.

I thought of the cops downstairs, the new locks, Ramirez' final sweep of the premises. "How the hell did you get in here?" I was still whispering. I don't know why, maybe because it seemed like the less I moved, the less likely the knife was to slip.

"I can see why you love this place," Erik said. "So full of history, so magnificent, even with what they've done to it. It was quite the masterpiece in its day. Von Strasser drew up the plans for the house himself, and only hired an architect to carry them out. You can find the originals at the Bayview, in their historical papers collection.

"The rough surgery they performed on this place left all kinds of hollow places inside, little nooks and crannies. They walled up the dumbwaiter completely. You know, it goes all the way to the basement."

He levered himself off the bed, never removing the blade from my throat. "Why don't you come see?"

He maneuvered me from the bedroom, walking behind me with an arm around my waist and the other holding the knife. "It was easy to get into the basement that first time: people forget their laundry soap, want to bring down another box of junk. They leave the door open more often than you'd imagine."

"How long?"

"Since Jason convinced Creider you had the film. After that it was just...a game. Tonight is was just a matter of patience. Your police woman didn't even hear me when she came to walk the dog."

That's what Sydney had been barking at. But where was he now? I turned my head slightly, the knife grazing the delicate flesh over my larynx. "What did you do to him?"

"He got into the walls, slippery little monster. But I'm sure someone will find him. Eventually."

We mounted the stairs slowly, Erik's arm hard under my breasts, a slow trickle of blood oozing past the sharp tip of the knife and down my neck.

I fought for a stalling tactic as we crossed the top of the stairs. "The house is surrounded, you know."

"Oh, yes. But having them be able to see you but not save you, don't you think that's dramatic? Very poignant, very tragic."

"I don't see why you just didn't run, Erik."

"Where would I run to? It's over. Isn't that what you think, Maddie? That I'm broken. There's no fixing me. First I thought of coming here to explain, to tell you, make you understand. And then I realized that I couldn't. I may be crazy, but I'm not stupid." He held me closer, leaning his head against mine, whispering in my ear. "I know it's over. I don't want to be a sad, frightened man in a cell, where people ask questions there are no answers for."

Erik had slipped over that fine line where madness is internal, confined within a framework of blood and brain and bone, to where it seeps out to tinge the world, changing everything. He forced me past the black square in the

220

wainscoting where he'd removed the paneling, and I felt anger well inside me. How had my sacred space so completely accepted him? I couldn't stand the thought of him in my house, Crieder in my house, coming and going as they pleased. There were hidden places in Erik I'd never suspected, and he had found the hidden places here that I was only now becoming aware of.

He tried to push me toward the turret window, but I balked. "If it's over, Erik, just let me go. You don't have to do this."

He sighed, his breath hot against my neck. "Do you believe in fate? I have to believe in something. Maybe fate put you in my path again. Maybe fate put us here. One last grand gesture. It has to means something. The story has to have an ending."

Erik pushed me forward with his knees, up near the darkened floor lamp that had been moved closer to the window seat. Lighting for his final act.

I gazed out the pane of glass, knowing that only it and a thirty-foot drop stood between me and rescue. I wondered if the police would see me in time, if they would look up and discern our shadows. Or were they just sipping coffee and talking about their kids or their girlfriends, oblivious to the premier that was about to take place?

What had Ramirez said? Scream and they'll hear you. But that wouldn't change the outcome now, only rush the last moments of my life to swift completion.

Erik dug his right elbow into my breast, trapping me against him, the blade still poised under my chin. He took his left arm from my body and caressed the glass shade of the lamp. As I strained against the knife to follow his movement, I caught fleeting glimpses of his plaster-dusted face, like a black and white image flashing and waning on one of Chaplin's early reels.

"It's time, Maddie."

I felt cold envelope me, raising goosebumps on my bare arm and legs as Erik slid his fingertips down the pull chain on the lamp. I flashed back to the alley, when I'd escaped Creider. I'd gotten away then. The combination of fatigue and medication was shutting down my mind. All I could think of was the light that would come on. I wished the same light would click on inside of me, but there was nothing. This would be the end of my ninth life.

I took one last, long breath, the air smelling of cinnamon. An unholy yowl filled the room, and before Erik could react, a white cannonball launched from the ledge above the windows, landing square on his head, a demonic fur hat. He released me and gave an inarticulate scream as Cat sunk her claws into his cheek and he tried to raise his hands to get a grip on her. The knife fell from his hands as he sent the lamp careening into the window seat, its glass shade shattering. Erik did a slow pirouette away from me, a grotesque ballet of man and cat, then dropped to one knee, flinging Cat away. She skittered across the floor, thudded against the wainscoting and sprung up, hissing. Erik began to rise, and that got me moving. He was between me and the path to the front door, so I sprinted to my left, over the remains of the lamp and through the jagged shards of glass. I made the bottom of the roof stairs and didn't look back.

I pounded up the stairs, slid the bolt and burst into the garden, screaming at the top of my lungs. The leaf rake was right where I'd left it, unfortunately. It caught my toes and I pitched forward, sprawling onto the dry remains of summer flowers, their corpses crackling beneath me.

Erik was faster than I thought, and before I could get to my feet he was on me.

The fear was gone, replaced by a dark, red rage, an ocean of hate. It was Erik's fault, all of it. He'd killed people I cared about, lied to me and tortured me, invaded my home and infected it with his disease. I rolled beneath him as he tried to pin my arms, felt his hot breath against my neck as he struggled on top of me.

"Don't make it this hard, Maddie," he panted. "Accept it. This is your destiny."

"You are not my destiny, you sick son of a bitch."

I brought my knee up as hard as I could, arching against him. It connected with his testicles and his face constricted in pain as he rolled away from me. I could hear shouts from the street below, but the sound seemed miles away. What was taking them so long?

I scrambled away on my knees. Erik's hand snaked around my ankle and I kicked back hard, feeling his grip release as I got to my feet. There was nowhere to go, just a shrouded obstacle course of potted trees and shrubs that ended with the sharp line of the roof.

I was trapped and rescue was three stories down. What did I have left but another lunge, another five feet of freedom? Maybe I could get their attention, at least let them know where I was.

I limped to the edge of the roof and saw lights dancing beyond the boundary of the back garden, lights coming on in the buildings around the house. I yelled and waved my arms, then heard a bellow of rage behind me. I turned to see Erik charging, blood streaking his face and chest like war paint. He hit me and drove me back against the parapet, knocking the breath from my lungs. Before I could lose my balance, he wrapped his arms around me.

His lips split in a demented smile, "One last dance?"

"Go to hell."

I stepped down hard on the bridge of his foot and twisted away from him, toward the center of the roof. I brought my left arm up as hard as I could and caught his jaw with the edge of the cast.

He had just a moment to register a look of surprise before he tumbled over into the darkness.

When I could breath again, I leaned over the half-wall and looked down, listening to clatter of police as they tried to find their way into the secluded square below.

It would have been like *Sunset Boulevard*, William Holden face down in the pool, but the pool had been dug up decades ago and Erik's lifeless body lay alone in the green glow of the garden, the heavy smell of oleander drifting by like it did on every other night about this time.

# CHAPTER THIRTY-ONE

Burton Willis had a heart attack three days after Thanksgiving. He dropped like a rock in the middle of a tirade aimed at the carpenters installing the walls of the juice bar. I made up a proposal and within a week and, to my complete surprise, the other owners accepted my offer to oversee the remainder of the renovation on the Orpheus. So what if I didn't have any experience? All I had to do was act like I knew what I was doing. Still, something told me their consent was influenced by the freak show factor. After all, in Hollywood, there is no bad publicity.

The books that were written were written without me, and I learned to avoid zealous reporters and roving cameramen. Otto's house was finally featured on the Haunted Hollywood tours, now part of the legendary and dark mystique of a hidden city, the grime beneath the glitter.

The police closed the case on Erik, even though the films were never found. There was speculation that the reels were in circulation in some elite power circles but, as Ramirez said, most people dismissed it as just urban legend.

Any hopes that the films were still hidden in the house became moot when a group of drunken revelers -- Malibu beach bums, socialites from up and down the street, hardcore star junkies -- set fire to the mansion. The orange glow drew a bigger crowd than any premiere had in weeks. As passing cars stopped to regurgitate everyone from prostitutes to powerbrokers, TV and radio people gathered in little nests working the throng. The crowd spilled from the massive front lawn, warding off any attempt by fire fighters to save the house. The fire burned through until morning, sending ash up to join the smog that would blanket the awakening city. There was no need for an arson investigation and no one was arrested. As far as I knew, Erik's parents never returned from Europe.

By Christmas the cast had come off my arm and, in between trips to the theater, I worked on physical rehabilitation. My first attempts at a swim met with feelings of claustrophobia, but eventually I felt at home again in the water. Sometimes Sam joined me, but we never talked about Erik or the wine cellar. That was a dark and uncharted territory best left unexplored. I was glad she stayed, that she broke up with Evan and was clean for now, but I wondered in the back of my mind how long it would take before her demon caught up with her again.

In March the renovation was complete, the old and new blending together in a glossy hybrid that still held the spark of the old building. I had managed that much anyway, and somewhere along the way I made peace with the new Orpheus. It had withstood and so would I, even though both of us were forever changed.

It was a clear spring day, the smog blown out to sea by winds from the east, when I stood outside the Orpheus with Sydney crouched at my feet. He was happy for the trip, but still resisting the leash. We watched as workers placed letters up on the old marquee, which was one of the things I'd fought to keep unchanged. The sun was moving in an arc behind the building, on its slow descent to the sea, and I felt that same old sense of awe, that conviction that the Orpheus was a place full of dreams, full of possibilities.

"I thought you might be here."

I turned toward Kyle and couldn't help smiling. He bent down and scratched Sydney behind the ears, straightened up and gave me a half-hearted grin.

"I just wanted to let you know that I'm back on full duty as of today, and I heard about the theater opening tomorrow and, well, I though you might like to go get a cup of herbal tea to celebrate."

I remember looking into those green eyes for the first time so many months ago. The same intensity was there, only softer, muted.

"Sure. I'd like that."

In a movie, this would be the scene where the hero takes the heroine in his arms and draws her into a long, passionate kiss as the music swells and the screen fades to black.

Life was never like the movies.

# ABOUT THE AUTHOR

## Susan Branham And Keri Knutson

Keri Knutson and Susan Branham have been writing together for more than 10 years, collaborating on the Maddie Pryce mystery series in between moving around the country with their respective families. Susan is a profilic essayist and Keri has published the novel Running Red and multiple short stories.

.

# BOOKS IN THIS SERIES

*Maddie Pryce Mysteries*

**Darker By Degree**

**Director's Cut**

Made in the USA
Middletown, DE
08 October 2022